Hide-away heart

CHERRY TREE HARBOR

Melanie Harlow

USA TODAY BESTSELLING AUTHOR

dear reader

In Hideaway Heart, I wanted the trust between Xander and Kelly to shine. That said, there is one intimate scene that may not be for everyone. If you're concerned, please use the QR code below to find out more information.

I hope you love their story as much as I loved writing them!

For Catherine Cowles,
who saw I was a woman in peril
and rescued me.

CHAPTER ONE

xander

I'LL JUST ADMIT IT. I've got an ego.

I'm not a jerk or anything—in fact, I think I'm a pretty good fucking time—it's just that I have a lot of confidence that if a thing can be done, I can do it. And I tell it like it is.

But I'm also a nice guy. I believe in fair fights, second chances, and paying my debts. So when Kevin Sullivan called me that Wednesday night for a favor, I didn't hesitate.

"You don't even have to ask twice, Sully," I said as I opened the sliding glass door and went out onto the patio, still sweaty from a run. "Name the time and place."

The voice from my past laughed. "Don't you want to know what it is first?"

"Won't matter. I know what I owe you." My right leg bore scars that served as a daily reminder of two things—the heroism of the man I was talking to and how close I'd come to dying six years ago.

"It's a job," he said.

"Talk to me." I grabbed the top of my right foot and stretched out my quad. Those five miles had been a little rough today, had taken me a little longer. I blamed the late August heat. Or maybe my injury. Definitely not my age—I might have been thirty-one, but I felt eighteen.

Mostly.

"I know you've been out of the game for a while, but—"

"Not that long," I told him. "I just left Cole Security about six months ago."

"That's what I heard. You moved back home? Opened a bar?"

"The bar isn't quite open yet. I bought it over the summer, but it needed pretty extensive renovations. If all goes according to plan, opening will be three weeks from tomorrow." Which meant I really didn't have time for a side gig right now, but that didn't matter. If Sully needed me, I was going to come through. "Tell me about the job. Is it domestic or international?"

"Domestic. Practically right in your backyard."

"My backyard?"

That didn't make much sense. Currently, I was living with my dad in the house where my four siblings and I had grown up. I glanced at the lawn I'd mowed a thousand times, at the rose bushes our mom had loved and our dad maintained in her memory, at the towering maple tree my brothers and

I used to climb while our little sister cried that she wanted to play pirate ship too.

My plan had been to move out over the summer, but the bar was eating all my savings. I even had my eye on a house not too far from my brother Austin and his family, but I'd had to choose between making a down payment and getting the sound system I really wanted for Buckley's Pub—and I went for the sound. I wanted the place to be comfortable but high-end, somewhere you could wear your ball cap and team jersey but drink expensive-as-fuck whiskey while you watched the game.

"I'm in Cherry Tree Harbor, Michigan, Sully," I told him, dropping into one of the chairs on the patio. "Who needs security way the hell up here?"

"My little sister."

I tried to remember if Sully had ever mentioned a sibling. We'd known each other a couple months before I got injured, but as the newest guy on our SEAL platoon, he'd understood he was expected to be seen and not heard. "I'm not sure I knew you had a sister."

"Her real name is Kelly Jo Sullivan, but professionally she goes by Pixie Hart."

"Pixie Hart, the country music singer? That's your sister? How did I not know that?"

"I don't talk about it much," he said. "People can get weird about it. And I'm protective of her."

"I get it." I was protective too, but fucking hell. *A celebrity?*

I scowled as I recalled the one and only time I'd

agreed to provide security for a rock band. They'd ignored every single safety precaution, trashed their hotel rooms, and generally behaved like drunk, entitled brats, making it impossible for me to do my job. I'd vowed I'd never take another celebrity gig again.

But it was Sully—I couldn't say no.

"So what's the deal?" I scrubbed a hand over my beard. "She need security for a concert or something? Music festival?"

"No. She needs a twenty-four-seven bodyguard during her two-week vacation."

"Twenty-four-seven for two weeks?" The job got even less palatable. "I want to help, Sully, but I'm about to open a business. I can't leave town."

"You wouldn't have to," he said quickly. "She rented a place outside Petoskey for the first two weeks of September. That's near you, right?"

"Yes," I said warily.

"She should not stay there alone, no matter what she says."

"And what does she say?"

"She's a bit resistant to the idea."

"What's 'a bit?'"

"I believe her words were, 'I don't want some Navy SEAL goon up in my business while I'm on vacation.'"

I laughed. "That seems like more than 'a bit.'"

"She needs you, Xander. Paparazzi follow her and bang on her car windows. Weirdos go through her trash. She just got back from a sold-out tour where she was mobbed wherever she went."

I frowned. "Didn't she have security?"

"She did, but they were a bunch of clowns hired by the label. At least one of them was selling information to photographers—what hotel she was staying at, when she'd be coming and going, where and when she had restaurant reservations, where she was shopping."

"Assholes," I muttered.

"They were all fired, but one of them is threatening to sue her. She's also got a dickhead ex-boyfriend who still thinks he owns her."

My hackles went up. "Who is he?"

"Duke Pruitt."

"That guy?" I could feel my face prune up like I'd smelled something bad. "His music sucks."

"I'm not a fan."

"Is he harassing her?"

"She says it's nothing she can't handle, but the guy's a dick. I don't trust him. He treated her like shit for years, and now that she finally left him for good, he wants her back."

"Maybe now isn't the best time for a vacation," I suggested.

"We've told her that, but she insists she's fine, even though she's five-foot-nothing and has zero self-defense skills, besides a loud voice. And the way she posts on social media all the time, I feel like people are going to figure out where she is."

I exhaled. "She should stay off social media."

"She claims that's impossible and unnecessary."

Of course she did. Because she was a celebrity

5

who knew everything. "Does she at least have security cameras at this vacation house?"

"Apparently not."

I exhaled again. Louder this time.

"Look, I know this is a lot to ask. If I was in the states, I'd go with her. But I'm deployed—about to go off the grid—and my gut is telling me it's a bad idea for her to be up there alone. I trust my gut. You would too, if it was your sister."

"You're right. I would."

"You're the only one I'd trust with her safety. Will you do it?"

Of course I would. Even if this gig was a total pain in the ass, I owed Sully my life. And his trust meant a lot to me. "I'll do it."

"Great." He sounded relieved. "I'm sure the place she rented is nice. We were raised poor, but she's got champagne tastes now. And you will be well compensated."

"Fuck off. You know I won't take your money."

He laughed. "You might want to meet her before you refuse compensation. She's sweet, but she's got some sass to her."

"Sounds like my little sister, Mabel."

"It's nothing you can't handle. No matter what she says, just don't let her fire you."

"When do you need me there?"

"She arrives Thursday."

"As in *tomorrow*?"

"Yeah—sorry about the late notice."

Fuck. This gave me less than twenty-four hours to prepare. "Text me the location."

"I will." He paused. "Keep her safe, brother."

With one last deep breath, I resigned myself to two weeks of babysitting a stubborn celebrity who didn't want me around. "I will," I promised. "You have my word."

Later that night, I drove over to my brother Austin's house. I found him in the garage, which functioned as his workshop. By day, he worked side by side with our dad running Two Buckleys Home Improvement, but recently he'd announced he wanted to leave that behind and start his own company making furniture out of reclaimed wood.

It had taken him forever to work up the nerve to tell our dad that's what he wanted, and even though I'd given him endless shit about that (what are siblings for?), I understood why he'd felt such loyalty to our father. Our mom had died when we were kids, and our dad had raised the five of us entirely on his own. Well, not entirely—Austin, who'd only been twelve when we lost our mother, had stepped up in ways no seventh grader should have to. I'd only been one year behind him, but he'd always seemed ten years more mature. While I spent my high school years chasing down girls and athletic records in cross country and swimming and track and field, he spent his working for our dad and helping out with the younger kids. He also kicked my ass regularly, probably because he had no other outlet.

I didn't mind. I liked a good scrap.

But that motherfucker was so talented. He could take a beat-up barn door and turn it into something so beautiful, you wanted to eat off it. I'd conned him into crafting a bar for Buckley's Pub by betting him he wouldn't be able to keep his pants zipped around the nanny he hired for the summer—he hadn't even lasted two weeks.

That bar was fucking *art*.

"Hey." I helped myself to a beer from his fridge and perched on the edge of his tool bench.

"Hey." He didn't even look up from measuring the planks across his work table. "Have a beer, why don't you?"

I grinned. "Thanks, I will. Can I get you one?"

"Nah."

"Veronica and the kids home?"

"They should be soon. They rode bikes into town after dinner for ice cream."

I took a swallow from the bottle. "I got a phone call from Kevin Sullivan today."

"The guy who saved your life?"

"Yeah. He needs a favor."

Austin finally looked up. "I hope you said yes."

"Of course I said yes," I scoffed.

He nodded his approval.

"But I wish he needed a different kind of favor."

8

"What's he need?"

"Security for his sister." I explained who his sister was and why he was concerned about her staying alone.

"Holy shit. So you're moving in with Pixie Hart for two weeks?"

"I'm not *moving in* with her," I said, annoyed. "I'm providing residential security. Close protection."

"For who?" Veronica strolled into the garage, followed by Austin's twins, seven-year-old Adelaide and Owen.

"Pixie Hart," I told her.

Adelaide let out an ear-piercing squeal. "Pixie Hart! I *love* Pixie Hart! You get to meet her?"

"He gets to live with her," said Austin.

I glared at him. "I promised my buddy I'd keep her safe, and that's all I'm doing. And I don't even want to do that."

"Why not?" Owen asked. "She's famous."

"Because famous people are a pain in the butt. They don't like being told what they can and cannot do, and they all think rules don't apply to them."

"So why do you have to do it?" Veronica asked.

"Because her brother saved my life in Afghanistan," I said. "Carried me half a mile, under fire, to safety after I'd been shot twice in the leg."

"He must be strong," said Owen. "You're even bigger than my dad."

"Not *that* much bigger," countered Austin, who continued to resent the two inches in height I had on him.

9

God, I loved those two inches.

"So are you going to Nashville?" Veronica asked, taking a seat in a wooden folding chair by the fridge. She was tall, blond, and blue-eyed, a perfect contrast to my brother, who had dark hair and brown eyes. He and I looked a lot alike, except I was taller, with more tattoos and a better beard.

"No," I said. "She's renting a cabin somewhere in the woods outside Petoskey, which means I'll probably have to delay the opening of Buckley's, even though I promoted the date already."

"Why?"

"Because I won't be around as much as I need to be to get it up and running. I'd need a temporary manager or something."

Veronica looked thoughtful as she hugged her knees to her chest. "Maybe I can help you out so you don't have to delay."

"Thanks, but you'll have your hands full with the new studio, won't you?" Veronica, who'd been a professional dancer in New York, had taken over an old dance school just outside town. Austin was helping her rehab it.

"It's only two weeks." Veronica lifted her shoulders. "And Austin is still doing the remodeling. I think I can manage both—just tell me what you need me to do."

"You're a life saver," I said gratefully. "Thanks."

Adelaide came over and stood in front of me, her expression hopeful, a mint green blotch on her white shirt from her ice cream. "Will I get to meet her, Uncle Xander?"

"Maybe." I tweaked one of her braids. "You excited for school to start next week?"

"Yes," she said. "Hey, maybe I can bring Pixie Hart for Show and Tell!"

"I think she probably needs to lie low," I told my niece, although I hated disappointing her.

"What's that mean?" asked Owen, who had a chocolate mustache. "To 'lie low.'"

"It means stay out of sight," I said. "So that her fans and the photographers who follow her around everywhere don't find out where she is and bother her. She doesn't even want *me* bothering her. Apparently, she's totally against the idea of security."

"Why?" Austin asked.

"Because she's probably delusional. They all are." I tipped up my beer. "Also, there was a breach on her previous security team, so I imagine she doesn't trust anyone right now. Her brother told me she flat out refused to have some goon up in her business while she's on vacation . . . right before he made me promise not to let her out of my sight."

"Oh dear," said Veronica.

Austin laughed. "Good luck with that."

"You know what? I won't need luck," I said, pushing my shoulders back. "I've got charm. I've got *magnetism*. She's gonna adore me."

"Oh dear," Veronica said again.

My brother shook his head. "What happens if she doesn't?"

"Nothing." I shrugged. "She's stuck with me."

After I packed a bag, I decided to do a little internet research on Pixie Hart. I Googled her name and clicked on some images that popped up in the search results.

Damn.

No denying it, Sully's sister was a bombshell.

Not my type—I wasn't into all the glitzy makeup and fancy clothes—but objectively, Pixie Hart was hot.

Tons of fiery red hair that fell halfway down her back, skin that looked like it might glow in the dark, giant green eyes flecked with gold, a megawatt smile with blindingly white teeth. She was short, like Sully had said, and she wore a lot of high heels, at least in these red carpet photos. She also wore a lot of glittery dresses, bright lipstick, and thick eye makeup. Her nails were long, pointy, and painted to match her outfits.

In some of the photos, that overrated dipshit Duke Pruitt stood next to her. He was a big name in country music, but he'd also acted in some movies. He was older, forty or so, and had a reputation for collecting vintage muscle cars and starry-eyed young singers. I was pretty sure he had at least three ex-wives.

Digging a little deeper, I discovered they'd had an on-and-off relationship for about three years. But the photos of the two of them were all at least six months old, and she had wiped her Instagram account clean of his existence.

Scrolling through her feed, I found some more casual photos of her. Boots instead of heels, jeans instead of dresses, cowboy hat and ponytail instead of all that big hair. There were also some pictures from photo shoots that showed her all dressed up in a fancy gown and running through wheat fields in bare feet (ridiculous), seated alone at a diner booth sipping a milkshake (she probably didn't even eat dairy), or splashing in a creek wearing very short denim cutoffs and a white bikini top. Her nipples were clearly visible in that shot, so I clicked away from it immediately. (And by that I mean immediately *after* I zoomed in to make sure I saw what I thought I saw).

But this was Sully's sister. And now she was my client. Everything, including my thoughts, had to stay completely professional.

Returning to my Pixie Hart search results, I clicked on news and checked out a few headlines. Beyond lots of gossip about her relationship with Duke Pruitt (consensus seemed to be that their troubles were due to his cheating), there were stories about her powering through a concert in Greenville despite having food poisoning, a piece about her visiting a children's hospital in Philadelphia, and something about her returning to her high school to

13

sing the National Anthem for homecoming in order to raise money for the marching band's new uniforms. She was often referred to as "country music's sweetheart."

I read all the way through one article that described her humble beginnings—the county fair circuit, wedding bands—until she won a reality show called *Nashville Next* at age twenty-two, which launched her career. After that, she spent a few years opening for other acts, and then finally began head-lining her own tours.

I peeked at a few reviews of her music, mostly positive despite some grumbling about her being a plastic doll propped up by the record label—all hat, no cattle—and how reality TV acts like her were ruining country music. But I saw plenty of praise for her "honeyed vocals with just the right amount of grit," her "winsome pop-country appeal," and her "balance of sparkling production and hell-raising fun." According to one critic, her guitar playing was only "passable" and she had a "limited range," but on the whole, most of the press was positive. Lots of writers mentioned her possession of that "it factor," whatever intangible star quality it was that made some people light up the stage and connect with an audience.

After about ninety minutes, I yawned, shut down my laptop, and went to the basement to retrieve my laundry. While I was tossing my clean clothes into a bag, a call came in from a number I didn't recognize.

I didn't pick up, and a moment later, I saw that I had a new voicemail.

"Hi, this message is for Xander Buckley."

The voice was feminine but feisty, with only the barest hint of a twang. *Honey and grit.*

"This is Kelly Jo Sullivan. I'm Kevin's sister? I just wanted to let you know that while I appreciate your offer to provide security for me on my vacation, it's not necessary. In fact, I'd prefer to be left alone. No offense or anything, but the place I've rented is tiny, and there really isn't room for two. Thanks anyway, and I hope you have a great night."

Right away, I called Sully, but he didn't pick up. Maybe he was off the grid already.

Oh well. I'd given my word to keep watch over her for those two weeks, day and night, whether she wanted it or not.

(And clearly, the answer was *not*.)

I wondered what would happen when I showed up. Would she accept the situation or would she insist on putting up a fight?

I remembered all that red hair and those loud ruby lips, and I had a feeling I knew what the answer was.

Fine by me.

I liked a good scrap.

CHAPTER TWO

kelly

TWO WEEKS TO MYSELF.

Two weeks of peace and freedom and reflection.

Two weeks of being plain old Kelly Jo Sullivan, rather than country music sensation Pixie Hart.

I could get up early or sleep 'til noon. I could spend my days hiking in the sun or reading in the shade. I could sip wine as I watched the moon rise and play my guitar beneath the stars.

I could listen to music or enjoy the silence. I could meditate or masturbate. I could ponder and plan what should come next for me without any other voices in my head.

I wouldn't have to wear sequins, put rollers in my hair, or sit through two hours of makeup. I wouldn't have to attend meetings with the suits at PMG Records who didn't like the lyrics I'd written, the haircut I'd gotten, or the five pounds I'd gained. I wouldn't have to tell anyone my plans.

If I wanted to go get a cup of coffee, I'd drive

myself. If I felt like cupcakes, I'd make them. If I wanted to leave my hair unwashed for a week, no paparazzi was going to catch it on camera.

Don't get me wrong—I thanked my lucky stars every single day for Pixie Hart's career, but after the last few months, I needed a little break from her. From everybody.

That's why I'd fired the security guard my brother had hired. I just wanted to feel *normal* for two weeks, and *normal* did not include an ex-Navy SEAL lummox following me around, watching every move I made.

I sat on my suitcase to get it closed, pumping a fist with triumph when I finally got it zipped. Rising to my feet, I dragged the suitcase into the hall and somehow managed to get it down the wide, curving staircase of my new Nashville home. At barely seven a.m., no one was up—my mom was a late sleeper, especially when my father was around—but I winced at the banging noise my bag made as it thumped on every marble step. I wanted to sneak out of here undetected.

After deactivating the house alarm, I opened the front door and slipped out into the damp heat of a late August morning. In the circular drive was the minivan my assistant, Jess, had rented for me in her name. It was a couple years old, gray and nondescript, with a dent in the bumper and a scratch on the driver's side door. It looked like a vehicle for a harried soccer mom with three young kids rather than a country music star, which was exactly what I wanted.

I rolled my suitcase down the porch steps—*thunk, thunk, thunk*—and popped the van's tailgate, but no matter how hard I tried, I could not lift the damn thing into the back. I was debating transferring some stuff to a second bag when a Chevy truck came careening around the curve of the driveway and screeched to a halt. The door opened, and a middle-aged guy wearing jeans and an ancient Willie Nelson tour T-shirt jumped out. My manager, Rick Wagstaff, or Wags, as everyone called him.

"I got your text." Wags shook his phone in my direction as he strode toward me. "What do you mean, you fired the bodyguard?"

I sighed. "I shouldn't have even told you."

"Kelly Jo, come on. You need security, even up there."

"I don't want a stranger with me on my vacation, Wags. And after everything I went through with Duke and then the leaks to the paparazzi on the tour, I'm in a serious no-trust zone right now."

"I don't blame you for that." He tucked his phone into his back pocket. "But this is someone your brother chose."

"I don't care." I paused. "You fix that thing with the disgruntled security guard threatening to sue me?"

"I'm working on it. I don't think he'll actually sue. He's sniffing around for a payout. Claims he was wrongly terminated."

"Is it possible he wasn't involved? Do I need to feel bad we fired an innocent guy?"

"Look, the photographer who came to me said it was absolutely happening and the entire team knew."

"Then I don't feel bad. Fuck him." I pointed at my giant, overpacked suitcase. "Can you help me with this?"

He folded his arms over his chest. "I will not aid and abet."

Rolling my eyes, I left the suitcase on the ground and went back into the house for my guitar.

Wags trailed me into the living room. "What about taking your mom with you?"

Grabbing my guitar case from next to the piano, I faced him. "You can't be serious. My mother's idea of relaxation is mani-pedis and massages, not hikes in the woods. I'd lose my mind, and so would she."

My manager exhaled and rubbed the back of his neck. "I wish your brother was around."

"Me too," I said, heading outside again. Kevin was the only person on earth I wouldn't mind being cooped up with for two weeks. No matter how tough things had been when we were kids, growing up had been tolerable because we'd had each other. He was two years older than me, and I'd never cried harder than the day he left for boot camp. "But he's not."

Wags stood by while I opened the sliding door on the van's passenger side and placed my guitar on the floor between the seats. "You need *someone* there with you," he insisted. "Can't you take Jess?"

"She's going to Colorado with her family while I'm gone." I went back into the house with Wags at my heels. In the kitchen's roomy pantry, I scooped up one of the brown paper grocery sacks I'd packed last night and handed it to him. "Here. Make yourself useful."

Wags followed me out to the van again. "I want it on record, I did not okay this."

I placed my sack of groceries in the back. "Wags, I have done *everything* you guys have told me to do over the past five years. I recorded the songs the PMG execs said to record, worked with every chauvinistic male producer in Nashville, did back-to-back tours with no breaks and no complaints, did all the publicity the label requested, and kept my nose out of trouble, even when the haters on the internet made me want to burn shit down. I have been a *good girl*."

"You have."

"So I need this break, Wags, or I'm going to snap."

He placed his bag next to mine. "I'm not saying you don't deserve time off, Kelly Jo. You do. But if anything happened to you . . . I'd never forgive myself."

His words softened the edges of my mood. Wags wasn't my father—a devilishly handsome, charming alcoholic with a weakness for women and gambling who'd been in and out of our lives since I was six—but he'd been my manager since before I won *Nashville Next*, and he was unfailingly loyal. "Nothing will happen to me. I'll be perfectly safe."

"Kevin doesn't think so."

"Well, he's an overprotective big brother who still sees me as a kid." I went around to the back of the van and tried again to lift my suitcase, but no matter how much I struggled, I couldn't get it into the cargo space. "Wags, can you *please* help me with this?"

His lips pursed beneath his bushy brown mustache. "If I do, will you say yes to security?"

I bent over and attempted to pick up the suitcase by the wheels, groaning with the effort.

"For god's sake, stop. You're going to hurt yourself." Wags gently pushed me aside, then heaved the suitcase into the van. "What the hell is in there that's making it so heavy?"

"Clothes," I said. "Hair products. Books."

And a few toys that vibrated, but he didn't need to know that.

He slammed the tailgate and walked me to the driver's side, opening the door. "Does this thing have a full tank? You're better off not stopping until you get way outside Nashville. Chances of you being spotted might decrease the farther you get out of town. Do you even know how to pump your own gas?"

"No," I deadpanned. "But I'm sure there will be someone there I can blow to pump it for me." I poked his chest and hopped behind the wheel. "Yes, I know how to pump gas! Lord almighty, I need to get out of here. Goodbye, Wags. I'll call you when I get there. Tell my mom I said bye and not to worry about me!"

Reaching into my purse, I pulled out oversized

sunglasses and slipped them on. Then I grabbed the baseball cap on the passenger seat and placed it on my head, hiding all my red hair beneath it. After starting the engine, I rolled down the window and smiled at my manager, who still stood on the driveway with his arms crossed, looking unhappy. "See? You can't even recognize me."

He shook his head. "This is a bad idea."

"I'll take all the blame," I said as I put the window up.

Then I put my old gray minivan in gear and headed for freedom.

I was about an hour into the drive when my mother called me. I really wanted to let it go to voicemail, but I knew she would probably just keep calling, and I didn't want her to panic and call the highway patrol. The last thing I needed was photos hitting the internet of Pixie Hart being pulled over by a state trooper.

"Hello?"

"Kelly Jo Sullivan! How could you?"

"Morning, Mama. How was your night?"

"Don't change the subject. You snuck out of the house just like you used to do when you were sixteen."

"Yeah, but back then I was sneaking out to clubs. This time I'm just going on vacation."

"Wags says you fired the bodyguard."

Dammit, Wags. "I don't need him."

"Well, don't come crying to me when you're attacked by a black bear. I told you about the premonition I had, didn't I?"

I rolled my eyes. "Yes."

"Do I need to tell you again?"

"No."

"Because you know I have the sight, just like Great Aunt Sissy."

"Yes."

"And this vision was *very clear*—there was this giant black bear just towering over you, looking like he wanted to tear you apart and eat the pieces. He wasn't even going to leave a crumb!"

"Mama, I promise you, if I see a bear, I will run the other way."

"No! That's the exact wrong thing to do! I looked it up, and you should just quietly back off. If you can't, you have to make yourself look big, make loud noises, and clap your hands."

"Make myself look big?" I was five-foot-two on my best big-hair days. "Not sure that's possible."

She sighed. "Your brother's going to be furious, you know."

"I'll deal with him when he gets back."

"I've got a mind to come up there and paddle your backside for making me fret like this. I can feel

24

the wrinkles forming! And your father is beside himself with concern."

Since when? I thought.

"He says he needs to talk to you. I'll put him on."

"No, don't! I have to—"

"Kelly Jo? That you, peanut?"

I grit my teeth. "It's me, Daddy."

"I was just making breakfast and thinking about how you and I used to get up early and make waffles for your mama and Kevin. What a mess we'd make." He laughed, and the sound took me back to our tiny yellow kitchen in the house where I'd grown up. Batter spilled on the counter. Syrup on my fingers. Comfort. Security. Love. *Before.*

"I remember."

"You sign that new PMG deal yet, peanut?"

"Not yet. I'm still thinking it over."

"It's a good deal. A lot of money. What's to think about?"

"I'd like more creative control. I want to work with some different producers, more women. I want to record my own songs."

"But the label knows best, peanut. They've got all the experience. You should do what they say."

Something dark in me wondered if the label had offered my father money if he could get me to agree to their terms. "I need to concentrate on the road, Daddy. I'll see you in two weeks." *If you stick around.*

Without waiting for him to argue, I hung up and put my phone on Do Not Disturb.

The trip took me almost twelve hours, but it was still light out when I arrived at my new home for the next couple weeks—an A-frame chalet nestled deep in the woods without a single neighbor visible in any direction.

Elated with the privacy, the mild temperature, and fourteen days of freedom, I tossed my hat aside, shook out my hair, and jumped out of the van. I was giddy with excitement—I'd stopped once for gas, once for a sandwich at a drive-thru, and once for a few fresh vegetables at a roadside farm stand, and I hadn't been recognized a *single* time. Twirling in a circle, I breathed deeply, taking it all in.

The air smelled like wet dirt and dead leaves and something tangy and herbal—like the dandelions you picked when you were a kid and thought were beautiful. I used to pluck tons of them from the vacant lot near our house and give them to my mom as a "bouquet." Poor Mama would dutifully put them in a mason jar with some water every time.

The A-frame was small, its façade painted moss green and its roof—which extended all the way to the ground—was a deep orange. A wooden porch ran the width of the front, with two rocking chairs to one side of the door and a large potted plant on the other.

Glancing to the left, I noted a fire pit surrounded

by four red Adirondack chairs. I wondered if I could figure out how to build a fire without accidentally burning down the house.

I approached the front door and quickly checked my email to find the code the rental company had provided to Jess, which she'd then forwarded to me. Punching in the numbers, the lock released and I opened the door.

Unlike my home in Nashville, which had been newly decorated in soothing whites and pale grays when I bought it, this place offered only comfy shades of brown. Knotty pine walls, coffee-colored couch, russet brick hearth, carpet the color of sand. I sniffed—it smelled slightly musty. Since the place had a screen door, I left the wooden front door open and cranked open the casement windows on either side of it to air out the room.

Straight ahead was a galley kitchen that would have fit within the breakfast nook of my Nashville home—just a dishwasher, a stainless sink, and a brown electric range that looked like it predated me. A butcher-block-topped peninsula jutted out from the wall, and two stools were tucked beneath it.

I wandered down the hall and found the bathroom on one side and the bedroom on the other. The white and yellow bathroom wasn't fancy, but it was bright and clean, and the towels folded on the vanity looked thick and fluffy. The bedroom was small, and the steep pitch of the knotty pine wall opposite the door made it seem even more confined, like a cross between a treehouse and a teepee.

The queen-sized bed had no headboard, but it was covered with puffy white bedding and plenty of pillows. The window above it looked out into the woods. Kneeling on the mattress, I cranked it open, smiling when I felt the fresh, cool air come through the screen and caress my face.

It wasn't the Ritz Carlton, but I didn't care.

I didn't need an ocean view or overpriced minibar or room service to relax. Happy with my cozy little hideaway, I hummed a tune as I headed outside to bring in my bags. (It took me a couple tries to get that damn suitcase out of the van, but I managed.)

After unpacking groceries, clothing, and toiletries, I stuck one vibrator under the bed and the other one in the shower, and traded my denim cutoffs, white T-shirt, and boots for running shorts, a sports bra, and Nikes. In the bathroom, I tightened my ponytail and smeared a little sunscreen on my face and arms. I was just about to stick my earbuds in and head out for a run when I realized I hadn't let anyone know I'd arrived safely.

I picked up my phone and noticed I'd gotten several text messages while I was on the road. One from Jess, one from Wags, and three from my mother, all wanting to know how the drive was. There was one from my stylist, Kayla, asking me to put a few fittings on the calendar. And I had two voicemails—one from Duke (which I deleted without listening to), and one from my dad. I wanted *so badly* to be able to delete that one too, but I couldn't. It was like no matter how old I got or how many times he disappointed me, there was a little girl inside me who held out hope every single time that he'd somehow magically become the daddy I wanted.

I took a breath and played it.

"Hi, peanut. I know you don't want to be bothered on your trip, so I won't keep you, but I didn't get a chance when we were on the phone earlier to remind you about that loan. I've got this new thing going that's gonna be huge, and I'm getting in on the ground floor. I won't bore you with all the details, but if you could just send me a check for, oh, twenty thousand—maybe make it twenty-five—that should be good. Thanks, peanut. You're my best girl."

I kept listening for a few seconds, almost like I expected something more, but of course, there was nothing else. He just wanted money, same as always.

I deleted the message. Took a deep breath. Counted to ten.

After I replied to my stylist, saying I'd add the fittings to my schedule and reminding her I was on vacation for two weeks, I sent a note to Jess.

> I made it! Got in about half an hour ago, and all is well.

> Yay! Place okay? I know it's definitely not the five-star hotels you're used to but you said you wanted something rustic where no one would find you!

29

> You did a great job! It's perfect. Small, hidden away, definitely rustic, but clean and cozy. I love it.

> Good. Enjoy your time off!

> You too!

Next, I texted Wags and my mom together.

> I'm here. I'm fine. I'm happy. No sign of bears or even humans nearby.

> I'm keeping my phone on Do Not Disturb so I can commune with nature, but I'll call you tomorrow. Don't worry about me.

Immediately, Wags liked my initial message and typed one back.

> I'll worry anyway, but thanks for letting me know, and keep in touch.

My mother replied with this:

> What about wolves? Google says Michigan has wolves. And something called a gray rat snake.

I shuddered. Gray rat snake?

I did not like the sound of that one little bit. Should I Google it just so I'd know what I was up against? I nearly typed the words into my phone, then I decided against it—better not to know.

I pushed open the door and stepped out onto the front porch, gingerly looking this way and that for any sign of slithering, and shrieking when a small brown bird landed in front of me. The bird flew away, and I laughed at myself. Taking a moment to snap a bunch of selfies, I chose the one I liked best and posted it for my nearly four million followers. *Grateful for the sun on my face,* I wrote.

Hopping off the porch, I spied a trail leading through the trees and followed it at an easy pace. In my ears was my favorite playlist, a mix of current and vintage country music stars, all women, all iconic, all badasses. As I worked up a sweat, I tried to channel some of their confidence and positive energy.

The truth was, the criticism of me and my music bothered me more than I let on. I hated being called a reality show hack, a sellout, pop-country window dressing. I hated that I'd let people tell me my real name was boring. I hated that in order to get ahead in this industry, you had to be a brand, not just a musician. I hated that I was starting to feel entirely manufactured.

I wanted to feel like my younger self again—the girl who stayed up late writing songs with a flashlight under the covers when she was supposed to be asleep. Those songs had meant something to me. Those songs were where I buried my deepest hurt, expressed my greatest joy, and dreamed my wildest dreams.

I wanted that girl's voice to be heard.

The trail ended at some kind of river or creek, and even though I was hot and sweaty, the water looked sort of green and scary. With visions of a slimy gray rat snake in my mind, I decided not to risk a swim and turned for home again. It was while I was on my way back that a song idea came to me—not fully formed or anything, just a few scraps of lyrics, a three-quarter time signature, and some chord changes I hadn't played with before.

I was so excited, I didn't even stop to wipe off the sweat, I just grabbed my guitar and a piece of paper. After scribbling down some notes, I recorded myself messing around with the chords and rhythm. It wasn't perfect, but when I played it back for myself I was happy. It was a good start.

My stomach growled as I stripped off my running clothes, and I realized I hadn't eaten in nearly eight hours. Between what I'd brought from home and my stop at the farm stand, I had enough on hand to make a nice little pasta dinner for myself. I'd even packed a bottle of wine. Tomorrow, I'd drive into town and stock up.

While I was in the shower, I kept trying out

different lyrics, and while I was rinsing the conditioner from my hair, the perfect lines came to me. Frantic to write them down, I jumped out of the shower and bolted from the bathroom naked.

That's when I discovered the bearded lummox in my living room.

CHAPTER THREE

xander

THE GIRL HAD SOME *PIPES*.

Her scream was so loud, you'd have thought I came after her with an axe. (Did I mention I know how to throw an axe?)

She also had a smokin' hot body with plenty of curves, and her long wet hair was clinging to her bare skin like vines. As quickly as I could react, I turned around and held up my hands so she wouldn't think I was there to harm her.

But the high-pitched shrieking continued as she ran back into the bathroom and slammed the door.

Then silence.

Except that my ears were ringing.

Tentatively, I turned around and called out. "Kelly Jo Sullivan?"

"Go away!"

"My name is Xander Buckley, I'm—"

"I know who you are—the bodyguard! And I already fired you, so *go away!*"

I moved closer to the bathroom door, so I wouldn't have to yell. "I can't do that."

Kelly, on the other hand, continued to shout. "Why not?"

"I made your brother a promise."

"What promise?"

"That I wouldn't leave no matter how hard you tried to make me."

"Damn him," she muttered quietly. Then louder, "What's he paying you to be here? I'll pay you double to leave!"

"He's not paying me."

"Then why are you here?"

"Because I owe him a favor." I paused. "Actually, I owe him my life."

A few seconds of silence passed. "What?"

"Six years ago, he saved my life in Afghanistan, and I've been waiting for the chance to repay the debt."

The bathroom door flew open. She'd wrapped one white towel around her head and a second around her body, which she held in place with stiff wooden-soldier arms. It struck me how much prettier she was without any makeup on. I noticed the ginger lashes and the dusting of freckles across her nose and cheeks, like cinnamon on whipped cream.

"Well, *I* am not that chance," she declared, lifting her chin. "So you can just march yourself right on out of here and wait for the next one." She pointed a finger toward the front door. Her nails were unpainted and trimmed short.

Exhaling, I shook my head. "I'm afraid I can't do that."

"Then I'm calling the cops," she announced imperiously.

"How? This place has no phone, and you left yours sitting over there on the couch." I jerked my thumb over one shoulder. "If I was a real threat, you'd be in big trouble."

Her emerald eyes blazed with fury. "This is breaking and entering!"

"I didn't break anything," I informed her calmly. "The door was unlocked, and every window in the place is open. You couldn't get any less secure if you tried."

She pursed her lips together and drew herself up with a deep inhale. "The fact remains. I don't want you here."

"Here's another fact that remains." I crossed my arms over my chest. "I'm not leaving."

We stood there in a stalemate for a solid twenty seconds, neither one of us willing to budge.

Finally, she shook her head. "I can't believe my brother would do this to me."

"What, try to keep you safe?"

"No! Stick me with a big, hairy jerk on my vacation!"

"I'm not a jerk," I told her. "I'm not even that hairy. And if you'd just give me a chance, I think you'll like me." I gave her my most winning smile, with just a hint of smolder. "Most people do."

She rolled her eyes. "Look, I appreciate that you

want to repay my brother and all, but he's overreacting. I'm not Taylor Swift. I don't need you."

"And I appreciate that you'd rather not have me around, but I gave my word to your brother, and I intend to keep it."

"Just because my brother trusts you doesn't mean I do!" She stamped her bare foot. "I am in a no-trust zone right now."

"I heard about the breach with your former security team. And that one of them is trying to sue you. All the more reason you need protection."

"It's not just that. I'm sick and tired of being pushed around and treated like my feelings don't matter." She was so worked up, her towel came loose, and she struggled to keep it in place.

I held up my hands. "I'm not here to push you around."

"Ha! Just the sight of you is nothing but a giant, tattooed reminder that I can't call the shots in my own life."

"I'm sorry to hear that. But for the next two weeks, you're stuck with me."

She took a breath and tried a different tactic. "Well, you'll have to sleep in your car, because there's only one bed."

"What about the couch?"

"Out of the question. This place is too small to share."

"Do I get bathroom privileges?"

"No. Find a tree."

I shrugged, pretty sure she was bluffing.

"And I don't want to see you creeping at the windows either. No spying on me."

"I'm not a spy, Kelly."

"Whatever. For my brother's sake, I will attempt to tolerate your presence as a sort of *guard dog*," she said, making it clear that was not a compliment, "but you will be an outdoor dog, is that clear?"

"Perfectly." Never in my life had I wanted to walk out on a job so badly, but I'd given Sully my word. Turning around, I pushed open the front door. "I'll be outside."

"Get used to it."

Jesus. This was country music's sweetheart?

I went out the door and assessed the outside of the place, noting all the doors and windows. I'd already looked up the address on Google maps and knew there were no close neighbors on any side. Then I looked over the gray minivan parked next to the house. When I'd seen it, I couldn't believe that was what Pixie Hart was driving. I'd been expecting a cute little convertible or some kind of pricey foreign car. Peering into the back, I wondered if it would be more comfortable to sleep in than my SUV. Had I known there wouldn't even be a couch to crash on, I'd have at least brought a tent.

For now, I decided to park myself on one of the rocking chairs next to the front door and try not to think about the fact that I'd seen her naked.

Wet and naked.

I shoved the image from my mind and dropped into a chair. As the sun began to sink behind the trees, I stretched out my legs and clasped my hands on my chest, running through my task list for the bar. I'd emailed everything to Veronica earlier, given her all the contact info, let her know when the beer and liquor distributors were coming, when the A/V guys would be there, when the final inspection would happen.

Thankfully, I already had bartenders, servers, and a chef lined up, but I was still going over applications for barbacks and other kitchen staff. It could probably wait until after the soft opening, but maybe I'd ask Veronica to look over the applications just in case there was anyone with awesome experience we didn't want to lose.

From inside, I heard a hair dryer running for a few minutes. After that, I heard the pop of a cork from a wine bottle, pots and pans clanking in the kitchen, and then music. Pretty soon, the smell of something good began wafting through the screens— something Italian maybe, with tomatoes and garlic and basil. I'd eaten a late lunch but no dinner, and my stomach started to growl. Dammit, why hadn't I brought a snack?

This whole thing had been so rushed, I hadn't been able to think straight while I was packing. To distract myself from hunger pangs, I went to my car and grabbed my laptop. Back in my rocking chair, I opened up my computer and realized I needed to ask her if this cabin had Wi-Fi.

Setting my computer aside, I stood up and peered through the screen door. She stood at the stove with her back to me, and the music was so loud, she didn't hear my knock. Opening the door, I poked my head inside. "Excuse me," I called.

She turned around and shrieked. "You scared me!"

"Sorry." Whatever she was making smelled so good, my mouth watered. "I knocked, but you didn't hear it. I just wondered if this place had Wi-Fi."

"Oh." She wiped her hands on a towel. "I think so. Hang on."

I closed the door and sat down in the rocking chair again, pulling my laptop onto my thighs. A moment later she came out onto the porch. "It's this," she said, holding her cell phone so I could see the screen.

I found the network and typed in the password. "Thanks."

For a moment, she just stood there, watching me. She was barefoot, wearing very short shorts and a black tank top with some writing on the front, which I didn't read because I did not want to be caught *spying* on her breasts.

(But for the record, they were a good size for someone so small—I'd even say pleasantly plump— and since I'd seen her naked, I knew her nipples were pale pink.)

"Do you need something?" I asked, without looking up from my screen.

"No." She remained where she stood, fidgeting a little. "Are you emailing my brother to tattle on me?"

If I'd have been in a better mood, I might have laughed. "No. I'm working."

"Oh yeah?" She sounded interested. "What do you do when you're not invading other people's vacation space and calling it security?"

"I'm not even in private security anymore. I own a bar. But it's not open yet."

"What kind of bar is it?"

"A sports bar."

"Of course it is."

I finally looked up at her. The dying sun lit her from behind, giving her red hair a hazy golden halo. "What's that mean?"

"Nothing." She shrugged. "You just look like the sports bar type."

"And what type is that?"

"Tall, muscular, varsity jacket in your closet. You know . . . sporty." A smile played on her lips. "I bet you really like playing with your balls."

I focused on my screen again.

She laughed, and it was a nice sound. Deeper and rustier than you'd expect from someone her size. "Oh, come on, I'm teasing. Are you hungry?" she asked.

"No," I said, pride talking over my ravenous stomach. Right away, my stomach chose revenge by groaning *very* loudly.

"I think your belly disagrees." She gestured toward the house. "Do you want to come in and eat with me?"

"And invade your vacation space? I wouldn't dare."

She held up her hands. "Let's call a truce so you don't waste away out here."

"No, thanks."

For a second, she seemed startled that I'd turned her down. Then she shrugged. "Okay. Suit yourself."

An apology was on the tip of my tongue—why was I letting her get to me like this?—but she went back into the house without another word.

So it surprised me when, a few minutes later, she came out with a bowl heaped with pasta in red sauce, topped with Parmesan cheese and a sprig of basil. She set the bowl at my feet along with a napkin and fork. "Here."

I glanced down at it. "Is that my doggie bowl?"

"You don't want it?" She bent down and picked it up again.

"I didn't say I didn't want it."

"So you *do* want it?"

"Yes."

She tilted her head, like something had just occurred to her. "How bad?"

"What?"

"How bad do you want it?"

I swallowed hard. *So bad.* "I don't know."

"Does it look good to you?"

"Yes."

"Does it smell good?" She sort of swung the bowl past my face, so the aroma of tomatoes and garlic and basil wafted toward me.

43

"Yes."

"It tastes good too," she said, almost flirtatiously. "I bet you haven't eaten in a while."

I was starting to sweat. Were we still talking about food? "What do you want me to say, Kelly? Please?"

"Hmm. Please is nice, but I was thinking maybe you could beg."

"Beg? Like, on my knees?"

"Oh, good idea." Smiling, she brandished the pasta again. "You want this, you get on your knees and beg."

She had a huge grin on her face, and yet I couldn't tell if she was joking. "I'm not getting on my knees for spaghetti, Kelly. Is this some kind of game?"

"What, you don't like being told that you can't have what you want unless you do it on someone else's terms?" Her eyes pinned mine, driving home her point.

I opened my mouth to argue, then snapped it shut. Focused on my screen again. "Forget it. I'm not hungry."

She stood there for another moment, saying nothing. Then she bent down, put the bowl at my feet again, and went into the house.

I thought about not eating it to make a point, but after precisely five seconds, I picked it up and scarfed down every single bite.

It was delicious.

I decided I would have begged.

44

CHAPTER FOUR

I COULDN'T BELIEVE I'd said that.

Beg on his knees?

What was *wrong* with me?

I made a beeline for the kitchen counter and picked up my glass of wine. Took a huge gulp.

Within seconds, I heard his fork clanking on the bowl out on the porch. It made me smile. Guess he was hungry after all.

Why did men have to be so stubborn? Did he really prefer eating alone on the porch with his food on his lap to sitting in here at the counter with me? Or had he rejected my offer for spite?

It was only because he'd given me so much attitude that I'd snapped. I wasn't even a temperamental person by nature. Passionate, sure. Feisty? Sometimes. Tenacious? Always. Despite the fact that I was scared to stand up to my label, I wouldn't have gotten this far without *some* spunk. But when you had to keep saying yes when you wanted to say no, swallow your opinions, and hold back your real feelings much of the time, they got all bottled up. The pressure built.

Just now, it had exploded.

But darn it, Xander didn't belong here! I'd wanted to be by myself. He'd let himself into my vacation home like he had the right. He'd announced he was staying like I had no choice in the matter.

He'd seen me naked.

I shivered on the stool, recalling the shock and humiliation of running into him in the living room wearing nothing but my birthday suit. I'd hightailed it back into the bathroom as fast as possible, but there was no doubt he'd gotten a good look.

I wonder how he'd react if I suggested he get naked and let me look at him just to even things out. Then I smiled, figuring he'd probably do it. I'd only known Xander Buckley for a couple hours, but something told me modesty was not his thing.

Still, as I finished my glass of wine, my conscience continued to nag me. I'd been rude, and that wasn't my style. It wasn't how Mama had raised me. *You don't need money to have class*, she always said. (Although now that we had money, she admitted having both was more fun.)

I supposed she'd be glad to know the lummox was here. So would Kevin, Wags, Jess, Kayla, and the rest of my team. I finished my glass of wine, picked up my phone, and sent a note to my brother.

I know you won't get this for a while, but your big beardy babysitter arrived and refuses to leave. Congratulations, you won this round.

I also sent texts to my mom, Jess, Kayla, and Wags, filling them in and letting them know that while I wasn't too happy about it, the guy was staying.

While my phone was still in my hand, I got a call from my dad. I nearly rejected it, but then I felt guilty. Maybe taking his call would serve as penance for telling Xander to bark like a dog.

"Hello?"

"Hey there, Pixie girl."

It took me a second. "Duke?"

"Surprise."

"Why are you calling me from my dad's phone?"

"We got together for a beer tonight for old times' sake. He said you're on vacation up north by yourself. We're both worried about you. Everything okay?"

"You got together for a beer with my dad?" The back of my neck prickled. My father had always been dazzled by Duke's fame and money and success, and therefore in favor of our relationship, but I'd had no idea they were drinking buddies.

"We've kept in touch," Duke said casually. "He reached out, said he was back in town, and I invited him over. We've had a nice time catching up."

Of course, said a cynical voice in my head. Of

course my father would keep in touch with my ex. Duke was probably giving him money for information about my whereabouts.

Thankfully, I hadn't told my parents my exact location—only Jess knew that. She wouldn't give Duke the time of day, let alone say anything about where I was. She'd been with me throughout the entire toxic relationship, and she couldn't stand him.

"What do you want, Duke?"

"I'm worried about you, baby. You should have told me you wanted to go on vacation. I'd have taken you to the farm, or my place in the mountains. I remember how much you liked that house."

"I'm good where I am."

"But are you sure it's safe there, sweetheart? Your dad told me about the trouble with the previous security team. Unbelievable. Didn't PMG vet those guys?"

"Not well enough, apparently. I have to go, Duke."

"That never would have happened if I'd been around. And who's this military prick your brother hired to provide security on your trip?"

My blood simmered. *Damn you, Daddy.* "He's not a prick. He's a friend of Kevin's."

"Listen, when you get back, let's get together, okay? I think this separation has gone on long enough."

"It's not a separation. We broke up."

He laughed. "Come on, Pix. Nothing's over 'til it's over, you know?"

It's over, Duke. It's been over. But as usual, it was like talking to a brick wall. "Goodbye, Duke."

I ended the call and sat there fuming for a minute. I didn't know who I was more mad at—my father, for colluding with my ex; Duke, for using my father to get to me; Kevin, for sticking me with Xander; or Xander himself for refusing to leave me alone. It felt like they were all on the other side of the room conspiring against me. Everyone knew better than I did. Everyone wanted a say.

No one was in my corner.

But while I was cleaning up the kitchen, I had a thought—maybe one of them could be persuaded to join my side. Maybe Xander and I could make a deal.

Determined to play nice, I went out to the porch. The sky was dark, and it was cool enough to raise goose pimples on my arms. Xander still sat with his laptop open, his expression serious as he studied the screen. His bowl and fork were resting on the second rocking chair. I smiled—not only was the bowl empty, but licked clean. There wasn't a single spot of tomato sauce left behind.

I hid a smile as I picked it up. "Did you like the pasta?"

"Yes. Thank you." Still no eye contact.

"Look, Xander, I'm sorry about earlier."

"No need to apologize."

I stood in front of him, holding the bowl against my stomach. "I just wanted to be alone up here, have two weeks of vacation like a normal person, and it's frustrating that no one will let me."

49

"I understand."

"And I'm guessing you don't really want to be here either, what with your bar opening soon and all."

He remained silent without looking up from his screen, so I assumed I was right—he didn't want to be here any more than I wanted him around. He was only doing this for Kevin.

"But since I'm stuck with you and you're stuck with me, maybe we could make a deal—you sort of leave me alone to do what I please, and I won't make you sleep outside. You can have the couch."

He finally shut the laptop and looked up at me. In the darkness, I couldn't really read his eyes—what color were they again? Brown? He was very handsome, I had to admit. Strong jawline, thick dark hair, wide, sensual mouth. I just didn't like what came out of it next.

"I don't think so."

"Why not?"

"That couch is really short." He folded his arms across his tanker chest. "I'd probably be more comfortable outside anyway. Or," he said, like he'd just thought of it, "in the bed."

"The bed!" Heat flooded my face. "Where am *I* supposed to sleep?"

"We could share it," he said, like it was obvious.

Outraged, I touched my collarbone, as if clutching my invisible pearls. "I'm not sharing my bed with you."

"Why not?"

"You're a complete stranger! Plus, you're huge! You'd take up all the space!"

He smiled and shrugged those massive shoulders. "Then I guess we can't make a deal."

Infuriated, I yanked the door open and went back inside.

I stuck his dishes in the dishwasher, used the bathroom, and shut myself in my room, making sure to slam a door whenever I had the opportunity. I undressed, tugged on an old T-shirt, and got into bed. Then I waited, staring at the sloping ceiling in the dark, listening for him to come in and use the bathroom.

But instead of hearing the screen door creak open, I heard footsteps through the window above my head, as if he was heading into the woods behind the house. Without hesitation, I popped onto my knees and peered out the window over the bed, my fingertips and chin on the sill. Through the screen, I saw him loping toward a nearby tree just at the edge of the clearing. He stopped with his back to me, plainly visible in the moonlight from my window. Spread his legs.

I gasped. He wouldn't.

I leaned closer to the screen, so close my nose touched it, so close I heard the zipper from his jeans going down.

Below the short sleeves of his dark T-shirt, his forearms and hands disappeared in front of him. I counted to twenty before I saw him do the shake, bobbing once on his heels before tucking himself back into his jeans and zipping up. When he turned around, he was facing me.

I dropped so fast, I banged my chin on the sill, then flopped onto my back, eyes wide open, heart pounding. Had he seen me watching him? No, it was completely dark in my room—he couldn't see in, could he?

I listened to his fading footsteps on the gravel as he walked back to the front of the house. Then I heard him let himself in and shut the door.

After that, it was silent—he must have decided to take the couch.

I lay there, rubbing my smarting chin, wondering about the tall, ship-shouldered bodyguard with the dark hair, inked-up arms, and chiseled jaw. Questions poked at my brain.

Was he single? What did he look like naked? What was he like in bed? Was he hot but selfish? Eager but clueless? Slow and thorough? Fast and rough? Those big hands . . . did he know how to use them? Parts of my body began to tingle beneath the sheets, and I thought about the vibrator under my bed.

No way—I couldn't risk it.

Instead, I grabbed my phone and Googled him. It took a bit of scrolling, but I finally found an article in a local paper about a former Navy SEAL named Xander Buckley who was restoring a decrepit old place called Tiki Tom's into a high-end sports bar called Buckley's Pub in the town of Cherry Tree Harbor. There were a few quotes from Xander and his brother, Austin, who was helping him with the renovation, and a photo of the two of them as well. I zoomed in, studying them both.

They looked alike, although Xander was smiling broadly for the camera and Austin had a more serious expression. Xander was also a little taller and broader through the back and shoulders. I wondered if his brother was older or younger, and if they were close. I wondered if Cherry Tree Harbor was home to him, and how far away it was. I wondered how well Kevin knew him and why my brother trusted him so much. Was it possible I could trust him too? I glanced at the empty space beside me.

Suddenly weary from the long day, I set my phone aside and lay back. As I drifted off to sleep, one last question popped into my head.

There were literally a hundred trees surrounding this place.

Had he chosen the one closest to my bedroom on purpose?

CHAPTER FIVE

xander

OF COURSE I DID.

CHAPTER SIX

WHEN I OPENED my eyes and checked my phone the next morning, it was just after eight. Sunlight streamed through the window above my head.

I smiled and stretched, realizing I could go back to sleep if I wanted, grab a book and read in bed, or take a cup of coffee outside and sit in the—

Shit! Coffee!

I flopped an arm over my head and groaned. I'd forgotten to pack coffee. Was there somewhere nearby I could grab a cup? Or should I just skip the lazy morning and go grocery shopping first thing? That way I could have my afternoon free, and it looked like it would be a gorgeous day.

Hauling myself out of bed, I threw on shorts and a tank top, pulled a hoodie on over it, and tugged on socks and sneakers. I loved my cherry red Lucchese boots more than anything, but since I was trying to go incognito for the next two weeks, I thought sneakers were a safer choice. I got recognized in those boots all the time.

Opening my bedroom door, I peeked toward the living room, but the couch wasn't visible. Quickly, I darted across the hall into the bathroom. When I was presentable—hair in a neat ponytail, a little concealer and mascara—I ambled casually toward the living room, uncomfortable with the way my pulse had quickened at the thought of seeing him asleep on the couch. Would he be shirtless? Was his chest all inked up like his arms? Were we still mad at each other?

But he wasn't there.

A black duffel bag was on the floor at one end of the couch, so I knew he had to be somewhere around here. I glanced toward the kitchen, but he wasn't there either. Pushing open the front door, I found him sitting in the same rocking chair as yesterday, looking at his phone.

"Morning," I said, my voice like sandpaper.

"Morning." He looked up at me. "Sleep okay?"

His eyes *were* brown. A deep, dark chocolate brown, framed with thick black lashes.

"Uh, yes," I said, clearing my throat. "I slept fine. You?"

"I've had better nights. But I've also had a lot worse." He stifled a yawn. "I could use some coffee."

"Me too. But I don't have any here—I forgot to pack it."

"Want to grab some in town?"

"Definitely," I said, glad he didn't seem to hold a grudge. "Let me get my purse."

He rose to his feet. "Would it be all right if I used the bathroom to brush my teeth?"

"It's fine." I went into the house, and he followed me, grabbing a small pouch from the black bag on the floor. That's when I blurted, "You could have used it last night, you know."

He straightened up and shrugged. "You said yesterday I didn't have bathroom privileges. I didn't want to assume anything."

"Well, just use the bathroom from now on, instead of a tree like some caveman."

He smirked. "Are you saying you didn't enjoy the view?"

My mouth fell open and heat rushed my cheeks.

"Funny that *you* were the one worried about spying." He gave my earlobe a little flick—a move straight out of the Older Brother's Handbook—and disappeared into the bathroom, closing the door behind him.

Snatching my purse off the kitchen counter, I stomped outside and shoved my oversized sunglasses on. Was it going to be like this for two weeks, him constantly antagonizing me? And then me trying to even the score?

Speaking of which.

I spotted my minivan parked there in the sunshine and got an idea.

A crazy, delightfully wicked idea that would drive Xander *nuts*.

Without stopping to think twice, I raced for my getaway car, started the engine, and peeled out, my

59

tires spitting gravel. I wound my way at a faster speed than was advisable down the driveway to the main road and turned right, even though I had no fucking clue where I was going.

Didn't matter—I'd ditched him! I'd won a battle!

I put all the windows down and cranked up the volume on the radio, taking it as a good sign that Shania Twain was on. With two hands on the wheel and my foot heavy on the gas, I sang along as loud as I could, bouncing up and down in the seat. When I reached the main highway, intuition told me to turn right again, and about half a mile up, I spotted a shopping plaza. On the off chance there might be a coffee shop among the stores, I pulled into the parking lot.

My spidey sense paid off when I spied the Starbucks mermaid. Gleeful with the joy of impending caffeine and having successfully evaded Xander, I parked my minivan and hopped out, strutting toward the coffee shop like a badass.

At the counter, I ordered a venti medium roast and paid for it with cash. "Thanks," I said as the teenage barista handed it over.

"You're welcome," she said. "Has anyone ever told you that you look like Pixie Hart?"

"A few times," I said with a wink.

Her eyes widened. "Oh my God."

I put my fingers to my lips and dropped a five-dollar bill in the tip jar. "Have a good one."

"Thanks," she said breathlessly.

With a smile on my face, I turned around to leave

and ran smack into a cement wall—Xander. I looked up at the scowl peeking through the dark beard. "Hey! You're lucky I didn't spill my coffee!"

"You're lucky I don't dump it over your head right now," he said through his teeth. He resembled a very large, very angry black bear—maybe my mom's premonition was right. He did sort of look like he wanted to tear me apart and eat the pieces. "You can't do that."

"I didn't do anything except go get a cup of coffee. And look!" Triumphant, I glanced around the busy shop. "Nothing happened!"

"Excuse me, Pixie?" The barista appeared at my side holding a napkin and a marker. "Could you sign this for me? My name's Lila. I'm a total Hart Throb."

"Sure." I handed Xander my coffee cup. "Can you hold this please?"

He grimaced, but he wrapped his big paw around my fingers and took the cup from me. I ignored the zing that shot up my arm at his touch.

After I scribbled my name, dotting the i's with hearts, I handed the napkin and marker back to her. "There you go, Lila."

"And could we get a selfie?"

"No pictures," Xander ordered.

Lila looked crushed.

"It's fine," I told him.

He inhaled through his nostrils, looking like an angry bull. "Your call, but I'd advise against it."

Ignoring him, I posed for the photo and smiled at the girl. "Nice meeting you. Take care." Turning to

Xander, I reached for my coffee, but he held it up high, well out of my reach. I jumped a few times, attempting to get a hand around the cup. "Hey! Give that back!"

"No," he said. "You're going to wait for me."

"You're holding my coffee hostage?"

"Yes." He ordered a venti dark roast and breakfast sandwich, and only when it was all in his hands did he return my caffeine.

"Rude," I huffed, hugging my coffee close as we moved for the exit.

"You sneak off on me, putting yourself in jeopardy and my promise to your brother at risk of being broken, and I'm the bad guy?" Xander shook his head as he held the door open for me.

"I was just having some fun," I said, stepping out onto the sidewalk. "What's the big deal?"

"The big deal is that I can't protect you if I'm not there." Xander looked both ways and then gestured for me to cross the lot toward my van. "I thought I could trust you for two minutes. Guess I was wrong."

"I'm sorry," I said. "I was just playing with you."

"This isn't a game, Kelly. We have to be able to trust each other. Or else the next two weeks are just going to be miserable for both of us. I can't be worried you're going to run off every time my back is turned."

"And I don't want to be told no every time I want to do something fun."

"I understand that, but you have to let me do my job," he said as we reached my van.

"How'd you find me anyway?"

"I fucking followed you." He frowned, his forehead wrinkling. "And the fact that you didn't notice makes me even more concerned."

"I wasn't looking," I said defensively. "I was just enjoying the ride."

"And when that *Hart Throb* posts her picture on social media and it's obvious to anyone that she met you at work, how long do you think before photographers realize where you are and show up here looking for you? Do you enjoy being followed with cameras?"

He was right. I'd probably blown my cover. "There are a gazillion Starbucks," I argued weakly.

"Kelly."

"Okay, okay." I gave him two thumps on the chest. Felt like granite under my hand. "Let's stop fighting. I won't take off again."

"Thank you." He opened the driver's side door for me, and I slid in behind the wheel.

"I need to go grocery shopping," I told him. "Should we do it now?"

"Yeah. Might be good to do it early—stores will be less crowded. But we need to talk about kitchen privileges." He held up the bag containing his breakfast sandwich. "I can't do this for every meal."

I tapped my lips with one finger, taking much longer than necessary to consider the issue. "Fine. You can have kitchen privileges."

"And I'll eventually need to take a shower."

Another deep drag of air and dramatic sigh. "Shower privileges too."

"I'll check for the nearest store on my phone and then I'll text you the location and directions. Don't leave without me."

I saluted. "Yes, sir."

He shut the van door and walked toward his SUV, parked across from me.

I watched him in the sideview mirror. "Xander Buckley, you totally ruined my plans," I murmured, taking a sip of my coffee. "But I gotta admit, you have a nice butt."

As he tucked his long, muscular body into the driver's seat of his car, I found myself thinking about those shower privileges. About him naked in my bathroom. Hot and wet.

I didn't hate the idea.

When we got back to the house after grocery shopping, I realized I'd forgotten the code for the front door. While Xander stood holding four grocery bags in his arms, I tried a few different number combinations I thought it might be, but nothing was right.

I turned to him sheepishly. "I forgot it."

"So now what?"

"I have to check my email." I dug through my purse for my phone and discovered it wasn't in there. "Shoot. You know what? I was so excited to escape you this morning, I guess I ran out without it."

Xander sighed heavily, setting down the grocery bags and reaching into his back pocket. "Can you log in on my phone?"

"Yes." I took his phone, logged into my account through the app, and located the forwarded email from Jess. Once the door was open, I handed his phone back to him. "Success!"

He looked at the screen and frowned. "You didn't log out."

"Do I need to? Are you going to steal my identity or something?"

That earned me a scathing glare. "Any time you log in on someone else's device, you should log out. Are you changing your passwords frequently enough?"

"Define 'enough.'"

"Every three months."

"Then no."

Grumbling, he tucked his phone back into his pocket and picked up the bags again.

After we put the groceries away, I found a blender in one of the cupboards and made myself a smoothie. Feeling magnanimous, I even offered one to Xander, who was back in his front porch office, but he declined. I noticed he'd kept his groceries separate from mine—he had his own little section in the fridge and kept the other stuff in plastic bags at one end of the counter.

Ridiculous. Did he think I was going to steal his eggs? His protein bars? Maybe he was worried I'd get my hands on his salami.

That actually made me laugh.

Smoothie in hand, I packed a bag with some sunscreen, a floppy hat, a beach towel, my notebook full of lyrics, a pencil, and a paperback. Then I went out to one of the Adirondack chairs at the side of the house and stretched out the towel.

After spraying myself down with SPF 50, I spent the next several hours happily reading romance in the sunshine. I only looked up when a huge shadow fell across my face.

Xander stood between me and the sky. "Hey."

"You're blocking my sun," I said, sliding my sunglasses to the top of my head.

"I'm going inside to make a sandwich."

"Okay. Maybe while you're eating your lunch, I'll get my run in."

"No." He shook his head. "You're not to take a run alone. I'll go with you."

"I can't even *jog* alone? Nobody's here! I didn't see a single soul when I ran yesterday." I gestured toward the woods.

Frowning, he scanned the perimeter. "This area isn't secure. There's no gate on the driveway. I have no idea where the fences are. Anyone could be lurking around here."

"So you're just going to trot along behind me? Lurking?"

"Yes."

I lowered my shades over my eyes again. "This vacation sucks."

"Don't be so dramatic," he said. "You won't even know I'm there." A hint of a smirk. "Unless you want to race me."

"Xander! I'm not racing you! Your legs are twice as long as mine!"

"Come on, I'll give you a head start."

"You sound like Kevin—who always lied about the head starts, by the way."

"Well, I play fair." The big oaf tapped my nose. "You know, you're getting kinda pink out here."

Swatting his hand away with my book, I touched my nose—it did feel tender and hot. "Dammit, I put sunscreen on."

"Maybe you should re-apply. Or wear a hat."

"Maybe you should stop acting like my mom and go make your lunch." I watched him walk away, and only when he was inside the house did I set my book down and pull out my sunscreen. And the hat.

I re-applied my SPF, plopped the hat on my head, then took the notebook and pencil from the bag. After rereading what I'd written last night, I found I didn't love it as much and turned to a fresh page. But instead of writing down new words, all I did was doodle.

Xander came back outside carrying a plate with a sandwich on it and an energy drink. He dropped into the chair opposite me. Since I was wearing dark sunglasses and the big hat, I pretended not to look at him while I surreptitiously let my eyes wander over his wide shoulders, broad chest, and big hands wrapped around the sandwich.

"Whatcha writing?" he asked. "New song?"

"Yeah. It's called 'My Vacation was Ruined by a Big Bossy Goon.'"

He laughed. "Sing it for me."

All I'd scrawled was nonsense, including a suspicious number of X's. Disconcerted, I flipped to the next page. "I'm still working on it."

"So you write your own stuff?"

"Yes. Not that the label lets me record any of it."

"Why not?"

I pressed my lips together and started scribbling again—spirals this time, not X's. "I don't want to talk about it."

"Okay."

But words came tumbling out. "They have all these bullshit reasons, and some of them contradict each other—this song is too country, that one isn't country enough, this one won't get commercial acceptance, that one is too off brand. It's so frustrating."

"I thought you didn't want to talk about it."

"It's like no one listens to me when I'm in the room," I went on. "I've always known that to succeed, you have to dream big, but you also have to be willing to compromise. You have to listen to the people who know better than you do about what will

68

sell records. You have to say yes to them. Sign their contracts. Sing their songs. Be easy to work with—especially if you're a woman. A man makes demands, he's a boss. A woman does the same, she's a diva. Or worse."

A big flock of birds flew overhead, squawking loudly. I watched them disappear over the treetops in a perfect V.

"What demands would you make?"

"For one, to record my own songs. For another, I'd like to choose my producers. I'd like more of a say in my cover art. My video shoots. My choreography. But I'm scared to stand up for myself," I said, and suddenly I was admitting to this total stranger what I couldn't even say to Wags. "I feel like I've become something I never intended to be and don't particularly like. But if I say that, I'll sound ungrateful."

"It's not ungrateful to want a say in your career." Xander set his plate aside and folded his hands on his chest. His long legs were stretched out in front of him, crossed at the ankle.

"I know, but they have all the power. They own me and all my music. My contract is up, and everyone is pressuring me to sign the new deal, and I don't know what to do."

"Sounds like you gotta tell them all to fuck off and sing what you want. That's what I'd do."

I shook my head. "You don't understand what it's like. I'm twenty-nine already. If I started pushing back, they can just move on to the next girl singing for a few bucks at the county fair. There's a hundred of them in every small town. And they're just as pretty, just as talented, and just as hungry as I was."

His shoulders twitched. "Guess that's a risk you'd have to be willing to take."

"It's not just myself I'd put at risk, but everyone who works for me too. I feel responsible for a lot of people." As always, when I let myself think about this stuff, my stomach began to ache. "If I get dropped from the label, what happens to them?"

"It's not like they're your kids."

"Many of them are *like* family, though. And they count on me. Abandoning people who need you is selfish and disloyal."

He tilted his head. "Who told you that?"

My father, I thought. "It doesn't matter," I said. "But I can't just blow everything up."

"Then it sounds like the price is giving up your own vision and doing what the label says." He raised his arms, locking them behind his head. "But I could never do that."

"You didn't follow orders in the Navy?" I countered.

"I did, but that was different. I wanted to be an asset to my team."

I grabbed the chair arms and sat up taller. "What do you think I'm *saying*? This isn't just about me! And stop with the whole 'price of fame' stuff. I'm not asking for all the pros and none of the cons. I just want my songs to mean as much to *me* as they do someone listening. I want the jerks who say I don't deserve to be where I am to eat their words. I want the producers and executives to stop saying no to all my ideas. I want a place at the table—I don't want to be the meal."

"You should be saying all this to them, not me."

"Gee, thanks." I shoved my things in my bag. "Why didn't I think of that?"

"You don't have to get mad about it," he said, infuriatingly calm.

"I'm not mad!" Slinging my bag over my shoulder, I stomped toward the house.

CHAPTER SEVEN

xander

I WATCHED her march off in a huff and wondered if she'd revoke my house privileges for hitting a nerve.

I hadn't meant to piss her off, but if she didn't like the way her label was treating her, why did she have to stay there? Weren't there other labels? Wasn't there such a thing as being indie? Those people who worked for her could find other jobs, couldn't they?

It *was* admirable that she felt responsible for people on her team—I liked loyalty. Probably, I should have just kept my mouth shut, like she said. The last thing I wanted was for her to report back to Sully that I'd been a dick to her. When she came back out, I'd apologize.

Inside the house, she rattled around in the kitchen —I could hear plates and glass and silverware clanking through the screens—and I figured she was making lunch. I was hoping she'd come outside to eat, but she didn't.

Twenty minutes passed. Thirty.

Pretending I had to get something from my car, I wandered past the front windows and saw her seated at the counter. Ambling back to the chairs, I sat down and scrolled through emails and texts. Read the news. Watched some replays from last night's baseball game.

Still no Kelly.

Fuck. Was she really that upset? Should I go in there? Had I said anything *that bad*? All I'd really done was suggest she tell the people controlling her career what she told me. I wasn't insinuating it would be easy, just that if she wanted those things, she needed to say them. It was fucking obvious, wasn't it?

Artistic types could be so sensitive. I made a mental note never to date one.

Instead of going in search of Kelly, I pulled out my phone to call Veronica.

"Hey," I said when she picked up. "How are things going?"

"Pretty good," she chirped. "Painters are here. New dishwasher was installed. But I was expecting the electrician today, and he hasn't shown yet."

"Dammit," I muttered. Finding reliable contractors had been a nightmare. "I'll try to get ahold of him."

"I also took a look at the applications you sent me and I'll reply to your email with the ones I thought looked most promising. Do you want me to give a couple of them a call? Set up interviews?"

"Yes, please. And thank you."

"So how's it going with Pixie Hart? I saw your picture with her."

"What picture?"

"It was online this morning. I'm not sure where it was taken exactly, but you're standing in a parking lot holding coffees."

I groaned. "Goddamn it. Can you send me the link when we get off the phone?"

"Sure. Adelaide got the biggest kick out of it. She's just beside herself with excitement that she's practically breathing the same air as her favorite singer. What's she like?"

Glancing at the house, I lowered my voice. "She's, ah, slightly difficult."

"Really? She seems so sweet in interviews. So down to earth."

"Maybe she's only sweet to people she likes."

Veronica laughed. "She doesn't like you?"

"Not a bit."

"What happened to your charm and magnetism?" she teased.

"I don't know, somehow she's immune to it." I left out the part where I walked in on her naked, peed on a tree close to her bedroom window, and insulted her. "Mostly she's just pissed to have security on her vacation. Not that I blame her—the cabin she's renting is small."

"How many bedrooms?"

"One. And one bathroom."

"Wow. That *is* small, especially for two people

who just met." She giggled. "Did you cuddle up last night?"

"Hell no. After threatening to make me sleep outside, she finally offered me the couch—which is too short for me. My legs are all cramped up today."

"You'll live," Veronica said cheerfully. "Try to see things from her perspective. She was probably trying to escape from being a celebrity and just be a regular person for a couple weeks."

"But you don't get to be a regular person if you want to be famous," I insisted. "Why is that so hard to understand?"

"It's not hard to understand, but it might be hard to live that way," Veronica said gently. "Imagine being surrounded by tons of people all the time who want a piece of you, but who don't really care. That has to be strange and lonely."

"Stop taking her side," I complained, even as my heart tugged a little in Kelly's direction. "She's mean to me."

Veronica laughed. "Poor Xander. But lots of people are mean to her too. Adelaide and I were looking at her Instagram earlier, and some people are just flat-out rude in the comments."

"She's not supposed to be posting on social media anyway," I said gruffly. "But she pays no attention to anything I say. And she tried to ditch me this morning."

"She did?"

"Yes! Took off in her car when I was in the bathroom."

Veronica laughed again. "How far did she get?"

"Not far at all—a Starbucks up the road. That's where the photo you saw was taken. She got recognized inside the place, so someone probably followed us out and snapped it."

"Well, I'd love to meet her," said Veronica. "Why don't you bring her over this weekend?"

"Because we're not friends, Roni. She's just a job." I said the words, but somehow they rang a little false. I *sort of* liked her.

And dammit, I wanted her to like me.

"Well, if you change your mind, we're planning to throw some stuff on the grill around four tomorrow, and you're both more than welcome. Adelaide would lose her mind if she got to meet Pixie Hart. And at least here you know she'd be safe and maybe even stay off social media."

"I'll think about it," I said, eyeballing the front door again. "Thanks for the help at the bar. I owe you."

After we hung up, I immediately opened Instagram and looked at Pixie Hart's most recent post. It was a photo she must have taken shortly after arriving here yesterday. I groaned—the house was right behind her, the numbers above the door slightly blurry but definitely visible above her head. Her face was tilted toward the sun, her eyes closed, her cheeks flushed, her lips curved into a smile. She looked natural and radiant and happy.

At first, I didn't see anything rude in the comments at all.

U r so pretty!!!
OMG I love ur top!
ILYSM!!!

ILYSM? What the fuck did that mean? I scrolled further.

Then I saw what Veronica meant. There were terrible comments about not only her music but her body, her face, her clothes, her former relationship with Duke Pruitt. I clicked on a few more photos in her feed and saw more of the same—mostly love and praise, but also a fuck ton of rudeness. My jaw tightened and my body temperature began to rise.

Why did people think they had the right? How did these assholes get through a day without being punched in the face? What made a person think it was okay to be openly cruel like that?

And if you knew people were going to act like this, why would you continue to put yourself out there? Why open yourself up to bored, miserable jackasses who had nothing better to do than spew their hate? Was her skin thick enough to withstand it day after day?

I looked again at the photo—no makeup, no stage lights, no sequins or glitter, her freckles clearly visible —and felt sorry for her. Beneath the fame and glittery façade, she was a human being like anyone else. Was Veronica right? Was she lonely? My chest tightened.

Deciding it was my protective instincts kicking up a notch, I navigated away from her account and did a quick search for #pixiehart and #hartthrob. Sure enough, the barista from this morning had posted the selfie immediately, along with the location. I frowned as I scanned the comments.

OMG where is this exactly?

WHATTTTTT she's here???

Not me getting in my car and driving 8hrs just to meet her.

A text arrived from Veronica—the link to the photo of Kelly and me in the coffee shop parking lot. It wasn't on a fan's social media account like I thought it might be, but a tabloid website called Splash that boasted the "Latest Celebrity News, Pictures, and Gossip."

Great. Now I was gossip.

Actually, I wasn't identified in the photo, but despite Kelly's big sunglasses, she was totally recognizable. To make things worse, the shot had been taken from an angle that showed the back of the minivan . . . and her license plates. "Jesus Christ," I muttered. "Could she make finding her any easier?"

The caption read, *Country music star Pixie Hart was spotted at a Starbucks in northern Michigan with a mystery man. What will Duke say???*

I rolled my eyes. Duke could fuck right off.

I studied the picture for another minute. It had obviously been taken by a photographer with a long-range lens and then sold to Splash. It wasn't just a fan who happened to see her at Starbucks. Given the previous leak with her security, it made me wonder who all knew she was up here. And how trustworthy they were.

Exhaling, I ran a hand through my hair and stood up, heading for the house.

She wasn't in the living room, and I didn't see her in the kitchen either. For a few scary heartbeats, I wondered if I'd been so distracted out there, I hadn't noticed her sneak out in her running clothes. Had she given me the slip again?

Then I heard her strumming chords on her guitar from the direction of the bedroom. As silently as I could, I slipped down the hall and listened for a moment. She began to sing softly, and chills swept down my arms.

I recognized the song, so I knew it wasn't one of hers—something about *why'd you come in here looking like that*—but she wasn't playing it how I remembered it. Her version was slower and sadder, like she was squeezing all the joy out of it.

Feeling guilty, I swallowed hard, then raised my hand to knock. But the next second, the music stopped and I heard her say, "Fuck you, Xander Buckley."

Shit—I'd been caught eavesdropping. I dropped my arm and squared my shoulders, prepared for her to open the door and take me to task.

But instead, she just kept on talking. "You're no different than any other man in my life, trying to cage me up and tell me what I can and cannot do. Or what I should do to fix things. Well, you don't know me at all. You don't know anything."

Offended, I pressed my lips together. I was guilty of some of that stuff, but I was also kinda mad that she thought I didn't know anything. *I knew some things.*

My arm shot up again, and I almost knocked.

"And fuck you for being hot too."

My hand stopped mid-air, my knuckles an inch from the door. She thought I was hot? I grinned. So when she yanked the door open a moment later, that's what she saw—me standing there smiling with a fist raised.

She yelped and clutched her chest. "Xander! Stop lurking!"

"Sorry." Playing it cool, I dropped my hand like I hadn't heard anything. "I just came in to see when you wanted to take that run."

"Now." She was already dressed in shorts and a sports bra. "Are you ready to go?"

"I just need a minute to change."

"Well, hurry up," she said tersely, shouldering past me toward the living room without so much as brushing against my shirt.

I watched her drop to the floor between the couch and the fireplace and start some kind of stretching routine. An apology for what I'd said earlier was on the tip of my tongue, but I got distracted when she bent forward over her straight, outstretched legs. Damn, she was flexible. Her nose was between her shins. Her breasts were resting just above her knees.

She spoke without looking at me. "You said a minute. You're down to thirty seconds."

Springing into action, I strode over to my bag, grabbed some workout clothes, and went into the bathroom. After I'd swapped my jeans for sweats and boots for running shoes, I couldn't resist peeking into the shower.

Immediately, I spied the vibrator.

It was dark pink, tall and thick, and it had what looked like a long-necked rabbit curving from the base of the shaft. What the fuck was that? And how was a regular dick supposed to compete?

I glanced down at my crotch. I felt pretty good about my size and stamina, and I definitely knew my way around a woman's body, but that contraption was giving me a bit of a complex.

And how did she use it? Standing up? Lying down? Kneeling above it? My eyes closed and images swam in the darkness, my cock surging to life.

Fuck you for being hot too.

I knew exactly how she felt.

From the front of the house, the door slammed. My eyes flew open, and I yanked the shower curtain back into place and hurried outside, tossing my jeans and boots on top of my bag on the way.

She was standing on the porch, twisting her torso from right to left.

More twitching in my pants. Uncomfortable tightness.

"You shouldn't be outside alone," I told her in my bossiest voice, to remind myself what I was—and wasn't—supposed to be doing here. "Paparazzi know you're in town. There's already a photo of us from the parking lot this morning online."

She stopped moving.

"And that picture you posted to Instagram yesterday while you were standing out here? The house address was visible right above your head."

Her shoulders drooped. "Sorry."

"If you're going to post to social media—which, for the record, I don't think you should do—I need to see the picture first."

"Fine," she said quietly. Stepping off the porch, she started out at an easy jog toward the woods.

I had to adjust myself before following.

She stuck to the dirt path and maintained her pace, never once stopping to catch her breath or massage an aching muscle. She was agile and light on her feet, gracefully sidestepping any rocks or sticks or fallen tree limbs on the ground in front of her. She ran all the way to what looked like a small river or large creek, where she finally stopped and did a few stretches. Then she immediately turned around and headed back into the woods at the same steady clip without speaking to me—or even looking at me.

It was starting to drive me crazy.

I fucking wanted her attention.

So I ran a little faster, like a middle school boy who likes a girl but doesn't know how to tell her. When she sensed me gaining on her, *she* ran faster. Smiling, I increased my pace again, so that we were running side by side.

She sent me an aggravated glance, pursed her lips, and shot forward with a burst of speed that seriously impressed me. Laughing a little, I let her take the lead and keep it once more, until I noticed her energy start to lag. Just barely winded, I lengthened my stride and caught up to her again.

"Stop it," she panted.

"Stop what?"

"Racing me!"

"I'm not racing you."

Jaw clenched and eyes forward, she gave one final effort, surging ahead of me as if she'd catapulted herself from a slingshot. I hit the gas as well, until we were running side by side.

It was *totally* unfair—she probably ran three steps for every one of mine—but I loved how determined she was, like if she just kept running and praying, she might actually beat me. Her arms pumped and her face turned red and her breath came in short, loud pants. When the clearing appeared ahead of us, I dropped back, letting her burst out of the woods first.

She lost her footing trying to slow down and tumbled onto the grassy patch behind the fire pit. Ending up on her back, she splayed her arms and legs like a starfish, her chest heaving.

"You okay?" I asked as I reached her.

She nodded. "I won."

That made me smile. "You won."

"Did you let me?"

"Do you really want to know?"

"No." She squeezed her eyes shut. "I can't breathe. I'm going to die now."

I dropped to the ground beside her and draped my arms over my knees. "Not on my watch."

She popped one eye open and aimed it at me. "Would you give me mouth to mouth to save me?"

Was she fucking *flirting*? "I'd do whatever it took," I said evenly.

"Hmm." She closed both eyes again.

We stayed like that for a few minutes, just resting in silence, our hearts slowing down, our breaths lengthening. The breeze was deliciously cool on my hot skin, and it ruffled the bottom of Kelly's shorts. My eyes traveled over her body, from her small feet up her pale thighs to the curve of her hips to her bare stomach to the sweat-stained sports bra covering her breasts. Her nipples were hard. I pictured them— lemonade pink—and my parched mouth longed for a taste. I could practically feel the shape of them on my tongue, their pebbled tips brushing against my lips. When my gaze finally reached her flushed, sun-kissed face, she was looking at me.

Fuck. I glanced toward the woods. A long beat passed, during which I waited for her to accuse me (rightly) of staring at her inappropriately.

Instead, she asked a question. "So what's your story, Xander Buckley?"

"My story?"

"Yeah." She rolled to one side and propped her head on her hand. "Your story. Where'd you grow up, how many siblings do you have, were you always so bossy? Your story."

I leaned back on my elbows. "I grew up not far

from here, in a town called Cherry Tree Harbor. I have one older brother, two younger brothers, and one little sister. As far as being bossy, Austin—he's the oldest of the five of us—was *way* worse. I didn't like being told what to do, so I never told anyone else what to do. I was more rambunctious than bossy. A daredevil."

She played with a few blades of grass in front of her. "Single? Married? Girlfriend?"

"Single." I paused. "What about you?"

She peeked up at me. "You mean you haven't done your research on my personal life?"

"I did, but the truth and the internet are not the same thing."

She snorted. "They sure aren't."

"That said, I did see quite a bit about you and Duke Pruitt."

"That's been over since last Christmas. He just can't wrap his brain around the fact that I won't come back to him this time. But that's my own fault —I went back plenty of times before."

"Why?"

She twisted a few blades of grass around her fingers. "You'll think it sounds stupid."

"You don't care what I think anyway."

She almost smiled, but not quite. "Sometimes I just like the idea of having a person in my corner, you know? Of feeling like I'm not alone."

"What would sound stupid about that?"

"What's stupid is that I knew I couldn't trust him,

but I let him be my person anyway. It's embarrassing."

"How long were you together?"

"About three years. On and off."

"That's a long time."

She sighed. "He's on the same label I am, so the suits liked it. The press liked it. Our agents and publicists liked it. Fans liked to obsess about it, which is always good for business. And sometimes we got along. He could be fun, when he wasn't being an asshole."

"Fuck that. You deserve better," I told her, and I meant it.

Her eyes flicked up to mine. "Thanks."

"So is Duke the reason for the no-trust zone you mentioned? Or was it the security leak?"

She rolled to her back again and flung an arm over her eyes. "He's part of it. The leak was part of it. But the no-trust zone has been forming around me like a force field for a long time."

I wanted her to elaborate, but it didn't seem right to poke at old wounds. I decided to shift gears. "Can I ask who knew you were coming up here?"

"My assistant, my manager, my agent, my parents, Duke."

"You told Duke?"

"My father told him."

"Duke is tight with your father?"

"Apparently." That arm was still draped over her eyes, so I couldn't see her expression, but her tone told me how she felt about it. "But I don't think he knew until today."

"Okay. And all those other people—you trust them? They wouldn't leak your location to media?"

Moving her arm up to her forehead, she looked over at me. "I don't think so. Why?"

"A photograph of us from the parking lot this morning is already online. It doesn't look like just a fan photo to me, so I wondered if maybe someone who knew where you'd be let it slip—for publicity or whatever."

"Oh. I don't think so. It was probably just a random person from Starbucks." She continued to study me, then switched topics abruptly. "You have very large shoulders. And hands."

"I've been told that helped make me a good swimmer."

"Were you a swimmer in high school?"

"Yes."

"Did you join the Navy right after graduation or go to college?"

"Right after graduation. I always knew I wanted to be a SEAL."

"How come?"

"Because everyone said how hard it was. I wanted to prove I'd be good at it."

"And were you?"

"Yeah," I said. "I was."

Her lips tipped up. "You've got a healthy ego, you know that?"

I gave her half a cocky grin. "Just telling it like it is."

She looked amused. "Do you still live around here?"

"Right now, I'm living with my dad in the house where I grew up. But I'm planning to move out as soon as the bar opens."

"Where's your mom?"

"She died when I was ten."

"Oh." The playful expression faded. "I'm sorry."

"It's okay."

She sighed. "My mom drives me crazy, but I can't imagine life without her."

"What about your dad?"

"My dad." She turned her face to the sky again, moving her arm down over her eyes. "He's around. Occasionally he even sticks around."

I waited for her to go on, but she didn't. "Sorry. Didn't mean to pry."

"It's fine. I've got Daddy issues, but who doesn't?"

"You don't have to talk about it if you don't want to."

She sighed, then rolled onto her side again. "You know what I *really* want to do?"

"What?"

"Go out for dinner. Like a normal person. Just go grab a beer, a burger and some fries, and relax. Is that possible?"

"It's possible," I hedged. "Will you take the precautions I ask you to?"

89

"Yes."

"Then let's do it." I popped to my feet and reached down to offer her a hand.

She took it and let me pull her up. For a second, we just stood there, chest to chest, her hand still in mine.

"I'm sorry about earlier," I told her.

"About what exactly?"

"Being a dick about your situation. Saying I'd never let anyone tell me what to do. I don't really know how I'd react in your place."

She looked surprised. "Thanks. I appreciate that."

I dropped her hand. "And I'm sorry I gave you shit about that Instagram post. I just want you to be safe, and now I'm expecting a tour bus full of Hart Throbs to pull up any minute."

Her expression turned sheepish. "I was so worried about what I looked like in the photo that I didn't even notice the house numbers above my head. You know what? I'll just stay off social media while I'm here. It's only two weeks. It will probably be better for my mental health anyway."

"I agree. People are assholes."

Her eyes met mine. She had to squint slightly in the sun. "Did you look at comments on my post?"

"Some of them," I allowed. "Do the negative ones bother you?"

"Sometimes."

"Is it worth it? I mean, why post at all? Why give millions of strangers a chance to pass judgment —*publicly*—on your life every day?"

"I feel like I have to, to stay relevant. And connect directly with fans. And at least I control that narrative. It's worse when those gossip sites just get hold of paparazzi photos and make shit up to get clicks. Last year, I had to have physical therapy for an injury to my foot, and the story accompanying the photos of me leaving the medical building was that I was getting my boobs done."

My eyes dropped to her chest. "Don't touch them, they're perfect." Then I squeezed them shut. "God, I'm sorry. I should not have said that. I'm a dick. You should fire me."

She started to laugh. "I already tried that."

"So posting to social media," I said, trying to swerve back onto the road of acceptable conversation. "It's about control?"

"Partly. Yes."

I understood a little better where she was coming from. I liked control too. "And is it worth it? All the shit you have to endure to feel like you have that control?"

"Sometimes," she said with a shrug. "Not all the time. But maybe that's all I can ask for, you know? Anyway, I'm going in to take a shower."

As I watched her walk away, I wish I could say that I was pondering the high price of fame, the invasiveness of paparazzi, or even the effects of social media on mental health.

Nope.

I was thinking about her perfect tits. I was looking at her magnificent round ass. I was wondering if she was going to use that rabbit thing in the shower. Did she use it often? Had she been with anyone since Duke? If not, she'd gone as long as I had without sex. Maybe she didn't miss it. There had to be something reliable about a vibrator. It was like jerking off, right? You knew it would get the job done.

But a toy didn't have hands to touch you, or lips to kiss you, or words that would make you blush. It couldn't make you feel wanted. It felt no desire. It wasn't personal. It wasn't like *being* with someone who wanted to put his hands in your long red hair or lick every inch of your radiant skin or hear you moan his name while he fucked you with his tongue.

Not that I was thinking about doing that *personally*.

I'm just telling it like it is.

CHAPTER EIGHT

xander

TO GIVE KELLY MORE PRIVACY, I waited on the porch while she took her shower. While I was out there, I texted a friend of mine from high school that bartended at a place called the Backwoods Bar and Grill that wasn't too far from here. Normally, I wouldn't have been too concerned about a crowd, but it was a holiday weekend.

> Hey Eric. You guys slammed already? Any way to reserve a table for two?

It took him a few minutes to answer.

> Place is packed. But text me when you're leaving. I'll see what I can do.

> Thanks man.

After that, I couldn't resist typing "pink rabbit vibrator" into Google.

Let me tell you, the search results were an education.

I didn't see the exact one Kelly owned, but many looked similar. And none of them looked like any human dick I'd ever seen. There were tickling rabbit ears, swirling beads, multiple speeds, curved shafts, dual motors. One of them had 36 vibrational patterns.

Thirty-six! My cock didn't even have *one* vibrational pattern. Would my tongue make up for it? My fingers? The rest of my body? Maybe my voice?

Dismayed, I closed the page and put my phone away. What got her off was none of my business, and I needed to stop thinking about it.

A few minutes later, I heard the water shut off and the hair dryer kick on. After that came the sound of one door opening and another closing. Only then did I go inside and knock on the bedroom door.

"Kelly?"

"Yes?"

"Is it okay if I take a shower now?"

"That's fine."

I pulled some clean clothes and my toiletries from my bag and headed into the bathroom, where I undressed with a pounding heart.

Was the vibrator still on the tub ledge? Would I have to shower with it standing there, mocking me? If it *was* still there, had she left it on purpose?

Counting to three, I swept the curtain open, relieved to see it was gone.

I came out of the bathroom just as Kelly was leaving the bedroom.

"Think I'm dressed okay?" she asked.

I scanned her denim shorts, sneakers, and Belmont University hoodie. Her hair was in two long braids. "Definitely. The place I'm thinking about is just a side-of-the-road bar and grill. But the beer is cold and the burgers are hot."

She smiled. "Perfect. Done in the bathroom?"

"Yeah."

"I just need a minute." She brushed past me, leaving the scent of her perfume in her wake—it was summery and sweet, and I wanted to bury my face in her neck and inhale deeply.

Disconcerted, I put my shoes on and went outside. While I waited for her, I shot a quick text to Eric and let him know we'd be there in about thirty minutes. He didn't reply, so my hopes that a table would be waiting for us weren't too high. I figured if the place was too jammed, I'd take her into Cherry Tree Harbor instead. It was a longer drive, but I felt more comfortable there than anywhere else.

The front door opened. "I'm ready," she said. "Let's go."

As she breezed by me, I smelled her perfume again. I followed her to my car, fighting the urge to throw both arms around her, pull her back against me, and let the scent fill my head. Dammit, I hadn't been this attracted to someone in *years*. Why the hell did she have to be Sully's celebrity sister?

After turning from the cabin's driveway onto the main road, I noticed a car parked on the shoulder about two hundred yards away. A beige Honda Civic. Dent in the left rear bumper. Michigan plates. It hadn't been there earlier, and my intuition told me to memorize the number. As we passed it, I saw a guy behind the wheel on his phone.

She reached for the volume knob on my radio and turned it up. An old Springsteen song was on. "Is this okay?"

"Sure."

"What kind of music do you like?"

"All kinds, really. Classic rock is probably my favorite."

"Do you listen to country?"

I shrugged. "Sometimes."

"Ever listen to me?"

"No." I felt sort of bad about it. "But my niece Adelaide is a big fan."

"Oh yeah? How old is she?"

"Seven."

"Does she live around here?"

"Yeah. My brother Austin's family—that's Adelaide's dad—also lives in Cherry Tree Harbor."

"I'd like to meet them."

I was thinking about asking her if she'd like to go to the barbecue tomorrow, but then she started singing along with the radio, and I got distracted. Her voice was warm and pretty—it sort of wrapped around you like a blanket—and I heard none of the mournful tone from earlier. She seemed like she was in a much better mood, and it made me feel good.

When we pulled into the parking lot of the Backwoods Bar and Grill, I could tell by the number of cars parked beyond the asphalt on the grass that the place was probably at capacity or beyond. "Got a hat in your bag, by any chance?"

She glanced at her shoulder bag. "Shoot—no. I forgot it."

"Let me see what I have." I got out of the car and opened the hatch in the back, spotting a black Two Buckleys Home Improvement cap. Grabbing it, I shut the hatch and walked around to the passenger side, where she'd just hopped out. "Here," I said. "Wear this."

She read the front of it. "Two Buckleys? Which two?"

"My dad and my brother Austin."

"Ah." She stuck the cap on her head, pulling it low on her forehead. "How's that?"

Fucking adorable, actually, but all I did was nod. "Keep your head down. When we get to whatever table they give us, take the seat facing the wall or window, not the door."

She saluted. "I'm ready to go in, coach."

As expected, the place was crammed with people. Keeping Kelly right in front of me, I maneuvered through the throng and had a quick word with Eric, who said he'd let the hostess know we were here, but it would be a few minutes. I bought a couple beers and tugged Kelly over to one corner of the bar. With my back to the wall, I instructed her to face me.

She stood close, her breasts nearly grazing my shirt. The scent of her perfume caused my body temperature to rise. Trying not to breathe in too deeply, I gripped my beer and concentrated on staying aware of our surroundings.

After a couple minutes, she started to laugh.

"What's so funny?" I asked, glancing down at her.

"Your face. You look like you're ready to kill somebody."

"I'm just trying to give off the vibe of an unfriendly, possessive boyfriend. I don't want anyone approaching us."

Her eyebrows shot up. "So we're pretending to be on a date, is that it?"

"*No*." I frowned. "That is not it."

She giggled again. "Oh, come on. I don't get to go on normal dates. It could be fun! We could make up little pet names for each other, like bear-bear and mudbug."

"We will not be doing anything of the kind."

"You're the worst fake boyfriend ever." She stuck her tongue out at me.

"Buckley? Party of two?" the hostess called from the entrance to the dining room.

She tucked her hand into my elbow. "Come on, bear-bear."

I scanned the crowd as we crossed to a booth in the back left corner of the restaurant. Mostly families at this hour. A few groups of friends. As instructed, Kelly slid into the side facing the back wall, and I took the side facing the room. "Thanks," I told the hostess.

"Sure," she said, handing us two menus. "Your server will be right over."

"So is this where you bring all your dates?" Kelly asked as I pulled out my phone and entered the info about the car I'd seen on the side of the road.

"I don't date much."

"Why not?"

I put my phone away. "I've been busy with the bar, and with my family—my dad had some health issues this summer."

"I hope he's okay," she said seriously.

"He's fine. I also spend a lot of time with my niece and nephew."

"That's right. You're an uncle." She tipped up her beer again. "Tell me about them."

"My niece is Adelaide—the one I told you about

99

—and she has a twin brother, Owen. They're a lot of fun."

The waitress came by—a twenty-something blonde with flushed cheeks and a tired smile from all the running around she was doing tonight. But she welcomed us warmly and took our orders, apologizing that our burgers might take longer than usual. Her eyes lingered so long on Kelly, I thought for sure she was going to ask if she was Pixie Hart.

When we were alone again, I said, "Listen, if you don't want to be recognized tonight, keep your head down. And if someone does ask, my advice is to say you're not her, but you hear that a lot."

She studied me. "You're very serious about this security thing, huh?"

"You should be glad about that."

"Do you have a gun?"

"Not on me."

"But what if something happens?" she persisted with a grin. "What if some kind of bar fight breaks out?"

"If something happens, my job is to get you out of here as quickly as possible. If I have to pull a gun or throw punches, I have not done my job."

Her expression turned coy. "But would you take a bullet for me?"

"Yes. If that's what I had to do to protect you."

"Seriously?" She seemed genuinely shocked. "You don't even like me. And you're not even being paid for this gig."

"How I feel about you is irrelevant. And this isn't

about money for me. I gave your brother my word I'd keep you safe, and I will." I paused, my beer halfway to my mouth. "I never said I didn't like you."

Her cheeks grew slightly pink. "Tell me about your little sister."

"She's twenty-three and crazy smart. She's in grad school at William and Mary."

"And you said your brother Austin is the oldest?"

I nodded. "He's thirty-two. One year older than me. Then comes Devlin, he's twenty-eight and works in Boston, but he's got a birthday coming up. He'll actually be home for a visit next week. And Dash is twenty-six. He's an actor."

"Like in Hollywood?"

"Yeah. Ever seen that show Malibu Splash?"

Her eyes went wide. "I binged all three seasons while I was on tour! He's on that show?"

"Yeah. He plays a lifeguard named Bulge."

She flapped her hands. "Oh my god—*Dashiel Buckley* is your *brother*?"

"That's him."

"You guys don't look alike at all! I never would have put it together."

"He looks like our mom. I look like my dad."

"Ever go out to Hollywood to visit him?"

"Once or twice when I was in the Navy. I was stationed in San Diego for a while."

"Okay, so those are all your siblings. What about Austin's wife?"

"He's not married. The mother of his kids lives in

101

California, and they visit her once a year. He's raising them on his own, although he *does* have a new girlfriend. They just met earlier this summer, but honestly, I think she's the one."

Kelly perked up. "Really? Why?"

I told her the story of how Veronica had shown up on my brother's doorstep in a wedding gown, stranded and broke, fresh from walking out on her wedding to a cheating bastard, desperate to convince him she'd make the perfect nanny.

Kelly listened with rapt attention. "This sounds like a song! And he fell in love with her right then?"

"Hell no. He thought she was nuts. I had to talk him into giving her a chance." I tipped up my beer. "As usual, he was wrong and I was right."

She rolled her eyes. "Of course you were."

Our food arrived, and Kelly picked up her burger and took a giant bite. "God, this is good. It's exactly what I wanted. This whole night is exactly what I wanted."

My chest swelled as I reached for the ketchup bottle and offered it to her. "Want some?"

She shook her head. "I can't eat ketchup anymore. When I first moved to Nashville, there were nights all I ate were ketchup packets for dinner."

"Seriously?"

"Yeah. I used to steal them from the bar I worked at. I'd go home and make soup with them—a little sugar, some water, stick it in the microwave, then drizzle it with a stolen coffee creamer and, if I was lucky, I might even have a pilfered package of oyster crackers to go with it."

"Times must have been tough when you were starting out."

"They were."

"Did you ever think about giving up?"

"Sure." She ate a French fry. "A few times I even packed my bags. Called my mom and begged her to send me money for a bus ticket home. But she always talked me into staying. She believed in me. That helped." She popped another fry in her mouth. "Then I got a manager who believed in me."

"Still, you had the talent. I mean, you *have* the talent."

She shrugged. "Tons of people have talent. I'm not an idiot. I don't think I'm the best singer that ever walked the earth. I just . . . I understand people. I can read a room—even a huge room—and I know how to make a person feel like I'm singing just for them."

I studied her across the table, thinking that it also didn't hurt she was so fucking pretty. I remembered the way she'd sung in the car, soft and low, and wondered about other sounds she'd make in other settings, such as a bedroom where she was naked and sprawled beneath me, my body moving over hers.

Quickly, I picked up my beer, looking away as I drank.

What was the matter with me? It was this damn dry spell. I normally didn't go so long without sex, but there hadn't been anyone in my bed since I'd moved home. Between living with my dad, wanting to avoid small town gossip, and working so much, I hadn't really had the opportunity. Maybe once these two weeks were up, I'd remedy that.

But messing around with Kelly was out of the question. It would break all kinds of personal rules and violate the trust her brother had placed in me.

I needed to keep my thoughts clean and my hands to myself.

We finished our meals and a second round of beers, and when the check came, I reached for it.

"You don't have to buy my dinner, Xander," Kelly said, trying to tug it out of my hands. "This isn't a real date, remember?"

"I remember," I said, winning the battle and holding it out of her reach. "But even on a fake date, I pay for dinner. Consider it a perk."

Her head tilted. "Any other perks I should know about? Massages? Manicures? Maybe a bedtime story?"

"No," I said emphatically, sliding my credit card into the holder.

"Well, at least let me buy you a drink at the bar before we go."

I shook my head. "I don't think so. It's too

crowded in there. And the later it gets, the more it will fill up with drunk assholes."

"Come on. Please?" She clasped her hands under her chin. "I never get to do this—just hang out on a Friday night. No one knows me here, I'll face the wall, I'll keep my little disguise on—" She lowered the bill of the cap and peeked right and left. "I won't even get up and dance on the bar."

Exhaling, I sat back and folded my arms. It was a bad sign that I couldn't say no to her. "If I say so, we leave immediately."

She made an X on her chest. "I will do as you command, cross my heart."

Great, now I had *ideas*.

When the bill was paid, we went back into the bar, which was hot, loud, and packed. I kept Kelly in front of me, steering her through the mob of people standing shoulder to shoulder, trying to get close enough to the bar to order. Every time some guy looked at her, I did my best to scare him off with a menacing glare. Possibly a growl.

I managed to get close enough to the bar to catch Eric's eye and signal for two beers, and he nodded, handing them over a moment later. Giving them to Kelly, I dug some cash from my wallet and shouted for Eric to keep the change. Then I took Kelly by the shoulders again and shepherded her back to our corner.

"You were supposed to let me pay." She pouted and hugged the beers to her chest. "I should refuse to give you one of these."

"Sorry." My eyes scanned the rowdy drinkers pressing close behind her. "I just wanted to get away from the bar quickly. Too many people."

"Fine. Have one." She relinquished one of the bottles to me and clinked hers to it. "Here's to our fake date—although it's the realest one I've been on in a long time."

"Me too." We each took a long pull.

"God, what does that say about us?" she asked.

"Huh?" My eyes were over her shoulder. There was a group of guys now standing *right* behind her, and I didn't like the way they were staring at her. Elbowing each other. Puffing up their chests. It was almost like they were daring one another to approach her. One of them rolled his shoulders and faced her. His arm came up, like he was about to tap her on the shoulder.

She looked up at me. "I mean why do you think we both—"

But before she could finish what she was saying, I grabbed her by the back of the neck and crushed my mouth to hers. A soft, surprised noise came from the back of her throat. I spun her so her back was to the wall, making it impossible for the guy to touch her or even see her. If he wanted to know if she was Pixie Hart, he was going to have to tap *my* shoulder.

He didn't.

I kept kissing her.

Five seconds went by. Then ten.

I lifted my head, our lips parting. The guy had

obviously changed his mind. The threat was gone. There was no reason to kiss her again.

I did it anyway.

In fact, I changed the angle of my head to go deeper, opened my mouth a little wider, eased my tongue between her lips. I tightened my grip on the back of her neck, holding her to me. I kissed her until I had to take a breath, and when I tore my lips from hers, I swear her knees buckled a little.

"Xander," she whispered. "What the hell?"

Those green eyes were looking up at me with wonder and confusion, but no anger—I had the feeling I could take her hand, take her home, take it all. And goddamn, I wanted to.

But I couldn't.

"Sorry." I dropped my hand from her neck and glanced over my shoulder. "There was a guy about to tap your shoulder. I didn't want him talking to you."

"Oh." She struggled to put it together. "So—so that was—that kiss was fake? It was like . . . a shield?"

Our mouths were still impossibly close. My eyes dropped to her lips. "Yes."

It wasn't a total lie—the first kiss had been a shield.

The second? That was a little more difficult to explain.

I decided not to try. "Come on, let's get out of here."

CHAPTER NINE

kelly

HE KISSED ME.

On the silent drive home, those three words kept running through my mind.

He kissed me. He kissed me. He kissed me.

He'd done more than that, actually. He'd stunned me. Stopped my breath. Spiked my pulse. Lit a fuse in me.

And I'd liked it.

Sure, we'd gotten off to a rough start yesterday, but by this afternoon it had felt like the last layer of ice had thawed. We'd actually warmed to each other. I liked hearing about his family and his bar. I liked that he took his job to protect me so seriously. I liked looking at him, the way it made my stomach go a little jumpy. Sure, he had an ego the size of Texas and issued his opinions like they were gospel, but he made me laugh. He made me feel safe.

And when he'd kissed me, I'd felt something real.

Had it really been just for show? I mean, maybe

the first kiss was a panic move. Maybe he honestly hadn't seen any other way to safeguard my identity.

But . . . twice?

And that second time, he'd kissed me like he *meant* it—hard and deep. The man put his *tongue* in my *mouth*.

So maybe it was possible both things were true. Maybe he'd kissed me once in order to protect me, but he did it again because he liked it.

Then again, maybe that was wishful thinking on my part.

I glanced over at him. He drove with one hand on the wheel, the other on the back of his neck. His bicep bulged inside the sleeve of his black T-shirt, sending a current of desire rippling through me. I wished there was a way I could just *ask* him for the truth—was he into me that way or not?

But of course, I couldn't.

I closed my eyes and tipped my head back, imagining what it would be like if we were just a regular couple on our way home from a Friday night date. Would he take my hand as he drove? Maybe I'd reach over and put a hand on his thigh. Tip my head onto his shoulder. And when we got home, we'd undress each other. Slip beneath the sheets. Cling together in the dark. I wondered what it would feel like to be held in those big, strong arms. Cradled against that hot, muscular body. Penetrated by his huge, hard—

"Kelly," he whispered.

That's when I realized we'd arrived at the cabin

and the engine was off. Just to mess with him, I didn't open my eyes.

"Kelly." Gently, he nudged my arm, but I continued to play possum. Could I get him to carry me to the house? Experience a small sliver of my fantasy?

He reached over and checked my pulse, which nearly broke me, but I kept it together.

"After two beers, you pass out?" he muttered. "Seriously?"

Grumbling, he went around to the passenger side of the SUV and opened the door. After unbuckling my seatbelt, he slid one hand behind my back and the other beneath my knees, then lifted me out. Feigning a deep sleep, I looped my arms around his neck and snuggled close—he smelled so good. Had he worn cologne tonight? Or was that just his natural scent?

He kicked the car door shut with one foot, then carried me like a baby toward the house. But after taking the steps up to the porch, he stopped.

"Kelly," he said, louder this time. "You need to wake up. I don't know the code."

I sighed dramatically. "But this is so nice, bear-bear. I like being carried around like your sweet little mudbug." As I dissolved into laughter, I was abruptly set on my feet.

"Open the door," he said gruffly. "And no more playing tricks on me."

"Why not? I particularly liked it when you took my pulse. Nice to know you cared that I wasn't

111

dead." We went inside, and he immediately started looking around, like he thought someone might have broken in.

"What are you doing?" I asked, removing my Two Buckleys cap and setting my purse down.

"I'm checking to make sure it's safe." He disappeared down the back hallway, and I went over to the kitchen.

"Want one more beer?" I called out, opening the fridge.

He appeared in the living room again, looking uncertain. "A beer?"

"Yeah. We didn't get to finish our last drink. I thought maybe if you know how to start a fire, we could sit out by the fire pit."

"I know how to start a fire."

"Great." Grabbing two beers, I shut the fridge with my hip. "Let's go."

"See? Isn't this nice?" Relaxing in my chair, just this side of tipsy, I stretched my feet toward the fire, which crackled and sparked.

"Sure." Next to me, Xander seemed anything but relaxed, leaning forward with his elbows on his knees, eyes on the flames when they weren't darting around like he was looking for photographers in the trees. Our two empty beer bottles lay on the gravel between us. He'd talked very little since we came out here, no matter how I tried to draw him out.

"What's got you so tense?" I looked around. "No paparazzi, no Hart Throbs, no bears."

"Bears?" He looked over at me, one thick dark eyebrow cocked.

I laughed. "My mom is convinced I'm going to be mauled by a black bear while I'm here. She had a premonition about it."

"Your mom has premonitions?"

"Yes. She calls it 'the sight.' She claims certain women in her family have this ability to see the future in these vivid daydreams they get. As soon as she heard about my plan to take this vacation alone, she had a vision of me being attacked by a giant, angry bear who wanted to eat me up, Little Red Riding Hood style."

"Interesting."

"I told her there are no predators here—of course, that was before I came out of the shower and found you standing in my living room." I gave him a pointed look.

"That was an accident. I'm sorry again for scaring you. And for . . . seeing you naked." His eyes darted toward my bare legs.

"Oh, come on." I used his words from earlier today to poke at him. "Are you saying you didn't enjoy the view?"

"I was just as uncomfortable as you were."

I looked over at him and smiled knowingly. "I doubt that."

113

"It's the truth."

"The truth, huh?" I looked at the fire again. "Should we talk about the truth?"

"What do you mean?"

"At the bar. That kiss." I kept my eyes on the flames. "Was it really fake?"

"Of course it was."

"Because it didn't feel fake." I braved a glance at him. "Especially the second time."

"Well, it was. Entirely fake. The whole thing."

Talk about protesting too much.

I smiled. "So you didn't want to kiss me back there?"

"Of course not."

"And you don't want to kiss me now?"

He hesitated just a second too long. "No."

I stood up. Moved in front of him.

"Kelly." He spoke my name, but what he meant was, *Don't.*

I leaned over and put my hands on his shoulders. Pushed him back against the chair while I straddled his thighs. "Are you sure about that?"

He didn't answer. But he didn't push me away, either. His forearms lay on the arms of the chair, his fingers curled over the edge. The fire popped and hissed behind me.

I flattened my palms on his chest and slid them down his stomach, muscles rippling beneath the cotton. I toyed with his belt.

"You should stop," he told me.

"I *should* stop?" I challenged. "Or you want me to stop?"

He swallowed, his Adam's apple bobbing in his throat. "You *should* stop."

"For my own good?" I laughed softly, putting my hands on the top of his chair, leaning close enough to brush my lips against his jaw. His beard was surprisingly soft.

"Yes. You don't really want this."

"I wonder," I murmured, rocking my hips gently over his, "if it ever occurred to you, or to any man, that *I* might know what's good for me. What I really want."

His breath drew in sharply.

"My God, what would that be like?" I whispered in his ear. "What would I *do* with that kind of freedom?"

"I have a pretty good idea." His voice was gravelly and thick.

"But you don't trust me." I pulled back slightly, looked him in the eye.

"Trust you?"

"To know what I want. You'd rather treat me like a little girl who needs a big, strong man to decide what's best for her."

"It's not about that."

"Then what's it about, Xander? Tell me."

"It's about honor," he said. "It's about your brother and the trust he has in me. It's about setting aside what I want and doing the right thing."

"The right thing." Closing my eyes, I sighed and

shook my head. "Okay. Fine. You win." I went to get off his lap, but his hands gripped my hips, locking me in place.

"Hey." His voice was gruff, almost angry. "You don't know how hard this is for me."

My eyes flicked down to his crotch. "I would, if you'd just relax and kiss me for real."

"I can't kiss you for real," he said, while his hands told a different story, rising to cradle my face. "I fucking can't."

Then he pulled me toward him, sealing his lips to mine. For a couple seconds, I was so surprised, I couldn't even move. But then his tongue slid between my lips, reigniting that spark I'd felt earlier in the bar.

I bunched my fingers into his shirt and held on tight, as if I was afraid he was going to push me away. His hands returned to my hips and set me in motion, rocking my lower body over his. Our mouths opened wider, his tongue growing more aggressive and commanding. I imagined what that tongue might feel like on the most sensitive parts of my body and felt the shock of it all the way down to my toes.

The bulge of his cock was thick and hard between my legs, and I rubbed myself along its solid length. The kiss grew reckless and messy. His mouth moved down my jaw and throat, and he unzipped my hoodie to my belly button.

"Fuck," he seethed, taking in the thin, low-cut tank top I wore without a bra. He tilted his forehead to my clavicle, and I felt his breath on my skin. *"Fuck. I can't."*

But then his mouth was on the upper curves of my breasts, his beard tickling my skin. Hooking his fingers over the top of my tank, he tugged it down, exposing one breast, and sucked hungrily on the puckered nipple. I cradled his head against my chest, my fingers threading into his hair. He moved to the other breast without even bothering to pull down my shirt, wetting the cotton, closing his lips over the stiff peak, drawing me and the material into his mouth with quick, hard pulls.

The fire popped and hissed, and the noise startled Xander to his senses.

Lifting me off his lap, he set me on my feet, drew my hoodie back over my shoulders, and backed away. "We have to stop."

"Why?" I looked around. "No one is here."

"We don't know that for sure. Someone could have followed us. This is reckless and unsafe and . . . wrong."

"Wrong?"

"Yes." He raked a hand through his hair. "I crossed the line. Your brother trusts me with you. He said I'm the *only* one he trusts with you."

"So?"

"So that means something." He spoke firmly, looking me in the eye. "Trust is important to me."

I stared at him in disbelief. "Me too, Xander! Trust is important to me too."

Next to us, the fire crackled again, sending sparks

shooting up into the dark. I shook my head. "Never mind. Let's just forget this happened."

"Thank you. I have to be able to do my job without distraction."

"Of course," I said, bristling at being called both a job and a distraction. I zipped my hoodie all the way to my chin. "I'm going into bed." Then I walked away without another word, not even *goodnight*.

Ten minutes later, I slipped between my sheets in the dark and curled up on my side. I felt cold and empty, a complete contrast to the way I'd felt sitting out by the fire, or even at the restaurant tonight.

It had been a long time since I'd spent hours on end with just one person, getting to know them, letting them get to know me, feeling a mutual attraction build, giving it room to breathe, testing its limits, sharing a first kiss.

And a second.

And a third.

Recalling the sensation of his mouth on my skin, the firm softness of his lips contrasted with the abrasive rub of his beard, that delicious tug on my nipples . . . I rolled onto my stomach, moaning softly into my pillow. Why did the guy assigned to protect me also have to turn me on so much? It was so unfair.

And yet, if I was honest, I had to admit that part of his appeal was that he was good at his job. For all the things I didn't like about him—and there were *plenty* of them—I did feel secure in his presence.

But I also felt sexy. Desirable. Wanted.

Me. The real me—Kelly Jo Sullivan.

The door to the house opened and closed. A moment later, I heard Xander's slow, heavy footsteps in the hall. He went into the bathroom. The faucet came on.

Was he thinking about me? Was he angry with himself? Did he regret putting the brakes on? The bathroom door opened and I listened for his footsteps thudding back down the hall again. But I didn't hear them. Just silence.

I propped myself up on one elbow, holding my breath. Was he on the other side of my door? Wondering if he should knock?

Knock, I thought. *Knock, you big lummox.*

A full ten seconds went by, my heart hammering wildly.

Then I heard the slow thump of his boots on the wood floor as he walked away. Flopping onto the pillow again, I frowned. Damn him for rejecting me! Didn't he understand how lonely I was? How long it had been since anyone had kissed me or touched me? How hard it was for me to be this vulnerable with someone?

If I was any other girl, I could just meet a handsome stranger and enjoy a sexy little vacation fling without worrying that he'd sell his story to the tabloids. Instead, I was *me*, stuck sharing this one-bedroom cabin in the middle of nowhere with a smoking hot guy I actually thought I could trust not to betray me, only he wouldn't come near the bed.

And he'd wanted me too. I knew that he had.

I rolled onto my back and closed my eyes, remembering in vivid detail the way I'd climbed onto his lap, feeling him hard and thick beneath me. I recalled the scent of him—tinged with smoke and fire—and the exhilaration of that moment when he'd grabbed my head and crushed his lips to mine.

Those strong hands on my hips, moving my body over his. His tongue in my mouth. The tingling warmth between my legs. Feeling it start to hum, again I slipped my hand into my underwear. As I moved my fingertips over my swollen clit, I pictured Xander out there in the living room, sliding his hand into his pants.

Behind my eyelids, I saw a huge fist working up and down a mammoth cock in the dark, the flexing abs, the quickened breath, the struggle to be fast and silent. The electric current surging through him, gathering heat and strength. That sensation of pressure rising and rising, until it couldn't be contained and came bursting forth in hot little pulses that would leave him sweaty and sticky and stifling a groan.

Fuck you, Xander, I thought as I took myself there while I fantasized about him jerking off. *Fuck you so hard*. As the throbbing between my legs subsided, I rolled onto my stomach, trying to smother my loud breathing.

And I wondered if he actually *was* out there on the couch, doing the same thing.

CHAPTER TEN

xander

OF COURSE I WAS.

CHAPTER ELEVEN

kelly

THE FOLLOWING DAY, I stepped out onto the front porch around ten a.m., both hands wrapped around a mug full of hot coffee. "Morning."

Xander looked up at me from where he sat in his usual rocking chair on the front porch, laptop open, cup of coffee in his hand. His dark hair was messy, making him look more rugged than usual, and there were dark circles beneath his eyes, like maybe he hadn't slept well.

"Morning," he said.

Still in my pajamas, I crossed in front of him and lowered myself into the other chair, crisscrossing my legs pretzel-style.

"You sleep okay?" he asked.

"Like a baby," I lied. I'd actually been pretty restless all night. "How's the couch treating you?"

"Fine," he said, taking a long sip of coffee. "It's fine."

I brought my cup to my lips and wondered if he

123

was thinking about the empty spot next to me in the bed, and how it could have been his last night. "Thanks for making coffee."

"I was up early. Decided to make myself useful."

"I appreciate it." A couple squirrels chased each other in circles on the gravel drive, then disappeared up a tree.

"Are you still mad?" he ventured.

"No." I'd had plenty of time during the night to think it over. "It's not like I don't understand where you're coming from, Xander. I get why you don't want to mess around with me."

"I *do* want to." He shook his head. "I just can't."

I sighed. "I suppose I should be glad someone assigned to watch out for me has such a strong moral code."

"My code obviously has a weak spot where you're concerned," he said. "But I promise, what happened last night will not happen again."

"And I promise, I will not try to tempt you."

"Good." He paused, eyeballing my bare legs. "I don't suppose you'd go put some pants on, would you?"

"I'll get dressed in a minute." I stretched my legs out in front of me, pointing my toes. "Looks like it's going to be another nice day."

He sipped his coffee and gave me a sort of grunt in response. "We made the news again."

"Huh?"

He rotated his screen so I could see the photo of us on Splash exiting the restaurant last night, Xander one step behind me looking warlike and furious, me looking shell-shocked and pale after the kiss. "Look at my face. That's me wondering what the actual fuck just happened."

He turned the laptop to face him. "Sorry."

"I'm teasing you. I'm sorry that you're being photographed like this."

"My fault. I thought we might be safe there, since it's so out of the way." He shook his head. "How do you ever get used to that, cameras in your face all the time? Not that this jerk was in our faces—he was obviously hiding across the parking lot."

"He might not be a jerk," I pointed out. "A lot of those paparazzi aren't bad. They're just doing their jobs. Trying to make a living like the rest of us."

"It's so invasive."

I shrugged. "Sometimes. But a lot of times, they treat you with respect. And some of them won't sell a bad photo. It's in their interest to play nice, you know? I'm more likely to give them a good shot if I like them."

"You know them personally?"

"Some of the Nashville guys, I do. In fact, it was one of the Nashville photographers that pointed the finger at the security team when it was obvious someone was leaking details about my schedule and locations to media. That was helpful. But . . ." I took another sip from my cup. "There are definitely bad apples who will do anything for a buck."

"Those guys are in every business."

I glanced over and noticed he was frowning at his screen. "Everything okay?"

"Just dealing with some issues at the bar."

"What issues?"

"You name it." He rubbed his temples with his thumb and forefinger. "I've got supply chain issues with the barstools, Wi-Fi problems that no one can figure out, and my electrician bailed."

"Where is the bar?"

"It's in Cherry Tree Harbor, just outside town."

"Can I see it?"

He leaned back in his chair and closed his computer. "I suppose I could take you to see it. But is that really what you want to be doing on your vacation?"

"Obviously, the kind of vacation I planned is not panning out."

"And what was it you'd planned, exactly?"

I twirled my hand gracefully through the air. "A sort of creative retreat where I'd get in touch with my inner child, which would inspire me to write soulful, introspective songs that would be lauded for their emotional weight and poetic lyricism."

He smiled, lifting his mug to his lips. "Instead, you wrote a song about me."

"That's right," I said with a laugh.

"So let me hear it."

"Now?"

"Yeah. Go get your guitar. Sing for me."

"I haven't even finished one cup of coffee yet," I

protested. "And I do *not* sound good first thing in the morning."

"Excuses, excuses," he scolded. "You think Dolly Parton worries about how she sounds first thing in the morning or how many cups of coffee she's had? I bet she wakes up and gets right to work lifting those emotional weights."

"Fine," I said, setting my cup on the ground and getting to my feet. "I'll sing you a song, but only if you promise to take me somewhere fun today."

"I might have an idea," he said, stroking his beard. "Depends on how much I like the song."

Laughing, I went into the house to retrieve my guitar from the bedroom. But first I ducked into the bathroom and peeked at myself in the mirror, pinching a little color into my cheeks. My hair was still in the braids I'd put in yesterday, but they were sort of ragged and frizzy from being slept on. For a moment, I debated taking them out but decided against it. I didn't want him to think I was trying to tempt him.

After rejoining him on the porch, I sat down and tuned my guitar. Xander's laptop was out of sight, and I noticed he'd refilled both our coffee cups. I took a sip of mine before playing a few warm-up exercises.

"Is that the song?"

"Hush," I told him, starting to strum a twelve-bar blues in E with a slow, shuffling rhythm. "Don't interrupt creativity in progress."

"A thousand apologies."

I closed my eyes, losing myself in the lazy groove. I played all the way through it once, the same simple form I'd taught myself as a twelve-year-old, back in my bedroom with a cheap guitar my dad had bought secondhand. Then I circled back around and added lyrics, doing my best impression of a broken-down, worn-out, fed-up woman who's had enough.

"Planned a vacation," I sang, my voice rusty with sleep. "Just to get some space." I finished out the first four bars and switched from the E to the A. "Planned a vacation," I sang a second time, "just to get some space. But what I got instead was just a bearded goon in my face."

Next to me, Xander burst out laughing. "Nice," he said, starting to applaud.

"I'm not done," I told him, bringing it around again.

"I've got the Xander Buckley blues, they haunt me day and night," I warbled plaintively, getting a little fancier on the guitar. "I got those Xander Buckley blues, they haunt me day and night. That's why I sat on his lap, but he left me unsatisfied." I finished with a walk down and resolved with two jazzy chords, humming a little riff on top.

Opening my eyes, I saw him sitting with his arms folded, a wry smile on his face. As the sound faded, I slapped a hand over the strings. "How was that?"

He gave me a few slow claps. "Very entertaining."

"Thank you." I set my guitar aside and picked up my coffee cup.

"Unsatisfied, huh?"

"Yes. Weren't you?"

"Yes."

"What did you do about it?" I asked playfully.

One eyebrow quirked up. "What did *you* do about it?"

Lifting my shoulders, I let his imagination run a little wild before taking a sip of my coffee. "So did I earn my field trip?"

"I guess we can go to the bar," he said. "It's not like anyone will be there."

"And I want to see where you grew up," I added.

"Fine."

"Can I meet your family?"

He gave me a warning look, like I was pushing my luck. "I suppose. Austin is having a barbecue—just his family—and Veronica invited us to come by."

"Yay!" My heels hit the porch with a thump. "But we should bring something. I don't want to show up to a barbecue empty-handed. Take me to the store so I can get some more groceries! I want to make a salad."

He frowned. "We don't need to—"

"I just need a few minutes to get dressed," I said, picking up my guitar. "I'll be ready in five."

I couldn't help smiling as I hurried back to my room. Going to a small-town, backyard barbecue wasn't something I got to do in Nashville, and I was coming off a tour where I'd spent most of my down-time alone on the bus or decompressing in a hotel room.

Glancing at my phone, I saw that my father had

called me again last night. He'd left me another voicemail, probably asking again about the "loan," as if he'd ever pay me back.

In the last five years, I'd bought my father a car, paid off his credit cards, settled his gambling debts, and financed two failed trips to rehab. My brother could not understand why I kept giving him money, but Kevin wasn't here—he didn't understand what it was like when our mom came to me crying, swearing up and down he seemed different this time, he was so sorry for what he'd put us through, he was back to stay.

Then there was the man himself. Handsome and charismatic, he'd been a musician too, with a deep, resonant voice that hypnotized his audience. A charmer through and through. Good with words, great with an apology, unrivaled at guilt trips. He could twist your feelings until you were wrung dry. In no time, you were convinced it was *you* who'd let him down.

You have so much, peanut. So much. And I know I haven't done enough to deserve your forgiveness, but didn't I take you on my knee and teach you to play the guitar? Didn't I bring you up on stage with me to sing duets when you were only knee high? Didn't I plant the seed, telling you you'd be famous one day? Have you forgotten your old man?

And couldn't I please help him out this one last time? Get him out of a jam? Set him on the straight and narrow so he could be the loving husband and father he knew he could be?

But no matter how much money I gave him or how many times my mother let him back in her bed or how hard we tried to help him slay his demons, it never worked.

I deleted his voicemail and texted my mother.

> Can you please ask Daddy to stop calling me? I'll talk to him when I get back.

I also had another voicemail from Duke, which I deleted without listening to, and one from Wags, which I decided to ignore. In fact, I decided I was going to ignore my phone for the next twenty-four hours. No texts, no voice messages, no emails, no social media. I powered it off and buried it in my suitcase.

After throwing on some jeans and a T-shirt, I pinned up my braids and—just for fun—put on one of the wigs I'd brought in case I needed a disguise. It was black with bangs and a blunt bob cut. Think Uma Thurman in *Pulp Fiction*.

When I came out of the room, Xander stopped and stared. "What the hell?"

"You like it?" I fluffed one side of the dark wig.

"I think I prefer the red."

"But the red might give me away. What if someone recognized me in the produce aisle? Or the frozen foods section? You might be tempted to kiss me again to protect my identity, and we can't have that." As I walked by him, I took the opportunity to smack him on the chest again.

He caught me by the wrist, his fingers like a padlock. "You're going to have to stop touching me."

"Jeez. 'No kissing, put on pants, stop touching me.'" I shook my head. "Are you this much fun in bed?"

He stared me down hard. "What I'm like in bed is none of your business."

"Okay, okay." Yanking my arm from his grasp, I headed for the door, but just as I reached for the handle, he spoke again.

"But for the record, I am a fucking *riot* in bed."

CHAPTER TWELVE

xander

"SO THIS IS IT, HUH?"

Kelly surveyed Buckley's Pub from the vantage point of the entrance, her eyes scanning the cement floor and brick walls, the huge TV screens, the curved booths upholstered in tufted leather, the industrial pendant lighting, the mirrored shelves behind the bar.

I stood behind her, my eyes greedily drinking her in from head to toe while she couldn't see me.

She wore a butter-yellow dress with flowers on it and these red cowboy boots that were knocking me out. Every time I looked at her, I felt like those boots were stomping on my chest.

It had taken every last ounce of my strength not to throw her over my shoulder and take her to bed last night. Even after I'd regained control of myself and reset the appropriate boundary, I'd watched her walk away with an ache in my balls and a gargantuan hard-on that refused to subside. Later, I'd stood outside her bedroom door, my fists clenched in agonized indecision, my head saying one thing, my body begging for another.

But in the end, my sense of right and wrong won out. She was under my protection. She'd been drinking. She might not even have meant those things she said.

I couldn't risk it.

So I'd taken care of business myself, desperately hoping she wouldn't hear me grunting out a fast, frantic orgasm on her couch, then quickly cleaned myself up with paper towels in the kitchen, which I shoved into a plastic grocery bag and buried deep within the trash.

She had me acting like a fucking teenager.

She'd only made things worse this morning, hinting that she'd done the same thing.

I wasn't sure I could survive two weeks like this. It had only been two days, and I was going out of my mind. How was I supposed to last?

"This is it." I moved past her, frowning at the missing barstools and hanging pendant lights that hadn't come on.

"I like it," she said, strolling across the floor toward the bar. "It's very . . ." She flexed one bicep. "Manly. Smells like wood and testosterone."

I walked behind the bar, irritated to see that someone had left trash from their lunch on the counter. I gathered it up and stuffed it into a garbage bag that had been left on the floor.

"No one's working today?" Kelly ran her hand

across the smooth surface of the bar Austin had crafted for me out of reclaimed wood.

"No. It's a holiday weekend."

She examined the bar closer. "Wow. This is *really* beautiful."

"My brother made it."

She glanced up at me in surprise. "Seriously?"

"Yeah. He makes incredible furniture—mostly dining tables—out of reclaimed wood. Barn doors, railroad ties, whiskey barrels—you name it."

Her eyes lit up. "*I* want a dining table made from reclaimed wood. Will he make one for me?"

"You can ask him. He's finally stepping back from running Two Buckleys with my dad to go into business for himself."

"That's awesome." She bellied up against the bar and gave me a devilish grin. "So make me a drink, barkeep. Let's watch some sports ball. Get mad and shout things at TVs. Root, root, root for the home team."

Laughing, I shook my head. "I don't even have any liquor yet, and the televisions aren't hooked up."

"Bummer." She sighed and turned around, ambling across the floor, her hand trailing along the back of a chair. "So did you always want to own a bar?"

"Not particularly." I was trying to keep my thoughts professional, or at least platonic, but my eyes kept drifting. That red hair. The curvy hips. Those fucking boots.

"Did you think you'd be in the Navy forever?"

She turned one of the chairs around and straddled it, elbows on the table, chin resting on one fist.

My throat was so dry. If I'd had any whiskey behind the bar, I'd have poured myself a shot. "I never really thought too far ahead."

"You were more of a take-each-day-as-it-comes kind of guy?"

"That's kind of how they trained us. To focus on the thing we're doing at the time and not stress about what was left to do or what was coming next. It would have been too easy to get overwhelmed and quit."

"Did you ever think about quitting?"

"During training? Sure. Everyone did. But I was a stubborn motherfucker."

One side of her mouth curved up. "Oh, I know all about that."

I couldn't stop thinking about those open thighs beneath the table, the way she'd straddled me last night. My mouth on her tits. Fuck.

"What about you?" I asked, trying to redirect.

"Me?" She touched her collarbone, right where I'd laid my forehead last night. "I was always focused on music. When I was little, my daddy used to play in local bars, and Mama would bring Kevin and me along to watch. I was mesmerized by the sound, the lights, the applause. He was having so much fun on that stage, and everyone loved him. Sometimes he'd bring me up there with him and we'd sing together. It just felt like magic to sing and make people smile or whistle or jump up and dance."

"Does it still?"

She looked surprised by the question. "Still what?"

"Feel like magic."

Her brow furrowed. "Why wouldn't it?"

"Maybe it does. I'm just asking."

"Sure, it does. I mean, maybe not every single night, but that's a lot to ask. Every performer gets tired. But I try to remember that even though I've sung a certain song hundreds of times, someone out there might be hearing it for the first time, or maybe hear it differently that night because of what's going on in their life." She shook her head. "I never want to let anyone down."

I studied her from across the room and felt the urge to take her in my arms and hide her away from the world. "That sounds exhausting. No wonder you wanted time away from that world."

"I'm fine." She got up from the chair and slid it beneath the table again. "I'm ready to go when you are."

"That's my house right there," I said as we passed it. "The red brick on the right."

"Wait, we're not stopping?" She turned to me, a look of distress on her face. "I want to see where you live. Where you grew up."

"You want to go *in*?"

"Yes." She tugged my sleeve. "Come on, please?"

Grumbling under my breath, I turned around in a neighbor's driveway and pulled into mine. My dad's car was gone, so I figured he was already at Austin's house.

"This is so nice," Kelly said as I led her up the front walk. She stopped to admire the hydrangeas, bending down to touch the silvery leaf of a lamb's ear plant.

"Thanks." I unlocked the front door and let her go in first. "Might be a little messy in here. My dad isn't the neatest housekeeper, and I've been gone for a couple days."

"That's okay." As soon as she walked in, my dad's dog, a German Australian Shepherd mix, came rushing over, excited about visitors. Kelly laughed, bending down to give him some love. "Hi, cutie. What's your name?"

"Fritz," I told her, shutting the door behind us.

"Hi, Fritz." She scratched behind his ears while he licked her knees and I tried not to be jealous of a dog. "What a handsome boy."

"Do you have a dog?" I asked.

"No. I want to get one, but my mom has bad allergies and she lives with me. Maybe someday. Kevin and I always wanted a dog." She began to wander through the rooms on the first floor, and Fritz stuck close to her side, completely devoted.

Trailing them from the dining room through the kitchen into the living room, I found myself slightly self-conscious about the well-worn furniture, the frayed carpet, the outdated appliances, the faded photos on the walls. For someone like her, who probably had a big fancy Nashville mansion, would a place like this seem shabby and run-down?

But Kelly seemed charmed, spinning in a slow circle in front of the fireplace. "What a great house to grow up in. It's so warm and homey. Were you close to your siblings?"

"Yeah. We're still pretty close."

She smiled as she looked closer at a family photo from Austin's high school graduation. Taking the frame off the mantel, she studied it. "So tell me who's who."

Standing slightly behind her, I pointed at each person. "That's my dad and older brother, Austin. That's me—I'm the tallest—and then my brother Devlin has the cast on his arm, my brother Dash has the blond hair, and Mabel is there in the front."

"So cute." She laughed softly. "You're so skinny. And it's funny to see you without the beard."

"Yeah, I didn't pack on any meat until later." I could smell her perfume again. It reminded me of a dessert I loved. Strawberry shortcake maybe. Or peach cobbler. Something sweet and summery.

She set the graduation photo down and picked up one that had been taken much earlier. "Is that your mom?"

"Yes." It was probably the last good picture of her before she got sick. She stood in the yard with Mabel on one hip, smiling broadly, the light catching the extraordinary blue of her eyes.

"She was really beautiful," Kelly remarked.

"She was."

Setting the photo carefully back on the mantel, she pointed at a wedding portrait of my parents. "Wow. You look *just* like your dad here."

"You think so?"

"Definitely. How old is he there?"

"I think he was about thirty when they got married."

She continued looking at the photo of my parents posing next to their wedding cake, broad smiles on both their faces. "They look so happy."

"They were. On their first date, he told her he was going to marry her. Six months later, he did it."

"Really?" She laughed. "I love that. I guess when you know, you know, huh?"

"That's what he always said."

She turned to face me. "Think you'll ever get married?"

I shrugged. "Yeah. I'd like a family. And my brother has two kids already. I hate it when he's winning, so I need at least three right away."

She headed for the stairs. "You'd have three kids just to beat your brother at something?"

"I'd do pretty much anything to beat my brother at something," I said. "But I do think I'd be a good dad."

Amused, she glanced at me over her shoulder. "Why am I not surprised?"

I grinned. "Just telling it like it is."

She started up the stairs, one hand trailing on the banister, Fritz at her heels. The steps creaked beneath her feet. "Three kids, huh? Boys or girls?"

"I'd like both. But I'll probably end up with three rowdy boys just like me."

"Your poor wife."

"What about you? Do you want a family?"

"Eventually." She reached the top of the stairs. "So which bedroom is yours?"

"Top of the stairs on the left."

As she reached the landing, I quickly raced into my room ahead of her to yank the bed covers up. "Sorry. I didn't make my bed before I left."

Kelly laughed. "A military man like you? No hospital corners?"

"I'm out of practice." I glanced around the room —was it presentable? I kept it fairly neat, although my dresser could probably use a dusting, and it was a little embarrassing that there were two twin beds with solar system bedding instead of something more adult. "This was Owen's room when Austin and his kids lived here," I said.

"They lived here?" She peeked into the bathroom Austin and I had shared with Devlin and Dash as kids and stuck her head into their bedroom on the other side of it.

"For a few years, before I moved back. Austin and the twins' mom were never really together, and she was going to give them up for adoption, but he said he would take them and raise them on his own.

They moved in with my dad so Austin would have help."

"Wow." She peered out the window that overlooked the backyard. "How old was he?"

"Twenty-five." I perched on the edge of one bed while she perused the items on my dresser top—a handful of change, a couple cologne bottles, a used dryer sheet, my camera.

"That's really mature and responsible for a twenty-five-year-old guy," she remarked, sniffing each bottle of cologne.

"Even as a kid, Austin was always mature and responsible."

"You make it sound like a bad thing."

"It's not a bad thing," I said quickly. "I've got a lot of respect for Austin. And I understand why he is the way he is. After our mom died, he had to pick up a lot of slack. He was the second parent in many ways. And for many years."

She turned around still holding one of the cologne bottles and leaned back against the dresser. "That had to be so hard for him. For all of you."

"Yeah." I thought for a moment. "We all kind of handled it differently. I think for Austin, bearing up and taking on that role of *rock* for the rest of us was how he coped. I never saw him break down."

Moving the bottle back and forth in front of her nose, she inhaled. "How did *you* cope?"

"The way you'd expect a ten-year-old kid to cope," I admitted. "I broke down a lot. I was a kid who wore my heart on my sleeve."

She blinked, and her eyes looked shiny. "That makes me want to give ten-year-old you a hug. Is he in there somewhere?"

I laughed and held up one palm. "No. He's gone. He grew up into a big bearded goon. Stay away."

Smiling, she held up the cologne. "This one is my favorite."

"Good to know. I'm never wearing it around you."

She set it down and picked up my camera. "Are you a photographer?"

"I wouldn't say that. I just like to take pictures."

"Of what?"

"Whatever. Places I visit. People in my life. Lately I've just been chronicling the progress at the bar."

She hefted it in both hands, then switched it on. Focusing on me, she clicked. "Gotcha."

"Don't," I told her.

"But it's fun to be on this side of the lens." Another click. "And you're kinda cute when you frown. Yes, give me mad—you're a tiger. Rawr."

"Will you stop?" I got up and moved toward her, reaching for the camera. She immediately ducked under my arm and sat on the edge of the bed, hiding the camera behind her back.

"Come and get it," she taunted.

I folded my arms and leaned back against the dresser, determined to keep my distance. "I'm not coming to get it."

"Why not?"

"You know why not."

143

"Because you're afraid of me?"

"I'm not afraid of anything."

She smiled, brandished the camera again, and clicked one more picture.

Kelly waited downstairs while I packed a bag with a few more articles of clothing, a better pair of running shoes, and my camera. Checking my reflection in the mirror over the dresser, I heard her singing to the dog in the front hall. I smiled—I really did like her voice.

And I liked her warmth and her sense of humor and her kindness. I liked her legs and her hips and her breasts. I liked the smell of her skin and the color of her hair and the gleam in those green eyes when she willfully pushed my buttons.

I liked that she'd climbed on my lap last night. I liked that she'd called me out on my bullshit. I liked that she wanted me.

What I didn't like was that nothing could come of it.

But I still sprayed myself with the cologne she said was her favorite before I left the room. I even stuck the bottle in the bag—along with a handful of condoms.

I was halfway down the stairs when I saw her bending over to play with the dog.

That's when I decided to go back for the entire box.

"You made it!" Veronica called, jumping up from her chair as Kelly and I walked into Austin's backyard. My brother waved from where he sat at a big table beneath an umbrella, and my dad called hello from the lawn, where he and Owen were playing a game of horseshoes.

Veronica came over to greet Kelly, a huge smile on her face. "Hi, I'm Veronica. Thank you so much for coming."

"Thanks for inviting me. I'm Kelly." She glanced down at the salad she'd made. "I brought a salad, but it's nothing much."

"This looks amazing!" Veronica took the salad from Kelly. "Is that arugula?"

"Yes. Arugula, strawberries, feta, shallot, pecans, a little mint." She made a face. "I've got the dressing in my bag—it's store-bought vinaigrette, sorry."

Veronica laughed. "Listen, a couple months ago, I would not even have been able to *identify* arugula, so don't feel bad. I'm still learning my way around the kitchen. Come on in the house, I'll get you a glass of wine."

"That sounds great, thanks." Kelly followed

Veronica, who belatedly looked at me over her shoulder. "Oh, hi, Xander."

"Hi, Veronica." But it was obvious she could not have cared less about me as she eagerly led Kelly toward the back door.

"Adelaide cannot wait to meet you," I heard her saying. "When she found out you were coming, she went into her room to get ready and hasn't come out since."

Kelly's laughter faded as they disappeared into the kitchen.

Fishing a beer from the cooler, I dropped into the chair opposite my brother and twisted the cap off the bottle. Took a long swallow.

"So how's it going?" Austin asked, glancing at the kitchen window. Through the screen we could hear Kelly and Veronica chattering a mile a minute, like they'd been friends forever.

I shrugged, scanning the perimeter of his yard. "Okay."

"Veronica said you and Kelly don't get along?"

"It's not that we don't get along."

"What is it?"

I tipped up my beer again. "The situation is just difficult."

My brother laughed. "Because she doesn't like you?"

"Turns out, she *likes* me just fine," I couldn't resist telling him.

"Oh yeah? From what Roni said, I thought she was giving you a hard time."

"She was, but we called a truce. Now she's . . ." From inside the house, I heard her laugh. "She's driving me a little crazy."

"In what way?"

I rolled my shoulders. "I know this is going to sound shocking, but I might have made a mistake."

"What did you do?"

"I kissed her."

His eyebrows shot up. "That *is* kind of shocking. I'm surprised you'd make a move on someone you're assigned to protect."

"It wasn't a move, okay?" I sat up taller in my chair. "It was a tactic."

"A tactic?"

"Yeah. I took her to Backwoods last night, and she wanted to have a drink in the bar before we left. Some asshole came up from behind and was about to tap her shoulder."

"Ah. Lives were at stake, and you had no choice but to kiss her." He raised his beer to me. "You're a hero."

"Don't be a dick. It was the only thing I could do in the moment to protect her."

He grinned and took a sip. "Of course it was. Go on."

"So even though I only kissed her in my capacity as her close personal protective agent, I believe she may have gotten the wrong idea."

"You didn't explain yourself right away?"

"I did, but . . ." This was the part that got tricky. "Then I kissed her again."

147

"At the bar?"

"Yes." I hesitated. "And later back at the house."

Austin burst out laughing. "Dude."

"Look, that one was not my idea," I said defensively. "*She* put the moves on *me*."

"Why'd she do that?"

I held out my arms, like *duh*.

My brother rolled his eyes. "You know what I mean."

"I don't know. It came out of nowhere! She was all, 'Let's go sit by the fire,' and 'Now I'm going to sit in your lap' and 'Don't tell me you didn't like seeing me naked.'"

Austin nearly choked. "You saw her naked?"

"It was an accident!" I glanced at the house and lowered my voice. "When I arrived on Thursday, the fucking door was unlocked and she wasn't answering my knock, so I let myself in, and she happened to walk straight from the shower into her living room *without even covering up with a towel*. Who does that?" I demanded.

"You must have scared her to death. No wonder she tried to fire you."

"She also threatened to make me sleep outside."

My brother laughed. "Did you?"

"No. She ended up giving me the couch, but it's like three feet too short, and my legs keep cramping up." As if to make my point, I massaged my left hamstring. "And there are already paparazzi up here taking her picture. Any minute now I'm expecting to see a camera lens pop up over your fence. I'm telling you, so much about this gig is a nightmare."

"But you have to do it."

"I have to do it." I leaned back and shut my eyes. "But I didn't have to kiss her, and I feel like shit."

"How come? Sounds like she was into it."

"Because it's a betrayal of the trust her brother placed in me."

"Did he tell you not to touch her?"

I shook my head. "Some things between brothers are just understood."

"I get that," he said, "but you and Kelly are also two grown adults who can make your own decisions."

"Excuse me," I said, pointing my beer at him, "I seem to recall you refusing to touch Veronica because she was working for you."

"And you were right in my face the whole time telling me I was being—let me see if I remember this correctly—a fucking idiot."

I smirked. "You were. It was so obvious what was going to happen."

The back door opened, and Adelaide came rushing out. "Daddy, look!" She ran over to us, and I noticed her shirt said *Hart Throb* in glittery pink and red letters. "She signed my shirt!" Spinning around, Adelaide presented us with her back, where Kelly had signed Pixie Hart, dotting the i's with hearts just like she'd signed the napkin yesterday, only much bigger.

"Pretty cool," Austin said.

"I'm going to wear it the first day of school," Adelaide announced, her cheeks flushed with anticipation.

Veronica and Kelly came out the back door, each holding a glass of wine, and made their way over to the table. My brother rose to his feet and held out his hand. "Hey. I'm Austin."

She smiled brightly as she shook it. "Nice to meet you. I'm Kelly."

"That's her real name," Adelaide said excitedly, hopping from foot to foot. "I thought her real name was Pixie Hart!"

Kelly laughed as she came around the table and took the chair next to me. "Nope, that's just a name a promoter liked back when he was booking me at county fairs and the like. Apparently, he didn't think Kelly Jo Sullivan was catchy enough."

"Does it bother you?" Veronica asked as Austin pulled out the chair next to him for her. She gave him a grateful smile as she sat down.

"It didn't back then. Now it kind of does," Kelly admitted. "Like I wonder if maybe I should have fought harder to keep my own name. But fighting doesn't come easily to me. I'm sort of conflict-avoidant."

"Could have fooled me," I mumbled, which earned me a sharp elbow to the rib.

My dad and Owen came over, and Kelly stood up to introduce herself, giving them both a handshake and smile. Owen mumbled his name and stared at the ground, while my dad doffed his cap, beamed excitedly, and pumped her hand up and down for a solid twenty seconds. Taking a seat at the end of the table between her and Veronica, he looked delighted with his luck.

"So how do you like our town?" he asked Kelly.

"Well, I haven't seen much of it yet," she said. "Xander is a bit of a dud when it comes to letting me get out and about. But from what I saw out the car window, it's lovely."

My dad scrunched up his face. "Why can't you let her out of the car?"

I gave Kelly a dirty look and saw her eyes were lit up with mischief as she took a sip of her wine. "I never said she couldn't get out of the car. I just don't want her driving herself or walking around alone or broadcasting her location to the internet."

"But this isn't some big, dangerous city," my dad argued. "It's Cherry Tree Harbor. It's perfectly safe to walk around alone."

"Not if you're Pixie Hart," I argued. "She's not the same as you or me, Dad. People follow her everywhere. And things can get out of control quickly."

"He's right," she said, forgetting the no-touching rule and patting my leg. "I just like giving him a hard time."

"But Cherry Tree Harbor is full of good people," my dad insisted. "You should take her around, Xander. I bet she'd like to see the lighthouse, take the ferry ride, have dinner at the Pier Inn."

"She definitely needs to eat some fudge while

she's here," Veronica said. "I highly recommend the ice cream too."

"And Moe's Diner!" shouted Adelaide, her mouth full of potato chips. "That's my favorite. It has a jukebox."

"All that sounds wonderful." Kelly gave me the side-eye. "What do you say? Will you play tour guide for me?"

"Not this weekend," I argued. "Cherry Tree Harbor is packed to the gills with tourists. Once they all go home on Monday, then I'll take you around."

"Deal," she said with a nod.

"You should take her out on the boat, Xander," said Veronica.

Kelly gasped and whacked my shoulder with the back of her hand. "You've got a boat? You never mentioned that."

"I just met you two days ago," I reminded her. "And I wasn't hired to amuse you, just to make sure you don't get into trouble."

"What kind of trouble could I get in out on your boat?"

I could think of plenty, especially if she was going to be wearing the skimpy white bathing suit I'd seen in that photo, but I kept my mouth shut.

"I think it's going to rain all day tomorrow," said Austin, "but Monday is supposed to be nice."

I looked up at the sky. Earlier it had been a bright, clear blue, but now I noticed clouds drifting in from the west. "I didn't realize it was going to rain."

"Yeah." Veronica made a face. "It's supposed to

be kind of a big storm. They were talking about it in town today. Such a bummer on a holiday weekend."

"When is the rain supposed to start?" Kelly asked. "I think we left windows open at the cabin."

"Not until tonight." Veronica looked at the sky. "Although those clouds are rolling in fast, aren't they?"

Austin stood up. "Guess I'd better get the meat on the grill. Xander, you want to give me a hand?"

"Sure." Rising to my feet, I followed him into the kitchen.

As soon as the door closed behind us, Austin started to laugh. "Dude."

"What's so funny?" I asked, bristling as he opened the fridge and pulled out a sealed plastic bag full of marinating chicken breasts.

"You are." He gave me a familiar smirk as he set the bag on the counter. His words were familiar too. "It's so obvious what's going to happen."

I folded my arms over my chest. "What do you mean?"

"I mean you and Pixie Hart."

"Don't call her that. It's not her name."

"Sorry." He grabbed a package of hot dogs and a plate stacked with hamburger patties from the fridge, kicking it shut with his foot. "You and Kelly Jo Sullivan out there."

"Nothing is going to happen," I said, thinking about those condoms in my bag.

"Oh yeah?" He pulled a glass baking dish from a

cupboard and dumped the chicken breasts into it. "Care to bet on it?"

I pressed my lips together. I rarely declined to take a bet, especially if winning it meant Austin would lose.

But I was nervous about my odds on this one.

"I don't think so," I said.

Surprised, Austin turned around and raised his eyebrows. "Why not?"

"Easy." I shrugged. "I'm not a fucking idiot."

CHAPTER THIRTEEN

kelly

"YOUR FAMILY IS SO NICE," I gushed as Xander turned around in his brother's driveway and I waved to Austin, Veronica, George, and the kids, who all stood on the porch watching us leave.

"Thanks for spending so much time with them," Xander said, switching the wipers on. Fat raindrops were just starting to splash onto the windshield. Lightning flashed in the deep gray sky. "My dad was definitely living his best life when you asked him for lessons on throwing horseshoes."

"Aww. He's such a sweetheart."

"I thought Adelaide was going to cry when you asked to see her bedroom."

I laughed. "I know how important a girl's room is. How she decorates it says a lot about her personality."

"So what does it say that she has a giant poster of you on her wall?"

"That she has good taste in music, duh." I reached

over and slapped his thigh. "Oops, sorry. I broke a rule."

"You've been breaking it all day," he complained. "Why do you have to be so touchy-feely?"

"It's not on purpose. I'm just a touchy-feely person. I'll try to be better." I put my hands between my knees and squeezed them. "How's that?"

He glanced at my legs, but his frown only deepened. "It's fine."

Hiding a smile by looking out the window, I noticed we'd turned onto the downtown main street, which looked straight out of a movie set—red brick sidewalks, charming little boutiques, quaint coffee shops, an ice cream parlor, an art gallery, a tiny movie theater. Even the old-fashioned streetlamps were adorable. Most of the businesses were closed, since it was close to nine o'clock, but through restaurant windows I could see people lingering over their Saturday night dinner tables.

"This town is so cute!" I said. "I can't wait to come back and explore." At the end of the business district, Xander turned left, and the street sloped down toward the harbor. The view was so pretty, I gasped. "Oh, look at the moon on the water! Is that the lighthouse your dad mentioned?"

"Yes." He slowed down. "This is Waterfront Park straight ahead of us. That big place on the right is called The Pier Inn. I used to work there every summer busing tables. The marina is on the other side of it." He turned left and we drove along the water.

"Is there a beach?" I asked, straining to see. "It's hard to tell in the dark."

"Not here. This is just a park and harbor. But there's a public beach up the road. On the left here— along the bluff—are big vacation homes that were built by rich Chicago families over a hundred years ago."

"Wow," I said, trying to lean over him so I could look out the driver's side window. Through the misty dark, I could see the hulking shapes of big old Victorians—turrets and gables and porches and witch hat roofs. "I wish I could see better."

"I'll bring you back during the day. I'm hoping to buy a house around here in a few months—not one of those, of course. Something smaller." As we left Cherry Tree Harbor behind us, the road became a highway, and Xander picked up speed. Rain drummed hard against the windshield.

"For your wife and three rowdy kids?" I teased.

"Ha."

"So Veronica lives in the apartment above Austin's garage?"

Xander laughed. "I think she *technically* lives in the apartment, but my guess is she spends a lot of nights in Austin's bed and sneaks out early."

"That's kinda fun."

"It's kinda ridiculous. Those kids *know* what's going on between them."

"Maybe, but having a secret makes you feel close to someone." I looked over at him. "Don't you think?"

He shrugged. "I don't really have any secrets."

"Oh, come on. Everyone has secrets. Stuff they bury way down deep."

"Not me. I'm an open book."

Shifting in the passenger seat to face him, I tucked one boot under the opposite knee. "An open book, huh?"

"Totally."

I rubbed a finger beneath my lower lip. "I disagree."

"What do you mean, you disagree?" He tossed a frown in my direction.

"I mean, I think you're one of those guys who *claims* to be an open book, and you keep everyone distracted with that cocky grin and easygoing charm, but you actually have a *second* book that you keep tightly closed, hidden from view."

"A second book?" He snorted. "And what's in this mysterious, hidden second book?"

"Your real feelings, of course."

He burst out laughing. "Like a little diary where I write down the names of all my crushes? Mabel had one of those she used to lock with an actual key. Except she hid it in the most obvious place ever, and Dashiel found it and cut it open."

I gasped. "He didn't."

"He did. And it turned out she had a huge crush on his best friend. We teased her about it mercilessly."

"That's awful," I said, shaking my head. "Boys are *awful*. Poor Mabel."

"She survived. But anyway, I don't have any secret diary of feelings. Sorry to disappoint you. What you see is what you get."

"Come on. We all have parts of ourselves we guard closer than others. We all choose which sides of ourselves to share and which to protect."

"Maybe I don't have a side that needs protection," he said. "Maybe I feel perfectly comfortable exposing all of my parts."

I laughed. "Except to me."

"Hey, listen." He got gruff with me again. "Protecting myself and protecting you are two different things. Don't confuse them."

"I'm not confused." I grinned and held out my arms, Xander Buckley-style. "I'm just telling it like it is."

By the time we got home, the rain was torrential, and the wind blew it in on a hard, pelting slant. We jumped out of the car and bolted for the porch, where Xander held his bag over my head while I typed in the code. "Shoot," I said as we rushed in. "We *did* leave the windows open!"

"Get the ones in the bedroom," he ordered, quickly turning a lamp on. "I'll get these."

I raced down the dark hallway into the bedroom, slipping on the wood floor in my wet boots. Luckily, the rain was angling away from the windows above the bed, so nothing had gotten wet. I cranked them shut, then sat down, tugged off my wet boots, and peeled off my damp socks. I thought about changing out of my soggy dress, but Xander seemed to like it. I'd caught him staring at me a lot today.

Heading back to the living room barefoot, I stopped short when I saw Xander's naked back across the room. He tossed his wet shirt aside and reached into his bag for another one. The muscles beneath his tattooed skin worked as he lifted the plain white T-shirt and pulled it over his head. He turned around before it was all the way on, giving me the briefest glimpse of his bare chest and abs. Lots of ink. Lots of muscles. Lots of delicious little hills and valleys I could imagine running my hands over. Or my tongue.

I might have licked my lips.

"Is anything wet?" he asked.

It took me a second. "Oh, you mean the bed? No."

"What did you think I meant?"

"Nothing."

Behind him, the lamp flickered. The house groaned in the wind. "Think we'll lose power?" I asked.

"We might."

A loud crack of lightning split the air. "Ooh!" Touching my chest, I laughed nervously as thunder shook the cabin walls. "That one spooked me."

He gave me a boyish smile that made my stomach flutter. "You okay?"

"I'm fine," I said. "Just a little jumpy, I guess."

We stood there for a moment, looking at each other from opposite ends of the room while rain hammered on the roof. *If my life were a movie*, I thought, *I'd rush toward him and he'd rush toward me and we'd close the gap between us in two heartbeats, our bodies and mouths colliding fast and hard.*

But I wasn't about to take that first step and risk his hand shooting out to stop me. He'd made his position clear last night, and I'd promised to respect it.

"Well," I said, "I guess I'll turn in and get cozy with a paperback."

"Okay."

I waved stupidly. "Goodnight."

He shoved his hands in his pockets. "Night."

Hesitating for a couple more seconds, I gave him ample opportunity to stop me, but he didn't. Rooted to the spot, his body was rigid and tense, the cords in his neck taut with restraint.

I could feel his eyes on me as I moved down the hall.

CHAPTER FOURTEEN

xander

SHE DISAPPEARED from view and I exhaled with relief. Only when I heard the bathroom door close did I pull my hands from my pockets. For a moment there, the compulsion to kiss her again had been almost unbearable. In three strides I could have crossed the floor and swept her into my arms, carried her off to bed, and stripped that wet dress from her skin.

My head could be buried between her thighs already.

Stifling a groan, I rubbed my face with both hands as the power flickered, then went off again. And this time, it didn't come back on.

The bathroom door opened a moment later. "Xander?"

Immediately I moved toward her worried voice. "I'm here."

"It's so dark. I can't see."

"I've got you." Trained as a combat swimmer, I

163

was used to navigating in total darkness. Reaching the bathroom doorway, I took her by the arm. "You okay?"

"Yeah, it just took me by surprise. And I don't—I don't *love* thunderstorms. I'm actually a little afraid of them."

"Yeah?" I led her across the hall into the bedroom.

"As a kid, I used to sleep in Kevin's room during the bad ones."

"He let you sleep in his bed?"

"No, he made me sleep on the floor."

I laughed. "Did he at least give you a sleeping bag?"

"Nope. Just a pillow and a blanket. But it was still better than being in my room alone."

I glanced at the bed. Swallowed hard. "Do you want me to sleep on the floor in here?"

"You'd do that?"

Realizing I still held her arm, I took my hands off her warm skin. "Sure."

"There's not much room."

"It's more room than I have on the couch."

She paused. "Do you want to just sleep in the bed?"

"I don't think that's a good idea."

"Xander, come on. Don't you trust me?"

"I trust you. Myself? Not so much."

She laughed softly. "Okay, fine. You want the floor, it's all yours."

"Give me a minute. I'll be right back."

I left the room and made my way out to the living room in the dark, my heart racing. Was she nuts? I couldn't sleep in her bed. It was hard enough keeping my tongue in my mouth when she was standing next to me, fully clothed. How was I supposed to behave when she was lying beside me, wearing next to nothing?

Fuck no. It was out of the question.

My eyes had adjusted well enough to find my duffel bag and root through it for some sweatpants. After trading my jeans for the sweats, I grabbed the little leather pouch with my toothbrush in it and used the bathroom. When I came out, the door to her bedroom was open, but I knocked anyway.

"You can come in," she called softly.

I entered the room and stood at the foot of the bed. She was already under the sheets, and my entire body yearned to join her, to hold her close during the storm. Take her mind off it with an orgasm or two. "Can you spare a pillow?"

"Of course." She sat up and handed me one. "There's an extra blanket in the closet."

"Thanks." Tossing the pillow to the floor, I opened the closet and pulled a thick fleece blanket from the shelf. Then I lay down on the rug between the dresser and the foot of the bed, spreading the blanket over my legs and tucking the pillow behind my head. "Night," I said.

"Night," she whispered back.

For a few minutes, I just lay there staring at the ceiling, listening to the steady hum of the rain on the roof, punctuated by the occasional rumble of thunder.

"Xander."

"What?"

"This is silly." She crawled to the foot of the bed and peeked down at me. "Just come up here."

"I don't think so."

"You can't be comfortable down there."

"My comfort isn't the issue."

"Come on, we can put all the pillows between us. The Great Wall. The Iron Curtain. Want me to see if there's some barbed wire lying around?"

"Yes."

A piercing crack split the air, followed by a roar of thunder that made the floor growl beneath me.

Kelly thumped the mattress. "Get up here, you big lummox. Or I'm coming down there."

Exhaling, I said a quick prayer asking for strength, then sat up. "Start building the wall." I grabbed my pillow and walked around to the empty side of the bed.

She placed pillows in a line down the center of the bed, on top of the covers. "There. See? You have your side, I have mine." She lay back and pulled the sheet up to her chin.

"You decent under there?"

"Define decent."

"Pajamas. Top and bottom."

She peeked under the covers. "Then I'm halfway decent."

I groaned. "What do you have against pants?"

She laughed. "Xander, I'm all the way over here! My leg isn't going to stray beyond the wall. And you're all covered up with sweats *and* a T-shirt. Just get in."

Taking the edge of the sheet in my hand, I hesitated before peeling it back. Because I knew—I *knew* —that if I got into that bed with her, something was going to happen. A fucking line of pillows wasn't going to stop me.

I got in anyway.

Laying on my back, I pulled the sheet to my waist and put my arms at my sides, stiff as a mummy. "Happy?"

"Yes." She rolled onto her side and propped her head in her hand. "Now let's stay up late and tell each other secrets."

"I told you, I don't have secrets."

"Oh, that's right. Xander Buckley: no secrets, no fears. Just telling it like it is."

"That's me."

"You should put that on a T-shirt. XB merch."

"Maybe I will. I could sell it at the bar." I stuck my hands behind my head.

She giggled. "So were you born fearless?"

I thought for a moment. "Maybe. Or maybe I was molded that way because I was the second kid. I was always trying to keep up with Austin. That meant I couldn't be scared of anything he wasn't scared of. And if he *was* scared of something, I had to prove I wasn't."

"Like what?"

"Like jumping from the garage roof into a small plastic baby pool with like five inches of water in it. He wouldn't do it, so I had to."

"Did you get hurt?"

"Fuck yes, I got hurt. Broke my arm."

"Ouch."

"I also had a big mouth, so I'd get myself in trouble by bragging I could do shit I couldn't actually do, but if Austin or anyone else called me out on it, I had to at least try to back it up."

"What would you say you could do?"

"Once, I said I could fly."

"Oh no." She started to laugh.

"It didn't end well."

"I'm afraid to ask this, but how did you try to prove it?"

"I stood on the back of the couch and tried to grab onto the ceiling fan. I figured the momentum would get me going and I might fly for at least a couple seconds."

"What happened?"

"I broke the fan. Got a bloody nose and a black eye."

"And yet you're probably lucky it wasn't worse."

"My mom was *so mad*. Even Austin got in trouble, for letting me do it." I paused as my mind wandered toward memories that were less physically harmful but had left me with deeper scars. "When she got sick, things changed. I changed."

In the silence that followed, the rain seemed louder. "How so?"

"I was afraid."

"Of losing her?"

"Yes." Thunder rumbled, shaking the knotty pine walls as I went on. "And then when my worst fear was realized, I started to be scared of everything. And I hated it. I was fucking mad. Then one day I decided enough was enough and if something made me afraid, I had to face it down. For instance, I never used to like deep water."

"Really?"

"Yeah. Especially in a lake where you couldn't see the bottom. Heights? I was fine. I'd climb any tree, scale any wall, ride the tallest rides. But that deep, dark water . . . it was the unknown. I was terrified of falling in and just sinking into oblivion."

"How'd you get over it?"

"I jumped into deep water at every possible opportunity. Practiced holding my breath as long as possible. Became a good swimmer—have I mentioned my swim team records at the high school?"

Her laughter was soft. "Not yet."

"A few of them still stand. Anyway, after high school, I did the thing I thought sounded the hardest and scariest—became a Navy SEAL combat swimmer. I was good at it because I knew how to overcome the panic and focus on the job."

"You learned to compartmentalize."

"I faced my fears." It seemed like an important distinction. "I'm not afraid of deep water anymore. Or anything else."

"Just me." She reached over the line of pillows and poked me in the ribs.

I grabbed her wrist. "Excuse me, ma'am, you've breached security one too many times today."

"I'm sorry! It was an accident!"

"I don't believe you." I kept my fingers locked around her arm, feeling the vestiges of my self-control crumble. "I think you keep trying to tempt me on purpose after you promised you wouldn't."

She giggled. "I swear I'm not. Please don't be mad."

"I'm not mad. But I can't let you off the hook without some consequence."

"Name it. I'll do anything."

"There you go again. Tempting me to do things I shouldn't. I wonder if country music knows its sweetheart is so evil beneath the sequins."

"They don't know anything about me," she said seriously. "What they get is an act."

"But they love it." I rubbed my thumb along her inner wrist, my body starting to hum. "And you're good at it."

"I've had a lot of practice. No one wants the real me."

"I wouldn't say that."

"Maybe one person does. But he's giving me some trouble."

"What a dick. Want me to fuck him up?"

"Yeah. Just enough to send a message."

"What's the message?" I brought her arm to my

170

mouth and pressed my lips where my thumb had been. Her inner wrist felt like satin.

"That he doesn't have to be afraid of me."

"Maybe you should be afraid of him." Tugging her closer, I kissed my way up her arm.

"Well, I'm not. I trust him."

"Why do you trust him? What did he do to earn it?" My lips reached the curve of her elbow.

"I don't know," she said softly. "I just feel safe with him."

Those words should have reminded me of my role as her protector, what my duty was, why I shouldn't touch her. But they had the opposite effect —they pushed me over the edge.

Hitching myself up on my elbow, I flipped her onto her back, the wall of pillows trapped between us. I looked down at her face, pale and hazy in the dark. I felt her breath on my lips. "You are safe with me."

"Xander," she whispered, curling her free hand around my jaw and sliding it to the back of my neck. "Please let me be close to you. Even if it's only for tonight."

She pulled my head down and I sealed my mouth to hers. Her fingers snaked into my hair as my tongue eased between her lips. As the kiss deepened, I grew frustrated with the sheet twisted between us, not to mention the barrier wall. Scrambling to my knees, I whipped the sheet back and threw every one of those pillows to the floor.

"No more wall?" she asked breathlessly.

"Fuck the wall." Eagerly, I ranged my body over hers again, but she stopped me with a hand to the chest.

"Take your shirt off."

I grabbed it at the back of my neck and yanked it off. Immediately, she got to her knees and put her hands on me, skimming her palms all over my stomach, chest, shoulders.

"I saw you," she breathed. "Earlier tonight, when you were changing your shirt. I saw you."

Her touch sent gooseflesh rippling down my arms. "I saw you too. Days ago. Completely naked and dripping wet. And I've been losing my mind ever since." I grabbed the bottom of her T-shirt and lifted it over her head, then wrapped her in my arms, our mouths colliding, our upper bodies pressing close. The skin-to-skin contact sent a jolt of arousal straight to my cock.

Our kiss was desperate and rough. Her palms on my back. My fists in her hair. My cock like a rocket ready to launch, trapped between us. I slid my hands down over her ass, inside her underwear, pulling her tight against me.

I'd never wanted so many things at once. I wanted gravity, heat, friction. I wanted to taste every inch of her skin. I wanted to feel her legs wrapped around me while I moved inside her. I wanted to make her come, hear the sounds she made as her body tightened around me, feel the pulse of her orgasm on my cock. I wanted to own her—the real her, the private her, the woman no one else knew.

But I had to make sure it was what she wanted too.

I tipped her onto her back and knelt between her thighs, bracing my hands above her shoulders. "Before we cross any more lines, I think we should talk."

Her hands skated up my chest. "You want to *talk*? *Now*?"

"Yes." But she was teasing my nipples with her fingertips, which made it difficult to use my words, so I sat back on my heels, out of her reach. "I need to know you're okay with this."

"You can't tell?" Sitting up, she took me by the wrist, bringing my hand between her legs. "Touch me."

Holding my breath, I caressed her through the silky material of her underwear, my cock surging as my fingertips found her swollen clit through the thin fabric.

"Inside."

My heart pumped hard as I inched my fingers beneath the silk and found her warm, soft, and wet. I slid one finger inside her, and she moaned. Or maybe that was me.

"Now do you believe me?" she asked.

"Yes. Lie back."

She did as I asked, and I slipped a second finger inside her, using my thumb against her clit. With my other hand, I reached for one nipple, teasing it with my fingertips, my cock aching as I remembered the pert feel of it against my tongue.

She lifted her hips, rocking them against my hand, her hands clawing the sheet next to her hips. "I want this, Xander. I want you. Tell me what you need to hear, I'll say it. I'll do anything you want me to."

"That's not how this is going to work, baby." I took my hands off her only so I could shimmy the damp silk panties down her legs and toss them aside.

"No?"

"No. I'm bossy, but I'm not your boss," I told her, pushing her knees apart and sliding down in the bed so my head was between her thighs. "I'm not the record label." I pressed a kiss to the soft warm skin at my left cheek. "I'm not your manager or your agent or your publicist." I rubbed my beard against the opposite thigh. "You don't have to worry about performing for me. I don't want an act. I don't want to fuck Pixie Hart."

She propped herself up on her elbows and looked down at me. "What do you want?"

"I want the real you," I said, slowly stroking up the center of her pussy with my tongue. I did it again, lingering at the top, swirling over her clit, making a little X just to feel like I was leaving my mark. I nuzzled the swollen little sweet spot with my nose. "I want Kelly Jo Sullivan. I want to know how she tastes, I want to know how she sounds, I want to know what makes her come."

"This is—this is a very . . . promising start." She gasped and cried out as I teased and licked and savored. After an entire day of fasting, I let myself feast.

"I want to make you forget everyone and anyone else," I said, easing my fingers back inside her, "because tonight, no one exists but you."

She tasted as sweet as the perfume she wore, and I devoured her with insatiable hunger. Caveman grunting. Greedy sucking noises. I knew she was getting close when her hips began to buck beneath my quicksilver tongue and her insides tightened around my probing fingers. Falling back, she clutched handfuls of my hair and held me to her as I sucked her clit into my mouth and flicked the tip of it with quick, hard strokes. Her cries grew louder as the climax hit, and I nearly came in my pants as I felt her body pulse and quiver.

The tremors had barely faded when I felt her yanking me up by my arms. "Xander." Her voice cracked over my name as she reached between my legs and stroked me through my sweatpants. "I want you. Now."

My pants were halfway to my knees when I realized I hadn't brought protection in here. "Hang on," I said, pulling them up again. "I'll be right back."

Thanking my earlier-in-the-day self for recognizing that my honor was bound to lose the battle to my desire, I fished a condom from the box I'd hidden at the bottom of my duffel bag and raced back into the bedroom. I stuck the packet between my teeth while I ditched my pants and underwear, then knelt on the bed again.

Kelly braced herself on her elbows and watched

me tear open the wrapper and roll the condom on. "Finally," she said. "I get to see *you* naked."

I fisted my cock, flexing my abs. "And?"

"And what?"

"What do you think?"

"I can't tell you that," she said, as if astonished I'd even ask. "Your ego is monster enough. It's almost as big as your dick."

"That's it." I grabbed her by the armpits and tossed her onto her back sideways across the bed, otherwise my head was going to hit the angled ceiling above us. Pinning her arms to the mattress, I buried my face in her neck and kissed my way down her throat to her chest, using my lips and tongue on each perfect breast, sucking the tight pink peaks into my mouth, biting them gently, enjoying the way it made her arch and moan.

"Enough," she said, trying to drag me back up her body. "I need you inside me. I can't wait any longer."

Since my patience had also reached its limits, I did as she asked, stretching out above her and positioning my cock between her legs. For a moment, I thought about teasing her, giving her an inch or two, making her beg for all of me, but as soon as I eased the tip inside her, I realized I didn't have the patience for any more games. I slid all the way home in one long stroke, both of us moaning at the sweet, sublime fit. She was warm and snug and velvety smooth, and I buried myself balls deep and stayed there for a moment, all my muscles tensed, body poised on the edge. If she'd moved, I'd have exploded.

But she stayed still too, breathing hard, her chest rising and falling fast. "Xander," she whispered, her eyes closed, her hands clutching my shoulders. "Give me a minute."

"I wish I could stop time right now. I'd give them all to you."

She opened her eyes and ran her hands down my arms. "God, this feels good. How is it possible that two days ago I despised you, and right now, all I want is you inside me?"

"I don't know," I said, my body aching to move. My thighs were burning, my stomach tight.

"But you didn't care what I wanted, did you?"

"I care now." I began to rock into her with slow, rhythmic strokes. "I care *deeply*. I care *hard*. Let me show you how much."

She moaned, digging her heels into the backs of my thighs. "Yes. Show me. Take me there."

I had every intention of going slow, of showing off my skills in the dark, the ones I'd bragged about this morning, but it was like trying to harness a wild horse at a full gallop. Within minutes, I was driving into her with vicious abandon, deeper and harder with every thrust. The bed jerked away from the wall. Her fingers raked across my back. Our skin grew slick with heat. The tension inside me raged like an animal behind bars.

Slow down, asshole, I told myself, recalling that

177

MELANIE HARLOW

pink vibrator. *She wants tickling rabbit ears. She wants swirling beads. She wants thirty-six vibrational patterns.*

Dammit, I didn't have any of those things! And all I wanted was to lose control, let go of this *feeling* for her—I didn't want it inside me anymore. It didn't belong there. It was confusing and infuriating and all her fault.

I slowed down and put my lips at her ear. "You're so fucking beautiful," I growled. "You make me crazy. I want to protect you and fucking tear you apart at the same time. I want to make you feel safe while I fuck you so hard it hurts. I want to be a good man for you, but I also want to feel you come on my cock."

"Xander," she panted. "Don't stop."

"You're so wet," I rasped, thrusting faster. "So tight. And I can still taste you on my tongue."

She grabbed my ass and rocked her hips beneath me, matching me stroke for stroke, murmuring incoherently as her body tensed up beneath me. *Yes, yes, yes, you're so good, right there, come with me, please . . .*

Staying tight to her body, I kept my rhythm firm and steady on her clit until her head fell to one side, her mouth opened in a silent scream, and her pussy clenched my cock with tiny little pulses that sent me shooting for the stars.

Letting go completely, I plunged into her again and again, making her cry out with every savage thrust, guttural sounds coming from the back of my throat as I powered through an orgasm so strong it paralyzed my muscles while rattling my bones.

Aftershocks reverberated through my body as I tried to catch my breath. Realizing I was probably smothering her, I lifted my chest and looked down. Her cheek was still turned, her eyes closed, her mouth open.

"You okay?" I asked.

Her insides squeezed me once more, and she shivered. "That. Was. Incredible."

"Look at that, we agree on something."

She smiled and looked up. "Who'd have thought?"

"I'll be right back," I said, rolling off her.

The thunderstorm had moved off, but I could still hear the rain as I headed into the bathroom. I remembered that Veronica said it was going to rain all day tomorrow, and I thought about spending the entire day in bed with Kelly. Was that allowed? Or was this one and done? She'd said something earlier like *only for tonight*. Had she meant it?

After cleaning up, I went back into the bedroom and pushed the bed back into place. "Sounds like the storm has passed."

Kelly rolled onto her side to face me. "I know."

"Do you still want me to sleep in here?"

"Depends."

"On what?"

"Do we still have the no-touching rule?"

I ran a hand through my hair. "Ah, I think we can bury that rule. It's good and dead."

She laughed and tossed the covers back. "May it rest in peace. But I won't miss it."

I climbed in next to her, and she immediately tucked herself against my side, throwing an arm across my waist and laying her head on my chest.

"I know you're probably not a cuddler," she said, "but can I just have a minute?"

"How do you know I'm not a cuddler?"

"Just a guess."

"Well, it's wrong. I happen to be a fucking great cuddler. It's my long arms." I wrapped one around her. "See?"

She giggled. "But that doesn't mean you *like* it. You can be good at something and not enjoy it."

"True. I guess you'll just have to trust me that in this case, I'm good at it *and* I'm enjoying it."

"I trust you." She paused. "It's actually strange how much I trust you. I wish you lived in Nashville so you could be in charge of my security team there."

"I'm not sure how well that would work," I said. "I'd probably punch anyone who got near you. And anyway, I'm out of the security business. This was just a favor for your brother." At the mention of Sully, I expected a stab of guilt. I was surprised when it didn't come.

We were both silent for a moment, listening to the rain drum softly on the roof. I stroked her shoulder and breathed in the sweet scent of her hair. Our breathing synced, and I found myself getting drowsy. My eyes closed. My hand stilled. My body relaxed.

"Xander?"

"Hmm?"

"I have to confess something."

"What?"

She sighed. "I'm not really afraid of storms anymore. I just wanted you to sleep in here."

"It's okay. I lied about something too."

"What?" She sat up and looked at me.

"I *did* want to kiss you last night. It wasn't all for show."

"Oh, that." She snickered. "That was obvious."

I pinched her butt. "Also, I saw your vibrator in the shower."

She gasped. "You snooped in my shower?"

"I wasn't snooping. I just sort of . . . peeked behind the curtain. But believe me, I was sorry I did it."

"Why?" She covered her bare chest demurely. "Did it ruin your image of country music's sweetheart?"

"No, but it gave me a slight insecurity complex. It has bits and bobs my anatomy does not have."

"Oh." She laughed, dropping her arms. "Yes, it does. But you've got nothing to worry about. It doesn't come close to you. I'd take your anatomy over a toy any day."

"Good."

"In fact, I shouldn't tell you this, because you'll get ridiculously smug about it, but I've never had two orgasms so close together before."

I pumped a fist in the air. "Fuck yeah. Want a third? I'll make it happen right now."

"I need a little break, overachiever, but maybe tomorrow you'll demonstrate more of your magic."

"Challenge accepted."

Her head tilted, and she spoke coyly. "I'll even let you play with my toys if you like. They're hidden under the bed."

"Toys? Plural?"

"Hey, I thought I was going to be alone for two weeks, remember? You were a surprise." She walked two fingers across my chest. "But since you're here, we can play together."

"So this isn't just for tonight? Earlier, you mentioned something . . ."

"I think I was just trying to get in your pants."

"It worked."

"So if you're up for it, we could continue exploring this new, *agreeable* side of our relationship while I'm here."

"I'm up for it. But don't be too agreeable," I told her. "I like a little bit of a fight."

"Challenge accepted."

She put her head down and snuggled up to me again. Her breathing slowed, and once or twice she sighed with contentment. I couldn't remember the last time I'd spent an entire night in someone's bed. My last few dalliances had been quick little one-night romps, the sexual equivalent of a candy bar. Good enough to take the edge off your hunger, but lacking the satisfaction of a full meal.

Kelly was something else entirely. My appetite was fully sated, and yet I wanted seconds. The fire was already building again. And those toys? I had so many *ideas* . . .

"Xander?" Her voice was soft and sleepy.

"Yeah?"

"I'm really glad my brother saved your life."

"I am too." In fact, I wasn't sure I'd ever been gladder. Life was pretty fucking great at the moment.

"And I'm glad you're here with me. I'm sorry I tried to make you leave."

"I was never going to leave," I said.

She held me tighter. "I know. I like that about you."

CHAPTER FIFTEEN

kelly

I WOKE up to the sound of drizzle on the roof and someone breathing behind me. A heavy arm circled my waist, and a warm, hard body curled around mine.

My eyes popped open. The first thing I saw was the knotty pine ceiling sloping toward me. When I looked down, I saw the ink on the thick, masculine forearm draped possessively over my belly. The previous night came back to me, and my body tingled right down to my toes.

I couldn't believe it—I'd had sex with the big bearded lummox.

Not just any sex, *good* sex. *Hot* sex. Mind-blowing, bed-moving, two-orgasm sex. Was I surprised? Not really. Xander moved in the world with the kind of confidence that came from knowing you could cash any check you wrote.

And that body, my God. The muscles. The ink. That mouth. Those hands. That cock. Between my legs, I felt that whoosh, followed by an involuntary contraction of my core muscles. A little memo from my body to my brain—*more please.*

Could I have more? It would be fun, but was it wise? Could this hot little vacation fling somehow come back to bite me in the ass?

I couldn't see how, really. I trusted Xander not to run to the internet tabloids or sell his story to the gossipmongers. We weren't making out in public. Photos of us in a clinch weren't going to pop up in entertainment news with a lot of speculation over who was banging Pixie Hart. Duke wasn't going to see them and come at me in a fit of jealous rage.

Not that I cared. I didn't belong to him. And he didn't really want me back—he just wanted the door to my bedroom to remain open for him. He liked the publicity we generated. He enjoyed me as candy on his arm.

Well, too fucking bad. I had no illusions he'd give a shit if I wasn't Pixie Hart. Maybe at first it was flattering to have the attention of such a well-known star, to feel special that you were the one who'd caught his eye when he could have anyone he wanted, to feel *chosen*, but reality had set in eventually. He hadn't chosen me. He didn't even know me. And he certainly hadn't been faithful to me.

I remembered Xander's words from last night. *You don't have to perform for me. I don't want an act. I don't want to fuck Pixie Hart.*

How could he have known I needed to hear those words so badly?

Suddenly the arm around me tightened. "It's tomorrow." His voice was gruff in my ear.

"Yes?"

"You said I could give you a third orgasm tomorrow, and it's tomorrow."

I laughed. "It's *barely* tomorrow."

"Does that mean you don't want one?" His hand snaked lower.

I was about to say of *course I want one, so keep going* when I remembered what he said about putting up a fight. I squeezed my legs together, denying his access. "You can't just give me an orgasm when you feel like it. You don't own me."

He froze. Then it clicked—we were playing a game. "You say bear, and it's over," he whispered.

"Okay."

Turning his hand sideways, he slid his fingers between my thighs. "You don't want this?"

"No," I said, tugging on his thick, sturdy wrist. It was like trying to pick up a cinderblock with my pinky. "I told you once before, I'm sick of being pushed around. I'm tired of everyone telling me what to do. This time, I'm putting up a fight."

In two seconds flat, he had me pinned beneath him, my stomach to the mattress, his body heavy on my back. "Do it. Put up a fight."

I squirmed and wiggled, as if I wanted to escape. One of my arms was trapped under my stomach along with one of his, but I swung at him with the other one—he laughed and let me flail before catching me by the wrist with his free hand and twisting that arm behind my back.

Placing his knees on either side of my thighs to keep them in place, he somehow captured my other arm, so he had both wrists crossed and pinioned against my lower back. "You're going to have to fight harder than that, baby."

I floundered and kicked and writhed, but it was like my upper body was encased in cement. "Not fair," I panted, turning my head to the side. "You're so much bigger and stronger than me."

"You're right. It really isn't fair at all." Somehow he locked one hand around both my wrists, holding them in place while he slid his other hand under my hips and hitched them up. Then he slipped a finger inside me from behind. Or maybe it was his thumb. "You're wet." His tone was cocky. "You want this."

"I don't," I lied, inwardly begging for more.

As if he heard me, he pushed in deeper, crooking his finger in some magical way that had my mouth opening wide on a fast exhale. "Liar," he rasped, now rubbing his fingertips over my clit in slow, sensual circles. "Now come for me."

"Never. Go to hell." I was panting with need, my nipples hard and tingling, my lower body surging with heat and pleasure. I wanted to move, to fuck his hand, to give up the fight. But part of what was turning me on so much was the game of resistance.

He flattened my body with his and spoke with a menacing tone. "Don't move, if you know what's good for you." Then he leaned down and reached under the bed. He felt around, and a moment later, he brought up his hand with my curvy little mini vibrator tucked in his grip. "What's this?"

It looked small in his wide, strong hand, but I knew how powerful it could be. "It's none of your business."

He pushed a button, switching it on. "Funny, I distinctly remember you offering to share your toys with me last night."

"I changed my mind."

A laugh rumbled in his chest as he slipped his hand beneath my hips again, yanked them up, and pressed the humming vibrator against my clit. "Too late now."

"Jerk." I pushed my forehead into the mattress. It felt so good, the way he was rubbing me with the rumbling little toy. I felt the vibrations in every fiber of my being. My body moved of its own accord as the tension pulled tight across my abdomen.

"That's it." His words dripped with self-satisfaction. "Just like that. Come for me. You want this."

"No!" I yelled, the mattress muffling the sound.

He laughed, holding it tight to my clit, the increased pressure and steady tremble taking me right to the summit.

Then his words pushed me right off.

"The only thing you want more is my cock."

"*Fuck you.*" My eyes closed and everything around me disappeared. There was only his scent in the air, his voice in my head, and the delicious, continuous burst of sensation beneath his touch.

When I stopped convulsing beneath him, he removed the toy, letting my hips collapse onto the mattress. Then he let go of my wrists and straightened up. "Three." Leaning forward, he whispered in my ear. "I'm gonna hit the shower. Join me if you want to fight about number four."

He sank his teeth into my shoulder before tossing the vibrator onto the bed and leaving the room.

The shower had only been running for a few minutes when I finally caught my breath and followed him into the bathroom. I noticed the light was on, which meant power had been restored at some point during the night. I took a minute to brush my teeth before I pulled back the shower curtain.

Xander looked like a god, bronzed and sculpted, water cascading down his tall, masculine body as he stood there slowly stroking his fully erect cock. "What took you so long?"

My eyes traveled down hungrily over his wet skin—the wide shoulders, the glistening ink, the towering erection—and back up again. With his hair all slicked back from his face, the chiseled jaw and cheekbones were even more arresting.

He was a work of art, and I'm pretty sure I drooled.

"Were you worried I ran off again?" I teased, stepping into the tub and pulling the curtain closed behind me.

His eyes narrowed as he caged me against the tiled wall with both arms. "You wouldn't dare."

"Oh no?"

"We've got an understanding now, you and I." He kissed me, teasing my lips open with his tongue. He tasted like toothpaste and smelled like his body wash, woodsy and clean.

"Is that what we're calling this? An understanding?" I sucked on his tongue and reached low, wrapping my fingers around his cock. His slippery flesh glided easily through my hand. I liked the way he immediately started to thrust into my fist, like he couldn't help himself, like he was already impatient for the release. I gripped him a little tighter, worked my arm a little faster.

"Fuck," he growled against my lips. "You better slow down."

"Why?"

"I'm about to come all over you."

"Maybe I want you to come all over me." When he groaned, I tortured him further by arching my back and brushing the pebbled tips of my breasts back and forth against his wet chest. Sparks of lust popped under my skin. "Maybe it's *my* turn to get what *I* want."

"Fuck me."

"We'll get to that." I rose up on tiptoe and ran my tongue along his bottom lip, then tugged it with my teeth. "We'll get to all kinds of things today."

"Christ." Xander was breathing hard, his jaw was clenched tight.

"That's it," I murmured as his cock thickened even more in my hand. It was dark in color and bulging with veins. "You want this. Stop pretending you don't. Give it to me."

"You want it?" His eyes closed, his stomach muscles flexing gorgeously as he neared climax. "You want my cum all over those perfect tits?"

"*Yes.*"

He had the audacity to count it off, as if to let me know he was still in control.

"Three." He wrapped his huge fist around mine, working my hand tighter and harder. "Two." His chest heaved. He pinned me with a hot, dark stare. "One." On the final word, he came in thick, white spurts that hit one breast like it was a bullseye. He pumped our hands a couple more times, each one bringing forth another shot that roped along my skin.

When he was spent, he put a hand on the mess he'd made and spread it around, rubbing himself into my skin, strumming my hard nipples with his fingers, then finally lowering his mouth to mine.

The kiss surprised me. It was deep but not hard, intense but not demanding. And it kept going. He wrapped one arm around my back and cradled my head with the other hand. His tongue was insistent but soft. My head began to swim, and despite the steam rising around us, my skin puckered with gooseflesh. My heart fluttered in an unfamiliar, all-consuming way.

"Hey." I pushed against his chest. "Give me some room. You're taking up all the space."

"I'm a big guy." He traded places with me. "Did I mention I'm two inches taller than Austin?"

"Once or twice," I said drily, moving under the spray. I wet my hair, then reached for my shampoo. Xander watched me intently as I lathered it up and rinsed it off. "What? Why are you staring at me like that?"

"You're nice to look at."

"Oh." My skin tingled. "Thanks."

"Plus my cum is still on your tits, which is really fucking hot."

I laughed. "You're a barbarian."

"But I was thinking that you're much prettier in person than in photographs."

I sighed, working conditioner through the long, wet strands. "Stop ruining the compliment, Xander."

"I'm not. I'm sweetening it. You always look good. Perfect, in fact. I just like you better like this."

"Because I'm naked."

"Because you're beautiful without any makeup on or your hair all done up." His arms slid around my waist, and he pressed his taut lower body to mine. "But yes. You're a fucking smoke show naked."

Our mouths came together, and I rose up on tiptoe, sliding my palms up his chest. His arms tightened around me, lifting me right off my feet. This time his kiss was more aggressive, his tongue more commanding. I was beginning to realize Xander had all kinds of kisses, and I liked every one of them.

"Hey," I said. "Put me down. I have to rinse my hair. And wash myself off."

He set me down and I rinsed the conditioner from my hair. When I opened my eyes, he was standing there working up a lather of my body wash in his hands. "Let me," he said.

"Use my soap?"

"Use it on you." He reached for my wrist and tugged me out from under the spray, then took his time soaping up every inch of my skin—arms, legs, hands, fingers, toes. My back, my belly, my breasts.

"You're good at this," I said as he crouched down to reach in between my thighs, surprisingly gentle considering he'd just assaulted the same place with a vibrator not even an hour ago.

"Thank you." He turned me around and moved my hair out of the way to rub my shoulders and the back of my neck. I laughed when he slid his hands into my armpits. "Stop it, you're like a kid," he complained as I wriggled away from him.

"I can't help it. I'm ticklish there."

He grabbed me by the hips and pulled me back into place, his hands skimming down my hips and the sides of my legs, then up the backs of my thighs and through the crack of my ass. Then he pressed up close behind me. "There. Squeaky clean."

I turned around and looped my arms around his neck. I had to tilt my head back to look up at him, he was so tall. "Is that just so it's more fun to get me dirty again?"

"Definitely." He locked his forearms around my lower back. "But I need food first. I'm hungry."

"Me too. Should we go out for breakfast?"

"I've got a better idea. I'll cook for you."

My eyebrows shot up. "You cook?"

"Don't look so surprised, princess." He pinched my butt. "We don't all have live-in chefs. And I lived alone for years. It was either cook or starve."

"What do you like to cook?"

"Meat. But I can also do some stuff with eggs."

"I like eggs and meat. Do you need groceries?"

"I think I can impress you with what we bought the other day."

I smiled. "Okay, then. Impress me."

Xander said he didn't want me in his way, so I stayed out of the kitchen while he made breakfast for us. With a cup of coffee in my hand, I stood by one of the front windows and watched the rain fall in heavy sheets. The world outside seemed dull and gray, even the vibrant emerald-colored pines had faded to a dreary shade of army green. The temperature had dropped too. I shivered as I brought my cup to my lips.

"Cold?" Xander called from the kitchen over the sizzle of bacon in the skillet.

I hadn't realized he'd been watching me. "A little."

"There's a sweatshirt in my bag there by the couch."

It was sort of ridiculous how giddy I felt as I set down my coffee and dug through his bag. I found the dark blue hooded sweatshirt and tugged it over my head. It was dark blue with NAVY printed in high-way-paint yellow block letters across the front. It was also gigantic—not only did it cover my tank top but my denim shorts as well. The thing fell midway down my thighs, and my hands were lost in its sleeves.

But it was cozy and smelled like him. Wearing it reminded me of being in high school when the boy you liked offered you his hoodie late one night at the county fair. Pulling it on for the first time was a little magical.

Careful to keep my back to him, I pulled the collar over my nose and mouth, inhaling deeply. The scent of him hit me straight in the lady bits and spread throughout my body from there, like streetlamps coming on one by one all the way down Main Street.

"Does it fit?"

"No. But I like it. Thank you." His bag was still open, and I noticed he'd brought his camera. I picked it up, switched it on, and focused on him working in the kitchen. "You brought your camera."

He looked up. "Hey."

"Come on. Give me a smile."

"Put that away."

"What'd you bring it for anyway? Are you going to take pictures of me while I'm sleeping and sell them to Splash!?"

"No!" He frowned. "I'd never do that."

"I know. I'm only teasing." I tucked the camera back in the bag and spied the box of condoms. Picking it up, I held it aloft. "Wow. The entire box, huh?"

"My instincts were telling me it was going to happen no matter what I said."

"That might explain sticking *one* condom in your bag. You brought thirty-six." I shook the box.

"I was fairly confident I'd enjoy the experience." He grinned arrogantly as he cracked eggs into a bowl. "And you would too."

"Oh, *now* he smiles." I shook my head, tossing the box back into his bag. "What are you making over there? It smells delicious."

"Denver omelets served with bacon and a side of arugula."

My stomach growled. "Yum." I wandered over and sat at the counter, watching him move confidently from skillet to mixing bowl to chopping board to fridge and back again. He looked even bigger because of the small size of the kitchen. "So how'd you learn to cook?"

"Just sort of figured it out, I guess." He took a sip from his coffee mug. "I was always hungry, and my dad worked long hours. Austin did a lot around the house and drove the younger kids to and from their activities, so unless I wanted to starve, I had to learn to cook. That was kind of the way I pitched in."

"So you cooked meals for everyone?"

"I wouldn't go that far, but if I made something— like spaghetti or chili or whatever—I'd make a lot so everyone could have some. I also worked at a restaurant."

"Oh that's right. The one we passed last night?"

"Yes, the Pier Inn."

"Maybe you'll take me there for dinner while I'm here. A *real* date this time." I watched him pour the eggs over the diced ham, red bell pepper, and onion in the skillet, then shake the pan to distribute everything more evenly.

He pretended to consider it. "Nah, I don't think so."

"Why not?"

"I'm working for you." After running a spatula beneath the edges, he sprinkled on some cheese. "Wouldn't be proper."

I laughed. "Oh, *now* you're working for me? I'll take care of that—you're fired."

"You wouldn't dare fire me now."

"Why not?"

He shook pepper on top of the omelet. "Because you like me. Just like I said you would."

I shook my head. "You're a smug, conceited pain in the ass, and I can't wait until I'm rid of you."

He smiled and gave the pan another shake. "But first you want me to take you to dinner."

"Only because I have no other prospects." I paused and conceded, "And I do *sort of* like you."

"Yeah?" He gave me a cocky, lopsided grin.

"Yeah. So will you take me to dinner?"

He carefully folded the omelet in half and then slid it onto a plate. "I'll think about it."

We ate breakfast sitting side by side at the kitchen counter, and I practically inhaled every single bite. Afterward, I told him I'd clean up since he'd done the cooking, but he wouldn't let me do it alone. I loaded the dishwasher while he scrubbed the pans by hand, then I dried them and put them away while he wiped down the counters.

"So what's the verdict?" he asked. "Are you impressed?"

"Totally. I have to admit, I didn't quite believe you when you said you could cook, but that was delicious." I wrapped my arms around his solid middle and rested my chin on his spine. Now that touching each other was okay, I couldn't seem to stop. "Thank you."

He rotated to face me and pulled me close. "What should we do today?"

"I don't know. With this rain, it looks like we're probably stuck inside."

"What a shame."

I smiled up at him. "I've got some ideas for how we might pass the time."

"Such as?"

"We could play cards. Read books. Do some yoga. Watch a movie."

He slipped his hands inside the sweatshirt I wore and rubbed the sides of my ribcage. "I have some ideas too."

"Such as?"

"You could get naked. Sit on my face. Let me fuck you with my tongue."

Arousal swooshed up my center, making my thighs tighten. "Is this before or after the movie?"

"How about during?"

"You know, for someone who was so against messing around with me, your ideas are *very* messy."

"I know." He fisted his hand in my hair and pulled my head to one side, fastening his mouth to my neck. His tongue tickled my throat as it traveled up to my ear, where he traced the shell. His beard rubbed against my jaw as he whispered, "I'll clean it all up."

I slid one hand between his legs, stroking the bulge in his jeans, excitement building in me as he thickened beneath my palm. His hands moved up to cover my breasts through my tank top. I hadn't bothered with a bra, so my nipples poked through the thin cotton, and his thumbs teased them until they were hard and almost painfully sensitive. Desire radiated outward from those two little tips, setting fire to every nerve ending in my body. It amazed me how he could use such a small body part of his to create such a powerful feeling in me. My clit ached for his touch. My pulse quickened with anticipation. His mouth covered mine in a searing-hot kiss that made me pant and writhe and want to lie down right here, right now.

Throwing my arms around his neck, I tried to pull him down, but he only laughed. "You want me to fuck you on the kitchen floor? Is that it?"

"Yes." And I was not above begging for it, but he didn't make me.

Reaching beneath the bottom of his sweatshirt, he unbuttoned and unzipped my denim shorts, then yanked them down to my ankles. As soon as I kicked them aside, he grabbed me and set me on the counter. Pushed my knees apart. Growled with animalistic hunger. Buried his head between my thighs.

Then he used his tongue and lips and fingers to drive me all the way to the edge of the orgasm cliff like five fucking times without actually sending me over. Propped on my elbows, I watched him delight in tormenting me, sometimes with his eyes closed in sensual abandon, sometimes looking up at me with smoldering intensity, sometimes focused on his hand as he fucked me with his fingers, slowly and expertly, with toe-curling patience and skill.

"Xander," I begged. "Please."

"Please what?" His breath on me was warm and tantalizing.

"Please let me come."

He backed off, pressing soft, wet kisses to my stomach, my hip bones, my clit. "You want to come?"

"Yes."

"What are you going to do for me?"

"Anything."

"Anything?" He bit my thigh. "Seems like a risky gamble on your part. You don't know me all that well. My mind could be a scary place."

"Xander."

"I mean, what if I want to tie you up?" He gave my clit the barest swipe with his tongue.

"Fine."

"Blindfold you?" Another agonizing, light-as-a-feather caress.

"Okay." My stomach muscles twitched.

"Fuck your mouth with my cock?"

I licked my lips. "Do it."

"You'd like that?" He pushed his fingers a little deeper and looked up at me with those dark, ravenous eyes. "Sucking my cock?"

"Yes." I tried to move my hips, get some friction.

"You want me to come in that pretty little mouth? Feel me dripping on your lips? Taste my cum on your tongue?"

"Yes. Goddamn it. Yes." Frustrated almost to the point of tears, I went to put my own hand between my legs, and he snatched both my wrists, pressing them firmly to the counter outside of my legs. My head fell back onto the butcher block with a thud, and I moaned with weary aggravation.

"Oh no," he reprimanded me with a harsh tone. "This is my orgasm to give, not yours to take."

"Then give it," I begged. "Please."

He exhaled, like I was asking too much of him. "Fine. But I might have to punish you later for rushing me."

"Deal," I said, positive the climax would be worth the cost. "Just don't stop this time."

He did as I asked, working his mouth and tongue and fingers together, taking me back to that edge and this time letting me sail over with blissful, pulsing relief, my thighs tight around his face.

I was still lost in the hazy aftermath when he tore his mouth off me with a grunt of frustration and left me on the counter. He was back inside fifteen seconds, undoing his jeans, tearing open the condom, sliding it on, pushing inside me. When he was buried deep, he put my legs over his shoulders.

"What's this?" I asked. "I thought you wanted my mouth."

"I can't see you like this and not have you."

"Like what?"

"Wet. Open. Bare." He grabbed my hips and gave me a few deep, bone-jarring thrusts. "Fuck. *Fuck. Fuck!*"

I watched him fall apart and thought I'd never enjoyed anything as much as the sight of big, strong Xander Buckley succumbing to his need for me, unable or unwilling to control himself. His eyes closed, his jaw clenched, and he cursed angrily and repeatedly, as if he was furious that the orgasm was gaining on him, about to beat him in the race. Then he scooped me up from the counter, put my back against the fridge and fucked me hard, driving into me with quick, deep jabs until finally he buried himself to the hilt. I gasped at the depth, at the shock of being filled so fully, but I barely had time to register the feeling because he began rocking his hips, his pubic bone rubbing my clit, his cock hitting that sweet spot inside me. Another blaze in me ignited, and we came together, his cock throbbing inside me, my insides tightening around him in a gorgeous tandem rhythm that beat throughout my entire body.

Bearing my weight beneath his hands, he turned and set me on the counter again. My forehead fell onto his sternum, my breath coming fast. His chest rising and falling quickly too.

Slowly, he stroked my back with both palms. Up and down. Up and down. Up and down.

"I like that sweatshirt on you," he said.

I smiled. "I can tell."

CHAPTER SIXTEEN
xander

SPENDING a rainy day stuck in a cabin with a celebrity client would have sounded like torture to me a week ago, but I had to admit, today had been pretty fucking fantastic.

After the kitchen sex, we took a nap, woke up, had bed sex, made lunch, and ate it on the couch while watching a movie. Then we had living room floor sex and a snack, and now we were stretched out on the couch watching a different movie, although I could not have told you what it was about, because I kept dozing off.

Kelly was lying on top of me like I was a mattress, her feet somewhere around my shins, her head on my chest. I'd undressed her completely after the post-nap sex, but it made me happy when she put my sweatshirt back on, along with her underwear and nothing else. I had no idea why it turned me on so much to see her wearing something of mine, but I'd had a hard time keeping my hands off her while we made lunch. And food is like my favorite thing on the planet, but I had to force myself to finish my sandwich before hauling her to the floor, turning her onto her hands and knees, and plowing into her from behind. While I was spent but still inside her, I reached between her legs and quickly got her off with my fingers, enjoying the way I could feel the pulse of her orgasm on my cock.

One of my arms cradled her back and the other was lost in her hair, which felt like silk around my fingers. My eyes closed, and my mind drifted. I wondered what it would be like if she wasn't Pixie Hart, if she was just a regular person I met in town, maybe a summer tourist or a new neighbor. For a moment, I experienced a quick spike of envy for my brother Austin, who'd lucked out so completely when Veronica knocked on his door.

I'd never really had a long-term girlfriend. Being a Navy SEAL was notoriously tough on relationships, and working private security had kept me away from home a lot. I'd had some friends with benefits over the years, which had suited me fine—I liked my own company perfectly fine and wasn't prone to feeling lonely—but ever since I moved back home, I'd been thinking more and more about settling down. Getting comfortable. Finding a groove. I liked the idea of being a protector and provider.

It's just that *thinking* it was one thing, and *doing* it was another.

Kelly twitched, and I realized she'd fallen asleep

in my arms. In a way, it was kind of amazing that we'd come so far in only three days, but I guess when you're forced to spend twenty-four seven with someone in a confined space, whatever chemistry you have is going to cause a reaction faster than usual. And our chemistry was pretty damn explosive.

Lying there holding her, I wondered if it would burn out completely by the time she had to leave. Actually, I hoped it would.

Missing someone was the worst.

"Hey."

I opened my eyes to see Kelly standing at the side of the couch, looking down at me. "Hey." Groggy, I propped myself up on one elbow. "What time is it?"

"It's almost five." She held out my phone. "I got up to get some water and saw your phone over there. You've got messages."

I took it from her and rubbed a hand over my face. "Thanks."

"You're welcome. Can I come back where I was?"

"Sure." I lay back and she stretched out on me again. I held the phone above her head and scrolled through my messages. "Oh. Shit. Devlin and Mabel are in town."

"Your brother and sister?"

MELANIE HARLOW

"Yeah. They arrived today. Devlin has some business in the area next week, but he came in a little early. And Mabel just decided on a spontaneous visit. Everyone's getting together at my dad's house for dinner at six."

"You can go if you want. I promise you, I'll be fine here. And I won't try to escape."

I laughed. "No?"

"No." She picked up her head and smiled at me. "We have an understanding, you and I."

My insides grew strangely warm when she said that. "You're invited too," I told her.

"To dinner at your dad's?"

"Yes. Do you want to go?"

"I'd love to!" She scrambled off me and popped to her feet. "Do you think I have time to shower?"

"You already showered today." I glanced at her bare legs. "But please put on some pants."

"Xander, I showered like *seven* orgasms ago! I've gotten sweaty since then."

I laughed. "Not sorry. But that's fine. We've got some time."

She went running down the hall, her bare feet thumping on the wood floor. The water came on in the bathroom, and I heard her pull the curtain aside and get in. Within seconds, she was singing.

I'd probably miss that too.

After dinner, we'd all gathered in the living room for a family game of Pictionary.

"Raccoon!" Devlin shouted while I tried my best to draw a fucking panda bear on a big white dry erase board. (Here's where I mention that art is not one of my talents.)

"Mouse!" My dad removed his glasses, wiped a lens, and put them back on, like maybe it was a smudge making my giant bear look like a small rodent.

Alas.

I stared at my shitty drawing. Did pandas have bigger ears? Why couldn't I picture one? I gave him a bushier tail and more black around the eyes.

"Platypus!" yelled Owen, the youngest member of the men's team.

"What the hell is that thing?" Austin muttered.

"Time!" Mabel called.

"It's a *panda bear*." I shot my team a grumpy look over my shoulder. "Obviously."

Everyone laughed as I scrubbed at it with the dry erase marker, then took my seat at one end of the L-shaped sectional couch. Austin was next to me, our dad on the other side of him. Owen, in charge of the timer, knelt by the coffee table.

"Okay, who's up?" Devlin asked, perched on the

couch arm next to me, a beer in his hand. He was tall, but built differently than I was. More like a runner—muscular, but long and lean. Not quite as wide through the shoulders. He had dark hair like Austin and me, but he had our mom's piercing blue eyes, which he was good at using to his advantage. He also had a way with words I'd always envied. Our dad always said he could sell water to a drowning man.

It was not, however, helping us at Pictionary.

My brothers groaned as Mabel's childhood best friend Ari jumped up and grabbed the marker. The women's team—Veronica, Kelly, Mabel, Ari, and Adelaide—was crushing the men's, largely due to the fact that Ari and Mabel obviously spoke some sort of telepathic language.

Owen started the timer. "Go!"

As Ari began to draw, I stole a glance at Kelly, who was seated between Veronica and Mabel on the couch, Adelaide and the dog by her feet. I liked that she'd put my sweatshirt on over her clean clothes after her shower. Now she was laughing at something Veronica had just whispered in her ear. It was like she'd always been around, the way she fit right in with my family. Not that I'd been worried she wouldn't, but—

"Bunk beds!" Mabel shouted.

"Yes!" Ari jumped up and down excitedly.

"What?" Devlin stared at the dry erase board. "Ari literally drew a bunch of lines and you guessed bunk beds? You guys are cheating!"

"We are not," said Mabel, pushing her glasses up

her nose. She had Devlin's coloring—the dark hair and blue eyes. "We're just more talented. You're lucky there's no singing and dancing involved." She gestured toward Veronica and Kelly. "This team is stacked."

"That's the game," my dad said, checking the score sheet. "Women, ten. Men, five."

My brothers grumbled as Veronica, Kelly, Mabel, Ari, and Adelaide all exchanged high fives.

"I want to be on the women's team next time," Owen said.

"Me too," Devlin chimed in, shoving my shoulder. "Or maybe just whatever team Xander isn't on. So who's up for hitting The Broken Spoke?"

"Tonight?" I asked.

"Yeah, why not?"

Because I want to go home and get laid again, that's why. "It's kind of late, isn't it?"

"It's only nine, Grandpa."

"It's Sunday."

"But it's a holiday weekend, so it'll be open late tonight, right?"

"Should be," said Austin. "Kids are gonna sleep here tonight, so we can go." He looked at Veronica. "If you want to."

"Sure!" She looked at Kelly. "What do you think? Too risky for you?"

Kelly looked at me before answering. "Maybe? I don't know."

"It's gonna be packed for sure." And I honestly didn't feel like sharing her.

"We can all go in together." Devlin sounded confident. "Keep her surrounded. It'll be like she has three bodyguards."

"Six," Mabel pointed out. "Ari and I and Veronica can help guard her too."

"What if you called ahead?" Austin suggested. "Maybe they'd let us reserve that table in the corner."

"They might have, if I'd done it earlier," I said. "At this point, I doubt they'd even answer the phone."

"I'm sure I'll be fine." Kelly smiled. "I'll wear a hat and keep my head down."

"I've got a hat I can lend you." My dad stood up, excited to help out. "Let me find it."

She came over and sat next to me, put a hand on my leg. "Is it okay? I don't have to go if you think it's a bad idea."

I liked that she trusted me to make the call. "It's okay. Let's head over there, and I'll assess the situation," I said. "If I go in and get a bad feeling, we'll go home."

"Okay." She smiled. "Home is fun too."

"I found one!" My dad shuffled over to us, proudly offering a Two Buckleys Home Improvement cap, much like the one I'd loaned her two nights before, only his was navy.

"Thanks." Kelly flashed him a grin and pulled the cap onto her head.

My father nodded his approval. "Looks good on you."

"All that red hair might be kind of recognizable," said Ari. "Maybe a ponytail?"

"Good idea." Kelly gathered her long hair at the nape of her neck. "Anyone have a ponytail holder?"

"I do." Veronica stood up and fished in her pocket, pulling out a little round elastic.

Kelly took it from her and wound it around her hair. Then she stood up and looked at us. "Better?"

Ari laughed. "That sweatshirt is gigantic. You could hide two Pixie Harts in there!"

"Is that yours, Xander?" Mabel asked.

"Yeah." And maybe I imagined the side-eye that accompanied the question, but I didn't want to draw any additional attention to the answer. "Let's head out."

The Broken Spoke was a few miles outside town, more of a local hot spot than a tourist destination. Kelly and I took our own car, Austin and Veronica took another, and Devlin drove Mabel and Ari. We met up in The Broken Spoke's gravel parking lot, which was packed, as expected. I scanned the rows of cars looking for the beige Honda with the dent in the left rear panel, but didn't see it.

As we headed for the door as a group, the women sort of flanked Kelly's sides while Devlin and I led the way and Austin kept an eye on everything from the rear. I'd called ahead, but as expected, I hadn't gotten an answer. We could hear the loud thump of the drums and wail of guitars as we approached the building, and after paying our cover fees at the door, we moved like a herd into the bar.

It was a huge rectangular space, a former barn on an old dairy farm. The stage took up most of the back wall, and a double row of round tables rimmed the perimeter of the dance floor in front of it. The bar ran almost the entire length of one side, and high-top tables were scattered near the entrance.

"I see a table emptying out!" Veronica shouted, and with the agility and grace of a dancer, she zigzagged, dodged, and ducked her way through the crowd and managed to snatch a round table at the corner of the dance floor. Reaching it just as a group of couples were leaving, she managed to snag a chair and sit down before anyone else could occupy it.

We made our way toward her, and I looked over the room the way I always did. I didn't see anything alarming—no phones aimed at us, no suspicious eyes glancing our way, no one young enough to be a Hart Throb squealing with excitement. Arriving at the table, I pulled out the chair I wanted Kelly to sit in and took the one next to her. Austin sat between Kelly and Veronica, with Mabel and Ari on Roni's other side. Devlin grabbed the seat next to me.

The server stopped by, we put in orders for drinks and some snacks, and I began to relax a little. The band was good, the beer was cold, the place was crowded but not out of control, I was surrounded by family, and I'd had sex more times in the last twenty-four hours than I'd had in a year. And there was more to be had when we got home tonight. I wondered how long we had to hang out here before I could suggest that we head back.

Not that I wasn't having fun. Veronica pulled Austin out onto the dance floor, and I thoroughly enjoyed watching him try to keep up with her. When he begged to sit down, she tugged Devlin's arm, and he reluctantly let himself be dragged out there. Ari and Mabel got asked to dance by some old friends from high school, and Kelly watched with obvious envy. "I wish I could dance too," she said loudly, so I could hear her over the music. "They're having so much fun."

Putting an arm around the back of her chair, I spoke in her ear. "Probably best if we just stay at the table."

"One little two-step? Please?" She clasped her hands beneath her chin.

"I don't think so."

"Why not? Don't you know any moves?"

"I know some moves," I assured her.

Placing a hand on my leg, she leaned toward me, her smile seductive. "I already know you've got rhythm. Don't you want to show it off? I'll be extra good to you later."

I couldn't resist her. "*One song.*"

"Yay!" She popped to her feet, whipped off my oversized sweatshirt to reveal a fitted white crop top, and slung it over the back of her chair. Then she took me by the hand.

"We'll be right back," I said to Austin, who gave me a smug, knowing look.

The singer counted off the next tune, which, lucky for me, turned out to be an up-tempo song I was familiar with. I'd told Kelly I knew some moves, but really I only knew three—I just kept repeating them in different directions. And not only was Kelly a good dancer, she was excellent at following my lead, so sometimes I could even get her to spin twice before switching to go back the other way. It helped that she was so much shorter than me, since she could easily turn under my arm whichever way I led her. When the song ended, she clapped for the band but turned to me with a hopeful smile. "Can I have another one please?"

I squinted at her. "Now you're pushing your luck."

The band struck up a ballad, and she gave me the big eyes from beneath the bill of her Two Buckleys cap. "Please?"

Exhaling, I took her in my arms, careful not to hold her too tightly. Without even looking, I knew my siblings were watching us with hawk eyes.

"You leaving room for Jesus, or what?" she said with a laugh.

"Huh?"

"You're holding me so far away from you! I feel like I'm back in middle school and boys don't want to touch me."

"That is not the case tonight, I promise. I just don't want to raise any eyebrows." But I pulled her in closer, tightening my hold around her lower back. My forearm rested along the warm, bare strip of skin between her jeans and her top, my fingers curling automatically around her waist. I could smell her perfume, and heat surged through me.

"You think your family would care?"

"Definitely," I said. "Austin already suspects."

"He does?" She arched back and looked up at me, pinning her hips against mine.

"We had a conversation about you yesterday at his house."

"Oh?" By her smile, I could tell she kind of liked that. "And what was said?"

"He bet me I wouldn't be able to keep my hands off you for two weeks."

Her head fell back as she laughed, exposing her throat. It took a lot of effort for me not to put my mouth on it. "Did you take it?"

"Fuck no."

She laughed some more, then pressed close again, her cheek on my chest, her head tucked beneath my chin. I happened to catch Austin's eye—he grinned wryly and shook his head. Devlin was staring at us like we were a math problem he was trying to figure out, and Mabel and Ari, also back at the table, were whispering back and forth as they observed us with keen-eyed glee.

When the song ended, the band announced they were taking a short break, and Kelly and I returned to the table. I pulled out her chair, and she sat down, fanning her face.

"Ooooh," she breathed. "Hot out there."

"Looked like it," said Veronica. "Hey, Kelly, I have to use the ladies' room. Would you like to come with me?"

"Yes." Kelly glanced at me. "I'll just be a few minutes. Is it okay?"

I stood up again. "I'll walk you."

"Xander, it's literally twenty feet from here," Mabel said, pointing toward the hallway next to the stage. "You can see the bathroom door."

Kelly tugged on my arm. "Sit. I'll be fine, I promise."

"We'll be with her the whole time," Veronica said, rising to her feet. Ari and Mabel popped up too, and the four of them hurried toward the women's bathroom. Kelly did a good job keeping her head down, but I could have sworn I saw heads turn in her direction as she made her way across the empty dance floor.

"So," Devlin said when it was just the three guys left at the table. "What's with you and Pixie Hart?"

"He doesn't like when you call her that," Austin said with a grin.

"Because it's not her name," I said testily.

"Sorry." Devlin leaned back in his chair and took a pull on his beer. "What's with you and *Kelly*?"

I shrugged. "Nothing much."

"Doesn't look like nothing much from where I'm

sitting," Devlin taunted. "You can't keep your eyes off her."

"That's not all he can't keep off her," Austin muttered, bringing his beer to his mouth. "And I'm not talking about his hoodie."

"We're just having fun together," I said. "It's not a big deal."

"So she's not in contention of the role of Mrs. Xander Buckley?" Austin asked.

I frowned at my older brother. "What the fuck are you talking about? I just met her three days ago."

"I know, but I distinctly remember you saying to me earlier this summer that you were looking for a wife."

Devlin burst out laughing. "Looking for a wife?"

"I never said that," I argued, but it sounded like the kind of thing I might announce just to mess with him.

"You absolutely said that," Austin countered. "We were in my garage. It was the night you bet me I wouldn't be able to stay away from Veronica for two weeks."

Devlin laughed. "How fast did you lose that one?"

"Lightning fast," I said. "I don't think he lasted more than a few days."

"We're not talking about me, we're talking about you." Austin pointed a finger at me. "You told me you were two-thirds of the way to respectable adult-hood, and a wife and some kids were going to be the final third."

"Maybe you should move out of Dad's house first," Devlin joked.

"Fuck off, both of you." Sweaty from dancing, or maybe the inquisition, I plucked my shirt away from my chest a few times. "All I meant was that I am now mature enough to handle the kind of committed relationship and responsibilities that come with having a wife."

"So romantic," Austin joked.

"Yeah, make sure you say it like that when you propose," Devlin joked. "But add in the part where she's going to bring you the last third of the way to respectability. That will really seal the deal."

"Good thinking." Austin pointed his beer at Devlin.

Devlin tapped his bottle to Austin's. "If there's one thing I know how to do, it's make a pitch."

"Speaking of pitching, what's the property you're in town about?" I asked, eager to change the subject.

"One of our biggest clients, a resort company, wants to acquire Snowberry Lodge."

"Seriously?" About twenty minutes from Cherry Tree harbor, Snowberry was one of the area's first ski resorts, maybe even one of the nation's first ski resorts. I pictured its dated Swiss Miss architecture and rickety old chairlifts. "That place has to be sixty years old. I didn't even know it was still open."

"It's almost *eighty* years old, and it's falling apart. Our client would tear it down. They just want the property it sits on for a new luxury hotel and winter sports complex. They've already acquired most of what's around it."

"Who owns Snowberry?" I wondered.

"The McIntyre family," said Devlin.

Austin huffed. "Good luck getting them to sell."

"You don't think they will?" I asked.

"Dad and I did some restoration work there about five years ago," said Austin. "They're just the kind of family that hangs on to the past. They don't want anything to change. I can't see them selling their family business to a resort company that's going to tear it down."

"They'd be crazy not to," Devlin said, pushing his wavy hair off his forehead. "Snowberry Lodge is a relic. Sure, it has some charm, but it's small and anti-quated. People are looking for luxury amenities these days, not just decent skiing. They want water parks and arcades, spas and upscale shops, multiple bars and dining options. In the summer, they want golf and tennis. Snowberry can't compete with the big modern resorts."

"Still," Austin said doubtfully, "people are stubborn and sentimental. They don't want to be told their family's dream is obsolete."

"I can bring them around." Devlin's tone was brimming with confidence. "The money is good."

Austin clearly wasn't convinced. "Money isn't everything to everyone."

"It will be something to them," Devlin insisted. "The fact is, they can't afford to stay open even two more seasons the way things are going. Why not sell now and at least make a good profit?"

"Pride?" I suggested.

"Pride won't keep the lights on," Devlin scoffed.

"I'm pretty sure Snowberry Lodge was the first ski resort in Michigan, maybe in the Midwest," Austin said. "The state might even have an interest in seeing it preserved."

"The state is going to like the tax revenue from all the conventions and tourism the new resort will bring. Trust me. Dollar signs are going to talk." Devlin gave us an easy, winning grin. "Plus, the patriarch of the family died last year, and Snowberry is now mostly owned by the grandmother. Little old ladies love me."

"Your pitch meeting is with the grandmother?" Austin asked.

He nodded. "I'm taking Granny to lunch on Tuesday. By dinnertime, I'll have it all wrapped up."

"Bamboozling little old Granny," I said. "Nice."

"I'm not bamboozling her, Xander. I'm trying to give her millions of dollars for something that's not worth half that."

"Maybe don't say it exactly that way," Austin suggested.

"I *know* how to say it. Talking people into things is my gift." Devlin spoke as if victory was already his. "Trust me. My pitch is perfect. This is a done deal." He rose to his feet. "And now, gentlemen, if you'll excuse me, I've just spotted a gorgeous brunette at the bar who might also enjoy a swing at my fastball tonight."

Austin laughed. "Ladies aren't that impressed with speed, Dev."

Devlin put a hand on his shoulder as he passed. "Not to worry, brother. Not to worry."

Just then, Ari and Mabel came out of the bathroom and headed for the bar area. I gave it ten seconds, but Kelly and Veronica didn't follow.

I got out of my chair too. "I'll be right back."

CHAPTER SEVENTEEN

kelly

THE SECOND THE bathroom door had closed behind the four of us, Veronica had leaned back against the sinks and crossed her arms. Her blue eyes were dancing. "Okay, Kelly Jo Sullivan. Spill."

"About what?" I said innocently.

"About what's going on with you and Xander!" Ari shrieked as she headed into a stall. "But talk loud so I can hear!"

I laughed, checking my reflection in the mirror. My face was flushed, and my head felt hot. I took off my borrowed Two Buckleys cap and yanked out my ponytail, shaking out my hair. "It's nothing."

"Um, it is *not* nothing." Mabel met my eyes in the glass. "I know my brother, and I have *never* seen him look at anyone the way he's been looking at you all night."

"That's what I told her earlier." Veronica nodded excitedly, her blond ponytail bobbing. "He cannot take his eyes off her. I'm expecting hearts to float out of them any second. And how about the fact that she's wearing his clothes?"

Laughing, Mabel went into a stall and continued talking behind the closed door. "I've never seen him dance that way with anyone either."

"We were just *dancing.*" But my cheeks grew warmer and pinker.

"Please." Veronica held up a hand. "He was hanging on to you like a kid hugs his teddy bear at night, like he was afraid someone was going to come along and steal you away."

"He's protective," I said. "He's always worried about me being recognized. Photos of me up here are already online."

"He still sleeping on the couch?"

"Um . . ." Should I lie? I wasn't sure what Xander wanted his family to know.

"You can trust us," she said. "We won't say anything."

"Definitely." Ari came out of the stall and went to the sinks to wash her hands. "When it comes to girls vs. the Buckley boys, the girls stick together. Cone of silence in here."

I laughed. "Okay. As of last night, he's not sleeping on the couch anymore."

Veronica squealed. "What happened? When I talked to him Friday, he said you two did not get along, and then yesterday at the house, you guys were adorable together."

"I don't really know what happened. We sort of

just . . ." My shoulders rose. "Talked. Tried a little harder to listen to each other."

"Talked?" Veronica squeaked. "*Talked?*"

"There may have been some other activities involved," I said, redoing my ponytail.

"Lalalalala, not listening," Mabel shouted from behind the stall door.

I laughed. "Sorry, Mabel. I know it's your brother we're talking about here." Sticking the cap back on my head, I ducked into the stall Ari had vacated. After finishing up, I went to the sink to wash my hands.

"I'm only teasing," Mabel said, drying her hands next to me. "I think it's great. Xander is a good guy."

"It must be hard to meet someone when you're so famous," said Ari. "You must have that suspicion in the back of your mind all the time, like does this person like me for the real me, or are they just dazzled by the celebrity persona?"

"It can be weird," I said, yanking some paper towels from the dispenser and drying my hands. "Although in Xander's case, he didn't like the real me at *all*, and he definitely wasn't dazzled by my celebrity." I laughed as I tossed the towels in the trash. "I kept trying to get rid of him, and he just kept refusing to leave. I've never met a more stubborn man."

"All my brothers are like that," said Mabel. "And as the baby sister of the family, I've experienced the full range of their bossy behavior. But they were also the best big brothers ever, so I can't really complain."

She turned to Ari. "Should we go back out and see if that one guy in the red shirt is still at the bar?"

"Sure." Ari smiled at me. "See you back at the table."

They left the bathroom, and Veronica came out of a stall and washed her hands. "Austin can be like that too. Bossy and demanding." She laughed as she pulled paper towels from the machine. "But I kinda like it."

I smiled. "You guys are so great together. He adores you."

Veronica lit up. "I'm madly in love with him. I wake up every day and pinch myself."

"Think he's the one?"

"I'm pretty sure," she said, her cheeks growing pink, her blue eyes bright. "I mean, it's only been a few months, so it's still a little new, but it just feels so right."

A banging on the door made us both jump. Veronica stepped in front of me like a shield, which I thought was so sweet.

"Kelly?" Xander's voice was muffled. "You in there?"

"Yes!" I shouted. "I'm coming out in a sec."

"I'll wait."

Veronica and I exchanged a look. "He's protective," I said again.

"Also kinda crazy about you," she whispered back. "I can see it."

"That was fun," I said on the way home.

Xander remained silent behind the wheel.

I leaned over and thumped his leg. "You didn't have a good time?"

"What?" He glanced at me. "Sorry, I was distracted. Yes, I had a good enough time."

"Just good enough?"

"I was on duty," he said. "It wasn't as easy for me to relax as it was for you guys."

"Well, thank you for letting us go." I left my hand where it was. "And for dancing."

He fell silent again.

"Austin and Veronica are perfect for each other. Think they'll get married?"

"Maybe. If my brother doesn't fuck it up."

I laughed. "He seems pretty taken with her. What about Devlin? I take it since he left with someone tonight that he's single?"

"As far as I know. He had a girlfriend for a while, but that ended earlier this year." He gave me the side-eye, thick with jealousy. "Why?"

"I want to bang him, obviously." I punched his shoulder. "I'm just curious! Jeez. Although he is very handsome."

Xander snorted. "Trust me, he knows."

"You're all handsome. Just in different ways." I

remembered what Ari had said about girls vs. Buckley boys. "You guys must have broken a lot of hearts around here."

"I don't know about that."

"Sounds like Mabel and Ari have been friends for a long time."

"They were inseparable growing up. Ari was always around."

"I wish I had good friends like that, from way back when. People you can just always count on, no matter how long it's been since you've seen them. People who will always be in your corner."

"You don't have good friends?" He sounded surprised.

"Not like that. I have my brother, but he's gone a lot."

"Are you close with your mom?"

"Yes," I said hesitantly. "We're close, and I love her, but I sometimes question her choices."

"What choices?"

I caught my lower lip between my teeth. "I feel bad judging her."

"You can say it."

"Because she always supported my dream. She was there for us growing up."

"Kelly. You're not a bad person for having a critical opinion about your mother."

"And I've got no room to talk. I took Duke back a bunch of times when I knew he wasn't faithful."

Xander glanced at me. "Is this about your dad?"

"Yes. He's . . . I'm trying to think of the word I

230

want to use here. Unreliable. He lets her down a lot. He lets us all down a lot."

Taking my hand in his, Xander stroked the back of it with his thumb. "Talk to me. If you want."

I took a deep breath. "He has a drinking problem. And a gambling problem. But he's also handsome and charming and funny and affectionate. He started leaving us for long periods of time when I was about six, but he'd always come back, full of apologies. My mom took him back every time."

"Wasn't she mad?"

"Oh, she was. And she'd freeze him out a little bit at first. But somehow, he'd charm his way back into her good graces."

"And yours too?"

"Sure. I was always just so happy that he'd come back, because I thought for sure it was my fault that he'd left in the first place."

"Why?"

"I don't know for sure. I just always thought, if I was better, if I was perfect, if I was *famous*, he'd come back for good and never leave."

He brought my hand to his lips and kissed it. "It wasn't true."

"I know that now." My throat felt tight. "I've gone to therapy and all that. I've tried hard to work through it. But certain things linger, you know?"

"I know."

"Even now that I have some fame, he still comes and goes. Only difference is, he wants money."

"Do you give it to him?"

231

"I feel obligated," I said. "I don't want to, but he's my father. He taught me to play guitar. He's why I love music so much. And he grew up with a terrible, angry father who hit him."

"That's fucking horrible. But it doesn't mean you have to support him if he keeps disappointing you."

"I know." I closed my eyes. "Kevin tells me this all the time. I just find it really hard to stand up to him."

"What would you say to him if you could?"

"God." I shuddered.

"Come on. Say the words to me. He's not here."

"I guess I'd tell him how much it hurt when he left us. How much it still hurts when he leaves again. I'd say that every single time he walks out the door, I wonder if I'll ever see him again. And how no little girl should have to live that way, wondering if her dad loves her enough to come back."

Xander was silent, like he knew there was more.

"And if he apologizes for not being the *perfect* dad, I'd say I was never looking for perfection. Just a dad. And when he says, 'I did the best I could,' I'd say, 'no, you didn't, Daddy. I love you, but no, you didn't.'"

"See?" He squeezed my hand. "You can do it. You can say the words."

"To you. Not to him."

"Maybe next time you have the chance, you'll do it. You've got the words in your head now."

"Thanks." I wondered if I'd ever have the guts to speak my mind to my dad that way. Xander was so lucky. His family was so great. "So did your brothers ask about us after we danced?"

"A little." He shrugged. "Mostly they just gave me shit about something I said a couple months ago."

"About me?"

"About looking for a wife."

"What?" My jaw dropped. "You're looking for a *wife*?"

"No! I mean, not *actually*. Not literally. I just feel like I'm at the age where if you're gonna do the whole white-picket-fence thing, you might as well get to it."

"Well, sure," I teased. "I mean, you're gonna need energy for those three rowdy boys."

"Exactly. I can't be old man dad. I need to be young, cool dad."

"I can see it very clearly. You are the cool, bar-owning dad with the tattoos and the swim records that still stand."

"That's fucking right they do."

I laughed. "The girls had all kinds of questions for me in the bathroom."

"I bet."

"Apparently, it's obvious you are no longer sleeping on the couch."

"Where I sleep is none of their business," he harrumphed.

"Oh, don't get grumpy about it. They were happy. They said nice things."

"Oh yeah? Like what?"

233

"Your sister says you're a good guy and I can trust you. She also said she had the best big brothers ever. It was really sweet. And Veronica said she'd never seen you with hearts in your eyes."

"I do not have fucking *hearts* in my eyes."

I laughed. "I think she just meant, she could tell that you like me."

He looked at me sideways. "Yeah, you're okay."

"So it's true?" My ridiculous heart was going pitter-patter like he'd just passed back the note with the YES box checked. "You like me?"

"I like you." He was silent as we turned into our driveway. "But when we get inside, I'm going to rip your clothes off and fuck you like I don't."

I lost my breath for a second. When I recovered, I put my hand on the door handle, ready to jump out. "You'll have to catch me first."

After an exhilarating chase through the dark, we ended up on the living room floor.

I'd bolted from the car and run into the trees, zigzagging this way and that, racing out into the clearing again, circling the house, and finally sprinting up the porch steps. Hot in pursuit, Xander caught up with me at the front door, locking an iron forearm around my middle and sinking his teeth gently into my neck.

"What took you so long?" I panted, my blood running hot and fast as I punched in the code.

"I'm a gentleman," he growled in my ear. "I gave you a head start."

In my addled mental state, the code took me several tries to get right, but finally the door gave way. Pushing it open, we tumbled to the floor, where Xander made good on his promise to tear off my clothes. He was rough with me, but maybe that was because I kept trying to escape. I'd only get about two feet—crawling on my hands and knees—before I'd feel his hand close around my ankle or his arm loop around my hips, and he'd drag me back to where he wanted me. I'd shriek and scramble and call him names, but it all seemed to turn him on.

He flipped me onto my back and went down on me, my thighs clamped tightly around his face, his beard deliciously abrasive on my skin. I thought he might play games with me again, leave me hovering on the cusp and pull back again, but he didn't. He came at me like a lion and didn't stop until my body was rigid with tension, then convulsing in sweet relief.

"Fuck, I love the taste of you." He gave me one final, bone-trembling lick up my center and jumped to his feet, yanking off his clothes. When he was naked, towering above me and stroking his cock, I got to my knees in front of him.

"My turn," I whispered, running my hands up his strong, muscular thighs.

"Who said you got a turn?"

"Come on." I looked up at him. "Play fair."

"You want me in your mouth?" He pressed the tip to my chin, brushing it back and forth along my jaw.

"Yes." My tongue darted out and licked the crown. "I want to make you come, just like you said." My hands replaced his. "Feel you dripping on my lips." I sucked just the tip, making him groan. "Taste you at the back of my throat."

He grunted and cursed as I lowered my mouth onto him, then slowly pulled the elastic from my ponytail. Sliding his hands along the sides of my head, he wove his fingers into my hair and fisted them. My scalp prickled as I worked my lips up and down his thick, hard shaft, ran my tongue over rigid veins and smooth crown, licked and sucked and teased. I gave him a taste of his own medicine, taking him to the brink of climax and easing off, torturing him the way he'd tortured me.

But Xander was not a man easily toyed with. As playful as he could be when he wasn't aroused, he was governed by a different side of himself when it came to sex. He liked control. He wanted to set the tone, the pace, the rhythm. He wanted to make the rules and enforce them.

"Kelly." His fists tightened in my hair. "Goddamn it."

I laughed, tasting the sweet saltiness of him on my tongue. His erection thickened and twitched once. I pulled him from my lips with a soft pop. "What?"

"You know what. Stop teasing me."

"But it's so much fun." I took him deep once more and slid my finger along the sensitive skin behind his balls, teasing at his tightly puckered hole.

He sucked in his breath. "Oh, fuck."

Suddenly I struggled to catch my breath between the quick, hard thrusts of his hips as his huge cock filled my mouth. Luckily for my lungs, he only lasted about eight seconds before I felt the hot stream at the back of my throat and the rhythmic throb of his orgasm between my lips.

"Jesus," he said as the spasms faded. He pulled out, loosening his grip on my head as I gasped for air. "Are you okay?"

I nodded, gulping in oxygen. "Yes."

"That was . . . *you* are . . . I can't even . . . Jesus."

Laughing, I wiped my mouth and looked up at him. "I like you too."

"So tell me about this wife." We were curled up in bed, Xander on his back and me tucked in along his side. "The one you're on the hunt for."

He groaned. "There's no wife, dammit. She's not real. It's just an idea."

"But she is real. That's the crazy thing, right? She's out there." I gestured grandly in the darkness with one hand. "Somewhere out there is the woman that will sweep you off your feet and make you fall madly in love with her."

"Eh . . . I doubt that."

"Why? Don't you believe in true love? Once-in-a-lifetime, struck-by-a-lightning-bolt love?"

"It's not that I don't believe in it. I just don't know if it's for me."

I slapped his chest. "That's so unromantic, Xander. Remind me never to marry you."

"Did I miss the part where I proposed?"

"I want my future husband to fall head over heels for me instantly, just like your dad fell for your mom. I want him to take one look and *know*. I want it to hit him like a hundred million volts."

He laughed. "No, you don't. It sounds good in stories, but if some guy took one look at you and announced he was in love because the sight of you electrocuted him, you wouldn't marry him. You'd think he was unhinged. You'd run in the other direction, and rightly so."

"Okay, maybe love at first *sight* is a bit much. But don't you want to fall deep and hard for the woman you're going to spend the rest of your life with?"

"I guess."

"God, you're so unenthusiastic! What's wrong with you?"

"Nothing! Look, if it happens, it happens, but I don't think it's a prerequisite to a successful marriage. Not everybody is cut out to have that kind of relationship. I've seen guys who fall in that kind of love, and it fucks them up. It's too unpredictable. Too volatile."

"What about Austin and Veronica? He's in love like that, and he's not fucked up. He's happy."

"Maybe, but Austin and I are different. Austin's a perfectionist, the kind of guy who has to have all or nothing. I'm more laidback. I'd rather be with someone I genuinely like, with an easygoing temperament and a good sense of humor. Someone who wants the same things I do. Someone who doesn't care that I'm not rich or famous or brilliant, just a good fucking time."

"Got it. So she can't be too picky."

He tugged my hair. "Smart ass."

I laughed. "I'm only kidding. I think you'll be a very good husband. You're protective and loyal and reliable. Plus, you give excellent orgasms."

"Thank you."

I snuggled up again. "What does she look like?"

"Huh?"

"This easygoing, funny, good-time future wife of yours. What does she look like? What's your type?"

He was silent for a moment. "I don't really have a type."

"But she'd be beautiful, right? She'd have to be, to catch your eye."

"Sure. I like beautiful." He paused, then flipped me over onto my back, settling between my thighs as he looked down at me. "And if she has great tits and likes to suck a dick on occasion, so much the better."

Grinning, I wrapped my legs around his hips and

my arms around his neck. "Good luck finding *that* wife. I don't think she exists."

"I'll find her," he said, lowering his mouth to mine. "I'm very resourceful."

I fell asleep that night happier than I'd been in a long time.

The next morning, I finally decided to look at my phone—mostly because I wanted to check the weather. Xander had promised me a day out on his boat if it was nice. I hadn't looked at my texts or peeked at my inbox or listened to voicemails or even glanced at social media in forty-eight hours, and given how good I was feeling, maybe I'd stay off the grid for the rest of my vacation.

When I tried to get out of bed, Xander's arm encircled my waist. "Where do you think you're going?" he mumbled.

I laughed, trying to pry his wrist from my hip, but he held me fast. "Let me up. I'm just going to grab my phone."

"You don't need that thing."

"You could be right. I haven't looked at it in two days, and I feel great."

"I'm always right." But he loosened his grip on me and I slid out of bed, went over to my suitcase, and dug my phone out. Powering it on, I slipped back into bed next to Xander, who was lying on his stomach, his head beneath the pillow.

"Ugh, I have forty-two texts," I said.

A muffled grunt was his response.

Ignoring the messages, I opened the weather app. "It's going to be a gorgeous day," I said happily. "Sunny and eighty-four degrees. That means you're taking me out on the boat."

He pushed the pillow off his face. "Remember how fun our rainy day was?"

"Yes, I do. But we can—oh no."

"What?" He picked up his head.

"Oh, God."

"Kelly, what is it?"

"Photos."

"Of what?" He sat all the way up and looked at the screen.

"Of us. Here at the cabin."

CHAPTER EIGHTEEN

xander

"MOTHERFUCKER." I reached over and scrolled through photos of us leaving the cabin last night hand in hand and dancing at The Broken Spoke. They'd been posted on a different tabloid site this time, one called Hot Shots that seemed to specialize in romantic speculation. The caption read, *Who's the local hottie that caught Pixie Hart's eye? Vacation fling or something more?* "Mother*fucker*."

From the angle and shitty quality of the photos, it looked like the guy had been shooting from the woods at a considerable distance.

But still. Someone had been here. Someone had been watching us, maybe all day. And I'd fucking missed it.

I jumped out of bed, glad to see we'd at least pulled the window shades down in here, but the living room had no window coverings—and we'd been out there last night. "Get dressed. We're leaving."

"Leaving? Where would we go? Xander, come on. It's not *that* big of a deal."

"It is to me." I hunted around for my jeans and yanked them on.

"You're not even identified."

"Doesn't matter. Someone was here," I said through clenched teeth. "How did I fucking miss it?"

"Because these guys are pros. They know all the tricks. They've got the equipment."

"They followed us to my dad's house. Then they followed us again. *Goddamn it.*" I stopped moving. "Is there a photo credit?"

"I don't know. What does it matter?"

"Because I'll fucking find him." I tugged my T-shirt over my head.

"And do what? Beat him up? Smash his camera?"

"That's a start."

"Do you know how many of these guys exist in my world? You can't beat them all up, Xander. You just learn to live with them."

"Bullshit." I knelt on the bed and grabbed the phone out of her hand, looking for the photo credit. All it said was Now News Media. "What's this?"

"It's probably a company the paparazzi sell to. There are tons of them."

I felt like TNT was running through my veins. How could I have been so fucking careless? I remembered the beige Honda Civic I'd seen parked on the road Friday night. Why hadn't I called someone to run the plates already? I knew fifteen people who'd have done it for me. Instead, I was busy thinking about my dick.

I tossed her phone onto the mattress and stood up. "Pack your things. We need to get out of here."

She gathered up the covers over her chest. "And go where?"

"For now, my house. This place is compromised."

"What about the boat?"

I raked a hand through my hair, thinking about all my mistakes. "Jesus, fuck, we were running around outside last night. He could have been out there."

"Xander, you're overreacting! This stuff happens to me all the time. It's just photographs."

Furious with myself, I scavenged around the floor for my socks, then pulled them on. "Anyone could have gotten photos of us through the windows last night. How much do you think a photo of you with my face between your legs would get? Or you on your knees with my dick in your mouth? Christ."

"They don't want to hurt me, they just want to get paid for the pictures."

"This wouldn't have happened if I'd been on my game. If I hadn't been distracted."

"Wait a minute. Are you blaming me?"

"I'm not blaming anyone but myself!" Roaring mad, I left the bedroom.

Out in the living room, I found my phone and texted a friend with contacts at the DMV, asking her to run the plates of that beige Honda. Then I shoved my feet in my boots and went outside, standing there on the porch, heels planted wide, fists clenched, chest expanded. "Are you there, motherfucker?" I muttered. My eyes swept the surrounding area. I cracked my knuckles. "Come on. Take my picture. I fucking dare you."

After a few minutes, the lava in my veins started to cool, and my heart rate slowed. Satisfied there was no immediate threat—but also kind of disappointed I wouldn't get to smash a camera—I went back into the house.

Kelly still hadn't come out of the bedroom. I owed her an apology, but I thought it might have a better chance of being accepted if I offered it along-side some caffeine, so I made some coffee first. When it was ready, I poured her a cup and took it with me down the hall.

She'd shut the bedroom door. Grimacing, I knocked on it. "Kelly?"

"Go away."

"I have coffee."

"Leave the coffee and go away."

"Can I please come in?"

A pause. "I don't care what you do."

I entered the room and saw she was still in bed, wrapped to her ears with blankets and curled up on her side, facing the wall.

"Hey." Careful not to spill the coffee, I sat on the bed.

Silence.

"I'm sorry, Kelly. I'm really mad at myself, and I took it out on you."

"You don't need to be mad at yourself. You didn't do anything wrong."

Setting the cup on the windowsill, I lay down behind her and wrapped my arm around her waist. "I did, but it wasn't your fault, and I treated you like it was."

"This is normal for me, Xander. People follow me around and take photos. Do I like it? No. Did I want this bullshit on my vacation? No. Do I want to try to have a good time anyway? Yes."

I kissed her shoulder. "Okay."

"I'm sorry your picture is being taken too. You didn't ask for this."

"I don't give a fuck about myself. But we're going to be more careful, okay?"

"Okay."

"Do you still want to go on the boat today?"

"Yes."

"I'll make you a deal. You agree to move into my house for the rest of your trip and I'll take you out on the boat."

She sighed. "Why do we have to move?"

"Because this place makes me nervous. It's remote—anyone could be staked out in those woods. There are no security cameras. There are no shades on the front windows—practically the entire wall is glass."

"Does your house have cameras?"

"No," I admitted. "But it has blinds and curtains. We have neighbors who'd notice a stranger lurking

247

around the house and report it. People look out for each other here."

"Is this going to be okay with your dad?"

"Are you kidding? He adores you. It will be just fine."

"We won't be able to sleep together."

"Why not?"

"Xander!" She rolled onto her back and looked up at me. "I can't sleep with you in your dad's house, while he's *there*. Mabel and Devlin are there too, right?"

"Oh yeah. I forgot about them." I thought for a moment. "I guess it's too crowded to stay at the house. I'll book a hotel room."

"Xander, we'll be fine here," she said, snuggling up to me. "I'm not afraid when I'm with you. And I will take all the precautions you tell me to. I won't stray from your side. You will truly be stuck with me from now until the moment I leave."

"Fine. But the other thing we're doing is working on some self-defense moves. I won't always be there."

"I don't need—"

"You want a ride on my boat, you learn the moves," I ordered.

She sighed dramatically. "Fine."

"And if I see that guy around here, I'm *going* to fucking smash his camera. Possibly his face."

"You have my permission," she said. "Although I'd like to remind you that just a few days ago, you said if you had to get into a fight for me, it meant you hadn't done your job."

"Well, things are different now." I looked at her messy red hair, clear green eyes, and freckled nose, experiencing a strange tightness in my chest. "And if someone I don't like gets near you on my watch, he's done."

She smiled, slowly, sweetly. "My hero."

It sort of hit me like a lightning bolt.

CHAPTER NINETEEN

kelly

WHILE XANDER MADE BREAKFAST, I sorted through my texts and emails. Much of it was unimportant, work-related stuff that could have waited until I got back—dates I needed to put on my calendar, collaboration pitches, songwriter suggestions for the next album—but no one seemed to understand the concept of "getting away."

Then there were my parents to deal with. My father wanted to talk over the PMG deal with me, review its many pros. And my mother had had another premonition—this time, the bear didn't eat me, it just carried me off to his cave and kept me there like a prisoner.

I ignored my father, texted my mother I was doing fine, took a few deep breaths, and moved on to my voicemails. Most were insignificant, but there was one from Wags that made me slightly nervous.

"Hey, Kelly Jo. Sorry to disturb you. But the situation with the disgruntled bodyguard—his name is

James Bond, believe it or not—is getting a little heated. He says he's going to sue for wrongful termination unless you want to settle with him privately for ten grand. He claims he can give you details about which members of the team were leaking info and why. Let me know what you want to do."

I called Wags back.

"Hey, Kelly," he said when he picked up. "You got my message?"

"I got it. I don't know what to do, Wags. I don't want a lawsuit, but silencing this guy with money doesn't feel right either. He obviously knew what was going on and didn't stop it or come forward."

"I agree with you. I think he's bluffing about the lawsuit. This guy doesn't have the money for attorneys and all that. Suing someone is a tedious, expensive pain in the ass."

"And what difference would it make to know who was leaking the info? It's not like I'd ever hire any of them again. I don't really care whether it was one of them or all of them. And I know why —money."

"So I'll tell him no private settlement."

"Yes," I said, feeling sure of myself. "Fuck that guy for thinking he can get money out of me. Let him come after me in court if he wants. I won't be bullied into paying him. If he knew it was happening and said nothing, he's guilty in my view."

"Mine too." He paused. "How's your trip?"

"It's good. But I was spotted pretty fast."

"I saw the photos. How many photographers are up there?"

"You know what? I haven't seen any, so I have no idea." I thought for a moment. "Which is kind of strange. I wonder if there's only one guy, and he's keeping his distance."

"Who's the guy with you in the pics? Is it the bodyguard?"

"Yes." I smiled as the scent of frying bacon wafted down the hall and into the bedroom. "Turns out, he's not so bad. But he's seriously pissed about the photos that were taken on the property here."

"Rightly so. I'm glad he's around. You be careful."

"I will. Bye, Wags."

We hung up, and I was feeling so confident and plucky, I decided I could even handle listening to Duke's latest voicemail, which he'd left yesterday.

His smooth voice made my shoulders tense up. "Hi Pix, it's me. I know you're on your little vacation, but I have an opportunity for you. How would you like to perform the opening number at the Music City Awards?"

I gasped. The Music City Awards were a big fucking deal.

"Rebecca Rose and I were slated to perform 'Back Where We Started.' But she has to have surgery on her vocal cords next week, and the show is a week after that. The producers came to me and asked if I had any idea who they should ask to fill in. Of course, I thought of you right away. If you're interested"—he laughed—"and I know you are, give me a call back."

Well, damn.

Performing the opening number at the Music City Awards would be amazing—bucket list amazing—and I wanted to jump at it. But filling in for Rebecca Rose on "Back Where We Started" would mean performing a romantic duet about a second chance at love with Duke. Could I stomach it? He was tricky and manipulative. What if he was dangling this opportunity with strings attached?

Phone in one hand, I picked up the cup of coffee Xander had brought me with the other and wandered out to the kitchen. After warming it up in the microwave, I sat at the counter and watched him scramble eggs and flip bacon. He had a kitchen towel tossed over one shoulder, and his hair was a mess.

"Are you going to make breakfast for your wife and three kids?" I asked.

"All the time," he said, adjusting the heat under the eggs. "It's the most important meal of the day." Then he turned around and noticed my expression. "What's wrong? More photos?"

"No." I exhaled. "It's Duke."

Xander's face darkened. "What about him?"

I told him about the offer to fill in for Rebecca Rose at the awards show. "It would be really hard to say no. Like, twelve-year-old me used to dream about this every night."

"So say yes."

"You think I should?"

254

He shrugged. "Do you want to sing on that stage?"

"Yes. With all my heart."

"Then don't let anyone stop you."

"You make it sound so simple."

"Because it is." He put some eggs and two strips of bacon on a plate and set it in front of me. "If something will make you happy, I think you should go after it. I used to have this argument with Austin all the time."

"Oh yeah?"

He put the rest of the eggs and bacon on his plate and came around the peninsula to sit next to me. "Yes. There's always going to be a reason why you shouldn't—and sometimes the reason is completely valid. But I believe in going after what you want. I think fortune favors the bold."

"Is that why you did things like jump off garages into baby pools and try to prove you could fly?"

"No. That was just ego." He ate half a strip of bacon in one bite. "But this isn't about ego, and it's not about Duke. It's about Kelly Jo Sullivan."

I sucked in my breath. "Xander! You're right!"

He held his arms out wide.

Laughing, I grabbed onto one. "I'm going to ask to perform not as Pixie Hart, but as Kelly Jo Sullivan! No gimmicky sets, no crazy costumes, no glittery makeup. No made-up, manufactured *character*. I just want to be me up there and sing from the heart."

"Then do it."

"I will." Sliding off the stool, I planted a kiss on

his temple. "I'll be right back. I'm going to call Duke."

Xander picked up his coffee cup, but he didn't say anything.

Back in the bedroom, I sat on the edge of the bed and made the call.

"Hey, honey. How's my Pixie girl?"

I cringed. "I'm fine."

"You get my message?"

"I did. I'd like to do it. I just have one request."

"And what's that?"

"I want to be introduced as Kelly Jo Sullivan. Not Pixie Hart."

"Why? No one knows who that is."

"I think it will be obvious when I walk on stage and start singing."

"But in terms of publicity and everything, Pixie Hart is a *name*."

I stiffened. "Kelly Jo Sullivan is a name too. I've just never been encouraged to use it."

"Because it's not memorable. And you're famous as Pixie Hart. Why change your name and confuse people?"

"It's important to me."

"Let's not worry about that minor detail right

now. I think we should rehearse as soon as possible. How quickly can you get back to Nashville?"

Annoyed that he'd dismissed my request as minor, I said, "I'm not back for another ten days."

"I know when you were *planning* to be back, but this is big, Pixie. We've never performed that song together. We can't just show up at the televised Music City Awards without practicing. Everyone who's anyone in the industry will be in the first three rows at Milton Auditorium that night."

"I'm not saying I don't want to practice, but I know the song, Duke. We'll still have a week once I'm back."

"I want you back sooner."

I flinched at the edge on his tone. "Maybe this isn't a good idea, us working together. You should probably find someone else."

"No, wait. Sorry." He exhaled and spoke more patiently. "I think you and I have the perfect chemistry for this song, and people love seeing us together. Our arrival alone will cause a media frenzy."

"Duke, I—"

"Don't worry, it will be strictly platonic behind the scenes. It's a musical collaboration between friends."

"Okay," I said warily.

"If you decide to come home sooner, let me know. Otherwise, I'll be in touch with details when I get them. Enjoy the rest of your vacation." He paused. "How's it going up there? I saw a few pictures."

"It's fine," I said. "I was hoping to stay under the radar, but it didn't happen."

"That's the worst. You can't relax when you know you're being watched."

"I know, but what can you do? I have to go, Duke. Thanks for the opportunity. I appreciate it."

We hung up, and I texted Wags, Jess, and my agent with the news, leaving out the bit about performing as Kelly Jo and not as Pixie. There would be pushback on that, but I'd deal with it later. I got immediate replies from Wags and my agent, who were thrilled with the idea and wanted to know when it would be announced. I told them I wasn't sure but would keep them posted. My assistant responded with more measured excitement.

> Wow! That's big. And you deserve that spot. But are you sure singing with Duke is the right call? Is he going to expect "payment" for this favor?

> He says it's just a collaboration between friends. Strictly platonic.

> Okay. I just know how he gets with you. And I could see him using this as a chance to pull you back into his orbit. He wants you to belong to him.

I know. Believe me, if it was anything less than opening the Music City Awards, I'd run in the other direction. I have no desire to let him walk all over me again. Been there, done that.

Okay. Well, I'm happy for you and so excited to see the show!! How's everything else going? I saw the photos. Is the security guard driving you crazy?

I had to laugh.

Yes. He is.

When we left the house, Xander hustled me from the front door into the car like I was the President of the United States. He made me wear another gigantic sweatshirt of his over my bathing suit, hood up, covering my hair. My oversized sunglasses helped hide a good portion of my face.

The drive to the marina was tense, with Xander constantly checking to see if anyone was following us. Not that he told me what he was doing, but he looked in the rearview mirror a lot, and he was unusually silent, his face uncharacteristically grim.

At the harbor, he parked, came around to get me, and once again shepherded me quickly onto the dock and down to his well. He got aboard the boat first, and then helped me on.

Only when we were heading out of the harbor and onto the open water did his shoulders relax and his jaw unclench. I shed the sweatshirt and my shorts, slathered myself in SPF 50, and spread out a towel on one of the reclining leather seats. Leaning back, I tilted my face to the sky and let the sun warm my skin. The bay was a little choppy, and every now and again, we'd hit a wave that would splash me lightly, but the cool water was refreshing in the hot air.

Eventually, Xander found a spot he must have felt was safely distanced from land and dropped the anchor. Only then did he doff his shirt, unfold a towel, and stretch out on the back bench seat, perpendicular to me. For a while, we just lay there like two turtles on a log in the sunshine. I breathed in —sunscreen, sea air, maybe a whiff of the woods that lined the shore. The call of the seagulls above us mingled with the soft lap of the water against the hull, and the boat rocked gently on the waves. It was blissfully peaceful, and my heart was happy. This was how I'd imagined feeling on my vacation.

I just hadn't imagined company.

My heels were propped up on the back bench next to Xander's. I picked up my head and studied our feet. It made me chuckle—Xander's were so huge compared to mine, his toes long, his ankles sturdy.

His legs were hairy, and my gaze wandered up toward his muscular thighs, causing a little involuntary contraction at my core.

I nudged him with my foot. "Hey."

"What?" He sat up immediately. "Everything okay? You see something?"

"No," I said, laughing. "I was just thinking how nice this is. And I wanted to thank you for taking me out on the water. I know it makes you nervous to be out and about with me."

He sat all the way up and moved to one side of the bench. "Come sit with me." I moved to the bench, and he reached down and took me by the back of the calves, swinging my feet into his lap. "Can I get you anything?"

"I'm good," I said. I could look at his body in the sun for hours. His skin kissed by gold, the ink gleaming, the rays glinting off the water behind him.

"So when is the awards ceremony you'll sing at?"

"It's in about two and a half weeks. Thursday, the twenty-first." Over breakfast, I'd told him that I'd agreed to sing with Duke on the condition that I would be introduced as Kelly Jo Sullivan.

"The night before Buckley's Pub will open—I hope."

"I wish I could be in two places at once," I said.

"Me too." His hand bracketed my ankle, his thumb rubbing the tendons of my heel.

"I'm expecting an argument with my label on the name thing."

"Fuck them."

261

I laughed. "I can't fuck them, but I'm going to fight for it."

"Good." He looked at me. "This is a big event?"

"Huge."

"And where is it held?"

"It's at the Milton Auditorium. Most famous stage in country music."

"That's a theater?"

"Yeah, but it's also got a museum, offices, and conference rooms on the upper floors. A lot of agents and publicists and even singers keep offices there."

"Does it have good security?"

"It will that night, I'm sure."

"What about you personally? What will you do?"

I sighed. "I guess I'll have to hire someone new. Oh—I forgot to tell you this. I spoke with Wags, my manager, this morning, and he said one of the bodyguards from the tour who was fired is trying to get money out of me."

His hand tightened around my ankle. "What?"

"He claims he was wrongfully terminated and in exchange for ten grand will provide the names of the guys who were really at fault."

"Fuck that guy. He knew what was happening and didn't say anything?"

"I guess. Want to hear the funny part? The guy's name is James Bond."

Xander didn't laugh. "He lives in Nashville?"

"I assume so."

He placed one wide hand over the tops of both my feet. "I hate that you're going back there without protection in place. Tell me you have cameras at your house."

"I do." I hesitated. "I think they work."

Xander groaned. "You don't know for sure?"

"Well, I never looked! I had people for that. Plus, I bought a house in this ritzy gated community, so I assumed it was safe."

His mouth assumed that stubborn shape again. "I'm going back with you."

"What?"

"When it's time, I'll go back with you. I'm going to do a security assessment, make sure those cameras are functioning, check out this gated community, and hire a new bodyguard for you."

"Xander, you don't have to do that." My heart was beating wildly in my chest.

"I want to."

"But how long will that take?"

"Depends. A few days, at least. Maybe a week."

"What about the bar?"

"I'll figure it out. But I need to make sure you're safe."

Moved that he cared so much, he'd follow me back to Nashville and do all those things when he had his own business to worry about, I felt my throat tighten. Pulling my feet from his lap, I got to my knees and swung one leg over him, straddling his lap. I placed my hands on his bronzed, sun-warmed shoulders and pressed my lips to his. "Thank you."

"It's not a big deal. Your brother would want it that way."

"So it's for him? Not for me?" I kissed him again, pressing my breasts against his chest. He grew hard beneath me, and I rocked my hips over his.

"I guess it's for you," he murmured against my lips. His hands wandered over my skin, slipping beneath the edges of my bathing suit.

"Did you bring a condom?" I asked in a hushed, breathless tone.

"No." His mouth moved down the side of my neck. "Guess I'll have to get you off another way."

"Xander?" I tilted my head, and he reached for the ties on my bikini top.

"Yeah?"

"I have a birth control implant."

His hands and his mouth stopped. "You do?"

"Yes. And I haven't been with anyone since Duke."

"I haven't been with anyone all year either."

"So . . ."

"So I'm okay with it if you are." He untied the top and let it fall, reaching for my breasts and lifting them to his face with both hands.

"Is this one of those times when you want me to put up a fight?" I asked.

"No," he said, his mouth buried.

I laughed, dizzy with desire. "Then I'm okay with it too."

The next five days passed in a warm, golden-hued, late summer haze. We slept in, sat on the porch with coffee, Xander with his laptop, me with a paperback. He cooked breakfasts for me, I made dinners for him. We spent a couple days at the bar when the beer and liquor deliveries were made, and I helped Xander get everything organized and inventoried. When the inspection was successfully completed, we celebrated with the first drinks poured at Buckley's Pub.

We took afternoon jogs, snuck out on the boat one night, worked on self-defense moves in the living room, and once the town wasn't bursting at the seams with tourists, he even took me on a tour, tolerantly stepping aside when someone asked for a selfie with me or an autograph for their child.

I adored Cherry Tree Harbor—especially with Xander at my side.

We climbed the lighthouse stairs, and finding ourselves alone, we snuck a quick kiss while the wind whipped my hair. We took a ride on the old ferry boat, admired the Victorian mansions along the shore, and listened to the guide tell stories about the past. We took his niece and nephew out for ice cream at an old-fashioned sweets parlor, and I got to taste the fudge Veronica had raved about. We shopped on Main Street, and I made Xander stand outside the fitting rooms while I tried on outfits. Then I'd come out and demand to know what he thought.

"Well?" I said, modeling a halter sundress in emerald green. "What do you think?"

"I like it."

I rolled my eyes. "You like everything. Scale of one to ten—and don't say ten. You've rated everything a ten."

"Eleven."

I clucked my tongue. "Never mind. You're no help." But I was smiling, and so was he.

"Get the dress," he said. "I'll take you to dinner."

The following Saturday night, he took me to the Pier Inn. Xander had called ahead and reserved a table, and when we got there, he introduced me to the manager, who happened to be his aunt.

"Kelly, this is my aunt Faye. And Aunt Faye, this is Kelly." He placed a hand on the small of my back when he said it. I liked that he didn't give me a label, like friend or client. That hand told me how he felt.

"So nice to meet you, dear." She gestured toward the dining room, where tables were covered in white linen and topped with flickering candles. "Your table is all ready."

We followed her to a corner table by the window, and Xander pulled out my chair before sitting across from me, facing the room. He looked gorgeous in a dark navy suit, light blue shirt, and maroon tie. We'd stopped at his house yesterday and picked it up, and I wondered if it would be strange to see his wide swimmer's shoulders restricted by a formal jacket, his thick neck enclosed by a stiff collar, his beard above the crisp knot of a tie.

It wasn't strange at all. It was breathtaking.

"You can't see the view from that seat," I scolded him. "And it's so beautiful." The sun was setting over the water, and the harbor shimmered with pink, orange, and amber light.

"My view is beautiful too," he said, his eyes on me. "In fact, I think it beats yours."

My cheeks warmed. "Thank you."

As we finished dessert—well, as *I* finished dessert, since Xander said he was full but I could not resist chocolate lava cake—his aunt Faye approached, looking nervous.

"I'm sorry to bother you," she said, wringing her hands together.

"What is it, Aunt Faye?"

"Word has gotten out that Pixie Hart is here, and some of the waitstaff and even a few tables of guests are asking if it would be okay to get a picture."

Xander looked at me. "Your call."

My eyebrows shot up. "Really?"

He shrugged. "It's obviously not a secret anymore that you're here. And maybe if you let fans post their photos, those jerks who hide out and take them in secret won't get any money for them."

MELANIE HARLOW

More photos of us had surfaced since Monday morning—getting out of Xander's SUV at the marina, strolling down Main Street, sitting on the rocks at the seawall. We saw nothing that had been snapped at the cabin, and Xander and I were very careful never to be affectionate in public, so the pictures were all pretty mundane, even boring. It didn't surprise me that hordes of photographers weren't flocking here to follow me around. It seemed like it was just one or two, and they were keeping their distance.

But the luckiest break was that another scandal was blowing up in Nashville—one of the most committed couples in country music had announced their split. The wife had evidently fallen for her trainer, and the husband had been carrying on with a nineteen-year-old backup singer, who was already wearing a big rock on her finger. I didn't wish anyone ill, but I was glad some of the heat was off me.

I touched my napkin to my mouth. "I don't mind," I said to Faye. "I'd just like a moment to use the ladies' room first."

"Of course," she said, looking relieved and grateful. "I'll show you where it is."

I stood up and looked at Xander. "Okay?"

He nodded. "Okay."

Faye and I walked side by side toward the restaurant entrance, where she gestured toward a door marked with a W. "There you are. Thank you so much," she said. "I hated to ask you. You two looked like you were having such a nice, intimate evening."

268

"It's all right," I assured her, glancing back at Xander. He lifted a hand. "It has been a lovely evening, but Xander understands."

She smiled. "I'm glad."

As I used the bathroom and freshened up, I thought about what I'd said. *Xander understands.*

And while I posed for photos for the next thirty minutes straight, he stood patiently to the side, always alert, always watching, always aware, close enough to step in if he felt someone was getting too familiar, but distant enough not to interfere.

Because he understood—this was part of my job, even when I was out for dinner, enjoying what should have been a private occasion. He understood that while it might not be my favorite part of the job, it was sometimes necessary. And he understood instinctively when I'd had enough, and he came forward and took my elbow. "We're done here."

With a nod to his aunt, he steered me through the room, out the door, and straight to the car. Once he'd tucked me safely in the passenger seat, he went around to the driver's side. But after sliding behind the wheel, he didn't start the engine.

"Is it always like that?" he asked. "Everywhere you go—coffee, shopping, ice cream, dinner . . . people are there wanting a piece of you?"

"Pretty much. But you know . . ." I lifted my shoulders. "It's the price you pay."

He looked at me. "I'm sorry I said that to you. This is a really high price. I don't know how you keep paying it."

"Sometimes I don't either." I reached over and rubbed his leg. "When it gets to be a lot, I think about when I was little and dreamed about hearing my songs on the radio, and signing autographs, and singing in front of huge crowds. Those dreams came true. So if I have to deal with some bad stuff in exchange, it's okay. I'd rather deal with fans than suits at the label any day. Or sleazy producers."

His expression angry, Xander started the car. "I don't blame you."

"Thanks for dinner," I said. "I loved it. I hope what happened at the end didn't spoil your night."

"Not at all. I guess I just feel a little . . . possessive of you." He shook his head. "Sounds shitty when I say it like that. I don't own you."

"Well . . ." I slid my hand up his thigh, grazing his crotch. "Sometimes you do."

CHAPTER TWENTY

xander

THE RIDE HOME seemed longer than usual. Unnecessarily long. Cruelly long. Something wrong with the time-space continuum long.

I think it was Kelly's hand on my cock.

The entire drive back, she kept stroking me through my pants, until I was so hard I thought my dick might bust right through the zipper.

I barely got the SUV parked before we were jumping out, racing for the cabin, and rushing for the bedroom. We no longer risked messing around in the living room, with no way to cover the windows. I loosened my necktie as I followed her down the hall like a predator.

As soon as I shut the bedroom door, I grabbed her from behind, hiked up her dress, fastened my mouth to her neck and slipped my hand between her thighs. "Fuck," I rasped. "You're not wearing anything under this dress."

"No."

"And you're already wet."

"Yes."

Normally, I prided myself on my patience and attentiveness during foreplay, but tonight I didn't have it in me to wait. I needed to get inside her. I needed to have her that close. I needed to feel like she was mine.

I spun her around, putting her back against the door, then quickly unbuckled my belt, undid my pants, and shoved them down just enough. After hoisting her up, I lowered her onto my cock, my hands gripping her ass. She was warm and soft and snug and clinging to me, crying out with every thrust, her back thumping loudly against the wood.

Perilously close to coming, I changed the angle so the base of my cock rubbed her clit the way she liked. It ratcheted me up even higher to realize I knew the way she liked to be touched. The way she liked to be kissed. The way she liked to be fucked.

Her little noises grew louder and more frantic. Her pussy grew wetter, slick with heat and friction. Then *thank fuck*, she cried out as her climax crashed through her and I let go of mine, my legs going stiff, sweat dripping down my spine beneath my suit, my cock surging inside her.

When I could control my muscles again, I gently set her on her feet and extracted myself. Leaning forward, my forearms on either side of her head against the door, I pressed my mouth to her forehead, her cheek, her jaw. She lifted her face and I kissed her lips.

"I'll be right back," she said quietly.

I nodded, giving her space to open the door. My heart was having a hard time slowing down.

While she was gone, I shed my jacket, slipped the tie from my collar, and peeled off my damp dress shirt. After hanging up the components of my suit, I stripped off the rest of my clothes.

She entered the room again, switched on the light, and shut the door. "Help me get this dress off?" Turning around, she lifted her thick red hair, and I worked the knot from the halter ties. Then I pressed my nose to the back of her neck and inhaled her scent. She must have washed her makeup off, because I could smell her facial cleanser and fancy moisturizer too.

"Can you bottle this please?" I asked, sliding my hands around her waist and holding her close.

She giggled. "Bottle what?"

"You." *Us*, I almost said, but caught myself. There wasn't an us, not an us that could be bottled. Kept. Saved. The thought caused a strange ache in my chest and I let her go. "Is there a zipper or anything?"

"I've got it. It's on the side."

I watched her undress, red hair swinging loose around her sun-kissed shoulders, breasts pale, nipples pink and tempting, tan line from her bikini bottom crossing her abdomen. I wanted to trace it with my tongue.

After hanging up her dress, she climbed onto the mattress, slipped beneath the sheets, and gave me an expectant look. "Are you coming to bed?"

"In a minute." I went into the bathroom and brushed my teeth, and when I was done, I surveyed all the girly shit on the sink. Potions and lotions and jars and tubes and compacts and brushes. It looked like five girls lived here, not just one. Would this be what it was like to live with a wife? And what if you had daughters? Would your bathroom look like the cosmetics aisle of the drugstore exploded inside it all the time?

Spotting her perfume, I picked it up and sniffed it. My pulse quickened, like my body thought she was near. I set the bottle back on the vanity and went to find the real thing.

The next day, I woke up first and used the bathroom. When I returned to the bedroom, it struck me how beautiful Kelly looked, lying there on her back, one arm arcing gracefully over her head, white sheet twisted at her waist, her copper hair flowing over the pillow.

The Sunday morning light was soft and pink, filtered through the thin shade covering the window above our heads. Her skin glowed gently. A few determined sunbeams snuck beneath the bottom of the shade, illuminating the freckles on her nose, and her lashes fanned like feathers over her cheeks.

She breathed in, her lungs expanding, and my eyes traveled down her body, over the feminine curves of her breasts, the softness of her middle. A breeze moved the shade, causing it to click against the sill.

She opened her eyes and saw me standing there. Her lips curved into a smile. Her voice was lazy. "What are you doing?"

"Thinking about how beautiful you look. I wish I could photograph you."

"So do it. You've got your camera."

I swallowed. "You want me to?"

"Sure." Her eyes closed again.

My bag was lying in the corner of the bedroom—Kelly had moved it in there earlier in the week. I pulled my camera from it and switched it on. But rather than focus the lens on her, I went and sat down at her side. Brushed a lock of hair from her forehead. "Hey."

She opened her sea glass green eyes. "Hey."

I braced my arm on the other side of her. "I want you to know I don't take this lightly."

"Me neither. And if these pictures pop up online without any Photoshopping, I'm going to be really mad."

"I'm serious, Kelly. I understand the level of trust this takes. And I know you're in a no-trust zone right now."

"You sort of exist outside the zone for me."

I half-smiled. "Yeah?"

She nodded. "It's like you're part of this other world, where there's just the two of us. And I'm safe in this world. I can't really describe it, but that's how I feel. Nothing that happens here can hurt me."

"It's the truth," I said, and I meant it. "You are safe in this world."

She smiled seductively. "Then take my picture, Xander Buckley. I want to know how you see me."

"I'm not sure any photograph I take will do you justice." I stood up and switched the camera on. "But I've never been one to back away from a challenge."

"Just tell me where you want me."

"Like that. Just like that." I snapped her lying there on her back with one arm curved overhead, the other at her hip, that sunset hair framing her face. I worked quickly, so I wouldn't lose that gossamer light.

Kelly was a gifted model—knowing intuitively how to angle her head, lift a shoulder, tilt her chin. She had graceful, supple limbs and beautiful lines. She revealed different sides of herself—wide-eyed and playful one moment, then heavy-lidded and provocative the next. Unabashed, she let the sheet fall away as she turned onto her stomach and looked over her shoulder, as she rolled to one side and lay her cheek on an arm stretched overhead, as she tipped onto her back and arched up off the mattress.

She was day and night. Light and dark. An angel and a temptress. As I clicked again and again, somewhere it registered that this was the hottest fucking thing I'd ever seen, but it didn't feel salacious or tawdry. It felt like the greatest gift I'd ever been given.

Eventually though, my body did respond to all her inviting poses and suggestive expressions, especially when she touched her bottom lip with a fingertip and rubbed gently.

"You're very good at this," I told her, setting my camera back in my bag.

"I've had some practice." She laughed. "Not that I've ever been photographed completely naked."

"Never?" I crawled into bed with her.

She shook her head. "What about you? Have you ever taken anyone's picture like you just took mine?"

"Nope." Stretching out beside her, I pulled her close to me, and she flung a leg over my hips and an arm over my chest. "I never even thought about it."

"Seriously? Why not?"

I had to think about the question for a minute. It's not like I didn't have an appreciation for female bodies before her. "Well, first of all, I've never seen anyone look as beautiful as you did in that light. I'm not really a stick-around-until-morning kind of guy. Not that I've been a jerk about it," I said quickly, "but I don't really stay the night."

"How come?"

"Gives the wrong idea."

"Ah." She ran her fingertip along my collarbone. "So I guess I was just lucky then, that you had no choice but to spend nights with me."

I laughed. "Pretty sure I'm the lucky one."

"You could have taken the photos at night. Before me, I mean."

"I guess I could have, but I'm telling you the truth when I say the idea never occurred to me. I've never wanted to capture someone like that before."

"Will you ever look at the pictures you took of me?"

"That depends."

"On what?"

"On what you do with them."

"What *I* do with them? They don't belong to me."

"Yes, they do." I rolled over and moved on top of her so she could see my face. "You let me photograph you—that took a lot of trust. To prove I'm worthy of that trust, I want to give you all the pictures."

"But the whole point is that I trust you to have them and never share them. Never betray me."

"I would die first."

She smiled, her eyes narrowing. "Or my brother would kill you."

"I'd deserve it. He should torture me before offing me. Make me listen to Duke Pruitt songs for hours on end."

That made her laugh. "Anyway, I don't want the pictures, Xander. You keep them. So you never forget me."

I buried my face in her neck and inhaled. "I could never forget you."

Actually, I was starting to think it might be a problem.

When I checked my messages that day, I had a voicemail from my friend with a contact at the DMV. She apologized for the delay—she'd been on vacation and was still catching up—but said she had an answer for me. The beige Honda was registered to a rental agency at the Traverse City airport.

Later that afternoon, I went out onto the porch while Kelly was in the shower and called up another friend of mine, a guy named Zach Barrett. He was also a former SEAL who worked for Cole Security. He'd worked out of the San Diego office and I'd been mostly east coast, but our paths had crossed every now and again, and I liked him a lot. Solid, trustworthy, and skilled. Plus, he could be a scary motherfucker.

Last I'd heard, he'd married a girl who lived not far from here, and he worked only part-time.

"Barrett here," he answered gruffly.

"Hey, Zach. It's Xander Buckley."

"Hey, Xander. It's been a while." His tone lost its hard edge. "How are you?"

We caught up for a few minutes, and I learned he lived about two hours from me, was married to a woman named Millie, and they had two kids.

"You've been busy," I said with a laugh. "Are you still working for Cole?"

"Here and there. I cut way back on travel because Millie—that's my wife—owns a business and with the two kids, it was hard being gone all the time. Plus, I don't want to be gone. I don't want to miss anything."

"I get it."

"What about you? Did I hear you're opening a sports bar?"

"Yeah. Hopefully, I'll be up and running soon. Just waiting on a few last-minute things."

"I'll have to drive up and check it out."

"I'd like that. So listen, I have a favor to ask." I explained what I was doing and why. "I've got no proof the car is connected to the asshole who was on the property taking photos or whoever snapped the shots at the bar, but I had a bad feeling when I saw it."

"I'd trust my gut on it too."

"Any way you can get the name of the guy who rented it?"

"Let me see what I can do."

After we hung up, I glanced at my screen and noticed today's date—it rang a bell in my head, like it was significant for some reason. Devlin's birthday—that was it. I decided to give him a quick call.

"Hello?"

"Hey, brother. Happy birthday."

"Thanks. How's everything going with the bar?"

"Okay. Still on track to open next Friday night."

"Can't wait to see it. I might be back next month."

"How did the lunch with Granny go? I never got

a chance to ask, you left town so fast. You sweet talk her into accepting your millions?"

"Ah, not exactly."

I had to grin. "*What*? I thought this was a done deal."

"It should have been a done deal. But there was a complication in the shape of a granddaughter who joined us for lunch."

"Granddaughter?" I pictured a child. "How old?"

"Late twenties, maybe. She grew up there and works there, and she's totally against selling. She's got some ridiculous notion she can get investors who will help turn the business around. My offer was much higher than anything else she'd get, but she refuses to listen to reason."

"You mean there are actually humans alive you can't sell to?"

"There's *one*," he clarified. "And it's only because she has the wrong idea about me."

"Maybe she noticed you were trying to bamboozle her granny over French onion soup."

"No, she arrived at the table with preconceived notions about my character. She was prejudicial and biased against me from the start."

"Why?"

Devlin exhaled loudly. "Because we'd met before."

"Where?"

"Remember that gorgeous brunette I left with the night we all went to The Broken Spoke?"

I started to laugh. "That was the granddaughter?"

"I didn't know it at the time, okay? We didn't get into a lot of personal details, we just had a good time. But no matter what I say, she doesn't believe me. She's convinced I sought her out and slept with her for nefarious purposes."

"So now what?"

"Now I have to figure out how to make this deal happen even though she's working against me at every turn. My boss won't accept anything less."

"You'll be fired if you can't make it happen?"

"I might not be fired, but instead of the promotion I want, I'd probably be relegated to sales manager in Bumfuck, Nowhere."

"Well, hang in there. I'm sure you'll find a way."

"I better. So how's everything going with you and Kelly?"

"Fine."

"Still strictly professional?"

"Uh, it's slightly less than professional."

Devlin laughed. "That didn't take long."

"But she's heading back to Nashville at the end of the week." I hoped I sounded more neutral than I felt.

"Will you see her again?"

"I doubt it," I said, again trying to come off like I didn't really care while a pit opened up in my gut.

"Why not? It's not like Nashville is that far. A couple hours on a plane."

"She's going on another tour soon, and I've got a business to open. We're just too busy. Our lives are too separate." The pit was starting to fill with an uncomfortable longing for something I didn't want to think about. And I was good at locking uncomfortable feelings away into boxes. "Anyway, I hope you have a great day. Enjoy the last year of your twenties."

"I'd enjoy it more if it ended with me getting that promotion. I can't believe how bad I fucked this up without even knowing it. I mean, what are the chances? Of all the gin joints in all the towns in all the world, you know?"

"I know. But hey, was it worth it?"

"You know what?" He was silent a moment, like he was into the memory. "It was."

Later that afternoon, I pinned Kelly to the ground, knees on either side of her hips, hands locked around her wrists, pushing them into the ground. "What do you do if someone gets you like this?"

"Bridge high, throw low."

"Do it."

She bucked her hips up hard, causing me to pitch forward—a guy would face plant above her head if he didn't release her wrists to catch himself. As soon as her arms were free, she swept them down to her sides along the grass snow-angel style, then immediately wrapped them around my torso, turning her face to the side to avoid my chest smashing her face.

"Tighter," I commanded. "You can't leave any space in between when you hug the tree, or he'll get an arm back in between you."

She squeezed harder, her cheek against my chest. "Like that?"

"Yes. Now what?"

"Climb the tree. Wrap the arm." She scooted up, hooked her left arm around my right bicep, and rolled me onto my back. "And from here . . ." Her elbow came slicing toward my face from the right, and after I blocked it, she jabbed the same elbow straight down, stopping just short of my gut. Then she jumped up and ran.

"Good job," I said, getting to my knees. "Now come back and let's do it again."

She hurried back to me and lay on the grass again, letting me pin her down. I didn't love being outside like this—I imagined photos were being taken of us right this second, and without the context of self-defense lessons, they'd look like something else was going on—but I *did* like knowing that the asshole with the camera would see she could protect herself. And fuck what anyone else thought. As long as she was safe, I didn't care.

"You sure you want me to escape this time?" she teased.

"Yes," I said seriously. "I want you to escape *every* time."

"Okay, but kiss me first."

"Kelly, I'm not playing. I want you to learn this stuff. I hope you never have to use it, but if you do, I want there to be no hesitation whatsoever."

"I am learning! And if anyone but you was pinning me like this, I would not hesitate. I promise." She smiled. "One kiss?"

"Earn it first. Go."

She thrust up explosively, forcing me to break my fall. She repeated the tree climb and the arm wrap, successfully getting me beneath her before fake-delivering the elbow jabs. But she didn't run this time.

"Now can I have my kiss?"

"Inside."

She looked around. "You really think someone is still out there?"

"I think we have to assume so."

"And would you be embarrassed to be seen kissing Pixie Hart?"

"Of course not. It's just nobody's fucking business. You don't have to give them that piece of you." *I want all of you to myself.*

"You're right. I don't." She smiled. "Let's go inside."

That night, we were invited for dinner over at Austin's. On the ride over, Kelly seemed distracted. Her hands were in her lap, and she kept scrunching up the material of her dress—this one was white with blue flowers on it, and it had ties on each shoulder and a flirty little skirt. Worried she was having second thoughts about those photographs, I asked her what was on her mind.

"I got a text from my manager while you were in the shower," she said. "The performance at the Music City Awards is a sure thing. One of the producers got in touch."

"That's great news, isn't it?"

"Yes, but Duke must be in everyone's ears, because now even my manager wants me to get back to Nashville immediately to start rehearsals."

"Like when?"

"Like tomorrow."

"Fuck that," I said, reluctant to end our private days and nights together. "They want you, they get you when they get you."

She laughed ruefully. "It doesn't really work that way if you're me. I don't have tons of leverage. And the thing is, it's not so much about going home three days sooner as it is about not wanting Duke to think he calls the shots for me."

I thought for a minute. "Have they approved your request to sing as Kelly Jo Sullivan?"

"Not yet."

"Okay, so maybe you offer a deal. You'll come

back to Nashville tomorrow if they approve that request."

"I could try that." She pulled her phone from her purse and stared at it. "It feels kind of scary though, to make a demand. They could find a dozen singers to replace me in an instant." She snapped her fingers, and I grabbed her hand in the air.

"Don't think like that. Be brave. Stand up for yourself."

"Okay." She took a deep breath. "Okay. I'll send the text."

"Good girl." I kissed her fingers and gave her hand back, and she typed a message.

A minute later, she dropped her phone into her bag. "Done. I sent one message to Wags, Duke, and the producer. Now I need a glass of wine."

"That can be arranged."

She looked over at me. "So would you be able to come back to Nashville with me tomorrow? I don't expect you to."

"I'll make it work. I'm going to talk to Veronica tonight about the interviews she conducted this week. I'm hoping to have the hiring done in the next couple days. And Austin found an electrician for me —retired guy, a friend of our dad's—who said he could finish the work this week. Barstools are scheduled to arrive on Thursday, and I think my brother or dad could handle that. Beer and liquor deliveries are complete. Point of sale system in. A/V is finished. If all goes well, I can still open next Friday night."

"All will go well," she said confidently. Her

phone lit up, and she looked down. "Fuck. It's Duke. He's calling me."

"Take the call," I told her, even though my gut told me to grab her phone and throw it out the window. "He can't hurt you."

"You're right. He can't." She sat up a little taller and tapped the screen. "Hello?"

kelly

"BABE, we talked about this. I said no." Duke's smooth baritone dripped with patronizing superiority.

"No, you said it could wait. And if you want me back in Nashville tomorrow, you'll say yes. Otherwise, I'm going to enjoy the rest of my trip."

"Stop playing around, Pixie." His voice lost some of its buttery charm. "We've got work to do."

"If you'll introduce me as Kelly Jo, I'll be home tomorrow," I said.

"The producers won't want that," he said. "They agreed to Pixie Hart and that's who you'll have to be. She's the name. And it makes no sense to me why you'd want to walk away from everything you've built."

"It doesn't have to make sense to you, Duke."

"Well, the answer is no."

"I'm going to wait to hear what the producers say."

"They'll say whatever I tell them to," he scoffed. "Don't forget who I am."

"I know exactly who you are."

"Good." And he hung up.

I dropped my phone into my bag. "That did not go well."

"I could tell." Xander's hands were white-knuckled on the wheel. "I'm sorry he's such a dickhead."

"It's okay. Let's forget about it for tonight."

While Veronica and Xander sat at the dining room table to work, I helped Austin out in the kitchen. At first, Austin had insisted he didn't need any help, but I told him I wasn't raised to sit around while someone else did all the work, and besides, I liked cooking. He eventually agreed to let me do some peeling and chopping, and we stood side by side in the kitchen, chatting amiably and watching Xander and Veronica go over her notes from this week's interviews.

I asked about his new business venture, if he planned to open up a storefront, how many people were on his wait list for a table and what a girl had to do to get on it.

He laughed. "I can put you on it. I just need some measurements, room size and all that."

"No problem. I'm heading back to Nashville within the next couple days, and Xander's actually going to come with me, so I'll have him take the measurements and get them to you."

"Xander's going to Nashville?" Austin sounded surprised.

"I think so. He wants to make sure the cameras at my house are working, hire a new security team for me, do a risk assessment on my property. I told him it wasn't necessary, but he's insisting."

"Xander's a stubborn son of a bitch."

I laughed. "He is. And it's such an inconvenience, with his bar opening soon and all."

"Then it must really matter to him," said Austin, right as we heard a sudden hammering on the ceiling above our heads.

"What's that?" I tipped my head back and stared at the plaster.

"That is my children practicing their tap dancing on Owen's bedroom floor. Ever since Veronica helped them create homemade tap shoes and taught them some steps, they've taken to rolling up the rug and letting loose on the oak, even though I've asked them to please use the basement instead." He shook his head and wiped his hands on a kitchen towel. "Excuse me for one second."

I laughed as he strode with long legs past the dining room table toward the stairs at the front of his house. He had a beautiful home, not super stylish or anything, but immaculately clean and full of warmth. Briefly I wondered if Xander would eventually have a home and family like this, but when I looked at him sitting at the dining room table, I experienced such a fierce longing for him that my chest ached. I was jealous of this future wife, this woman who would get everything.

His sunny afternoons on the boat and his rainy days on the couch. His lazy smile over coffee in the morning. His Denver omelets and sizzling bacon. His Sunday dinners with extended family. His boyish laugh and his possessive growl. His wide, strong palms on her stomach. His beard prickly on her thighs. His voice deep and gravelly in the dark. His camera focused on her as she luxuriated in warm white sheets on a soft Sunday morning. His time. His attention. His protection.

I had to stop there. I wasn't normally a jealous person and didn't particularly enjoy envying the life of some woman I didn't even know—for fuck's sake, even Xander didn't know who she was. She wasn't even real yet.

But she would be. Someday, she would be.

The feeling stayed with me, and it put me on edge. By the time we got home, it had driven a wedge of tension between us. I'd been silent the entire drive back, and now we were in the bedroom. Door closed. Light on. Shades down.

I toed off my sneakers and kicked them aside, frustrated I hadn't been able to wear my boots in over a week. I removed my earrings and bracelets and tossed them in my suitcase, not even bothering with my jewelry bag.

"Are you okay?" Xander asked from behind me.

"I'm fine," I said. "Just a little tired." It wasn't like I could tell him that among other bullshit problems I had at the moment, I didn't like the thought of sharing him with his future wife. That was insane. What Xander and I had was a vacation fling, not a forever thing. It would never work. Our lives had crossed like railroad tracks, but each train was heading in a different direction.

"Their house can be a lot, with two kids." His tone was apologetic.

"No, no, it's not that at all—the kids are adorable. Austin is so nice, and Veronica is wonderful." I turned to find him leaning back against the door, sizing me up. "I think I'm still aggravated from that phone call with Duke. And the fact that Wags thinks I should just do what the producers want. And of course, the producers will do whatever Duke tells them to, because he's the big name." I threw my hands up in surrender. "It's the same old, same old. The men are in charge."

"I'm sorry. I wish there was something I could do."

"You don't know what it's like." I didn't want to take it out on him, but I couldn't stop the words from spilling from my mouth as I stood there studying him. His shoulders were like mountains. His legs like Sequoias, his chest like the side of a cliff. "You're big and strong. You're always in control. You have no idea what it's like to feel powerless."

He studied me for a moment, then pushed off the

door and took a few steps forward, so we were chest to chest.

Then he dropped to his knees. "Show me."

Right there on the bedroom floor, he went down on his knees for me.

"What?" I whispered.

"Show me," he urged, and his voice was so deep and his shoulders so wide and his height so excessive that even on his knees, he hardly seemed any less powerful.

But it was enough.

He understood.

Rushing forward, I cupped his bearded face in my hands and pressed my lips to his. Penetrated his mouth with my tongue. Controlled the angle and depth and heat of the kiss in a way I couldn't have done from beneath him. Need for him surged within me, and I thought maybe my plan had backfired, because I felt even more helpless than I had before.

Falling to my knees in front of him, I pulled his black T-shirt over his head and unbuckled his belt, unbuttoned his jeans, and tugged down the zipper. After wriggling one leg out of my panties, I left them hooked around one ankle and pushed against Xander's chest. He lay back on his elbows obligingly, and I straddled his legs, dragging his jeans down to his thighs. Unbound, his cock sprang free and I took it in my hand, slipping it through my fist a few times. With the light on, I could see how different parts of his body reacted to my touch. I liked the way his abs flexed and his eyes darkened and his chest rose and fell in quick succession. I liked the way his hands curled into fists. I liked the tension in his jaw. I liked the deep purple color of his erection as it thickened and lengthened further in my hand.

Most of all, I liked that his body was mine tonight, that he'd surrendered it to me. That he'd ceded control. For Xander, that didn't come easily. It took trust, the way this morning's photographs had for me.

I lowered my mouth onto him, licking the warm, smooth crown and sucking the tip. He groaned with tortured delight. "I wish I could get my hands on you."

"Not yet. I get to have my way with you first." Suddenly I had an idea.

"Your way?"

"Yes." I picked up my head and smiled coyly at him. "Don't move, if you know what's good for you."

One of his brows quirked up.

Popping to my feet, I went over to the side of the bed and reached beneath it, pulling out my mini vibrator. Returning to him, I pulled his jeans all the way off and knelt between his legs. My thumb hit the button on the toy, bringing it to life. It hummed in my hand as I lowered my head again, running my tongue from the base of his shaft to the tip. Then I did it again while gently pressing the vibrator to his balls.

He inhaled sharply. "Oh, fuck."

I took the head in my mouth and sucked while

295

moving the toy along his shaft, careful not to press too hard or go too fast. But judging by the sounds he made and the way his dick was reacting in my mouth, he found the sensations pleasurable. I moved it between his legs again, farther back this time. He cursed and groaned, his body growing tense, his breath coming fast.

I used firmer pressure with the toy, and his climax erupted suddenly, a grunt tearing from his throat as he grabbed my head and fisted a hand in my hair, his hips bucking off the floor as his cock surged again and again in my mouth.

When the spasms faded, he moved away from me and the vibrator, which had probably become unbearable. "Christ. What did you just do to me?"

I sat back on my heels, switching off the vibrator and wiping my mouth with the back of my hand. "Did you like it?"

"Yes. No. Yes. *Fuck*." His eyes closed. "I don't generally like the feeling of not being in control, but that felt amazing."

"Good." I tossed the vibrator onto the bed.

"Now come here." He sat up and reached for the front of my dress, pulling me toward him. As I crawled up his body, he lay all the way back. Then he hooked his arms beneath my thighs and snaked beneath me so my knees were on either side of his head, his face between my thighs.

I held my dress up so I could watch him, gasping at the first smooth stroke of his tongue. His eyes stayed locked on mine as he licked and sucked and teased and flicked. But before long my eyes closed in surrender, and my body began to move to its own rhythm, slowly at first—deliciously, delectably slow, riding his tongue, his lips, even his nose. The velvet texture of his tongue played nicely with the scratch of his beard. His greedy moans vibrated through my lower body. His hands clutched the tops of my legs, pulling me to him.

Balling up the front of my dress in one hand, I slid the other into his hair and closed my fingers, gripping tight, as if I was afraid I'd fall off this ride. His mouth fastened on my clit and sucked hard, and I lost whatever control I had left, the orgasm splintering me into a million glittering little pieces.

When I regained the use of my legs, I scooted down his body and collapsed on his chest.

"Thank you," I said.

"For what?"

"For understanding me. For knowing what I need. For being willing to give it to me." I closed my eyes. "For being in my corner."

He stroked my back and spoke quietly. "It's a nice place to be."

Our breathing synced, and I wondered if I'd ever felt such peace. "Xander?"

"Hmm?"

I think I'm in love with you. But I bit my tongue rather than risk saying the words out loud. "Nothing. Never mind."

I couldn't. I just couldn't.

In all my life, I'd never told someone I loved them without hearing it first.

Pictures of the outdoor self-defense session were published by the following morning. And of course, it did not appear as if the activities we were engaged in were of the educational sort.

Xander was livid. He stormed out onto the porch and stood there scanning the trees and cracking his knuckles for a solid twenty minutes. I knew better than to talk to him when he got that way, so I gave him some time to cool off. Sipping coffee at the counter, I was sifting through my inbox when the text from Duke came in.

> Sorry about how I acted last night. I had a rough week, but that's no excuse for what I said. You can be introduced with any name you want. What matters is the song, us singing it together. I'll let the producers know it's fine with me.

> I agree completely. It's the music that matters. Thank you!

The moment I saw it, I jumped up and ran outside.

"Guess what?" I said excitedly, tapping his shoulder.

"What?" He stood like a sentry keeping watch, not even turning to look at me.

"It worked."

"What worked?"

"I can perform as Kelly Jo Sullivan."

He finally faced me. "Really?"

I nodded happily. "Really. I just got a text from Duke. He apologized and said what matters is the music." Then I jumped up, throwing my arms and legs around him, pressing my lips to his. "I did it! I stood up for myself!"

"You did it." His hands were solid and strong beneath me. "I'm proud of you."

I kissed him again, not caring who saw, not caring about anything except sharing this amazing moment with the one who'd encouraged me to make it happen. Not because he'd get anything out of it, but because he cared about me. He wanted me to be happy. He understood the way I—

Suddenly he set me on my feet and launched himself off the porch.

"Xander?" Totally confused, I watched him sprint into the trees.

I ran down the steps and followed him as quickly as I could in my bare feet, wincing as I stepped on rocks and sticks and prickly things.

"Motherfucker!"

I followed the sound of Xander's angry voice and found him screaming obscenities at a man lying face down on the ground while Xander pinned his arms behind his back.

"Gimme my camera back," the man complained. "I've got a right to do my job."

"You've got a right to shut the fuck up," ordered Xander. "You trespass on other people's property, you lose your other rights."

A few feet away, I saw the camera. I picked it up and moved closer to them. He swung his head to look at me.

I recognized him. "Hoop?"

"See? She knows me!"

Xander looked at me. "You know this cocksucker?"

"I know who he is," I said. "He's one of the Nashville paparazzi."

"That doesn't sound like a reason I shouldn't kick his ass." Xander looked down at Hoop. "The fuck are you doing up here?"

"My job! I told you!"

"How did you know where to find her?"

Hoop said nothing at first.

"Answer me, you piece of shit." Xander put more pressure on Hoop's arms.

"Ow! I just figured it out!" Hoop blurted. "We do it all the time."

"Xander, it was probably my stupid Instagram post," I said, uncomfortable with the violence. I didn't want to see anyone in pain because of me.

"Exactly," said Hoop. "It was Instagram."

Xander refused to let up. "That still doesn't give you the right to come up here and harass her."

"I wasn't harassing her! I was just trying to make a buck. I've got five kids, okay? And one of them has medical problems. I've got a lot of bills to pay."

"You should have thought about that before breaking the law."

"Xander, just let him go," I said.

Xander looked up at me. "Seriously?"

"Yeah." I don't know whether it was the fact that it was my fault he'd located me, or the mention of his five kids or the medical bills, or if I was just feeling generous because I'd just scored a big victory right before this happened—but I simply wanted this situation over so I could celebrate it.

"Can I at least smash his camera?" Xander asked.

I shook my head. "No. But you can delete all the pictures before we give it back to him."

Hoop started to whine. "But I have some nice shots of the sunset over the harbor in there."

"Fuck off, Hoop," I said good-naturedly. "What you're doing here is illegal, and you know it. You're lucky I'm in a good mood today. Now stay where you are." I handed the camera to Xander, who deleted all the photos at once before allowing Hoop to get up. It was almost comical looking at the two men standing next to each other—no wonder Xander had subdued him so quickly. Standing chest to chest with Xander, he looked like a flabby weasel facing off against an angry grizzly.

Xander gave him the camera. "Now get the fuck out of here."

Hoop seemed eager to obey that command and scurried off toward the driveway without argument.

"Bet you anything he's driving a beige Honda rental," Xander muttered, watching Hoop disappear into the trees.

"How do you know?"

"Just a hunch."

"Doesn't matter," I said, tugging his arm. "Come here. We were celebrating, remember?"

"That's right." He wrapped me in his arms. "You okay?"

"I'm great." I held him tightly, my ear pressed to his chest. I closed my eyes as a breeze cooled my skin. "I'm happy."

"I'm sorry it took me so long to find that guy."

"Don't worry about it," I said. "Hoop's annoying, but he's harmless. I'm frankly shocked he had the wherewithal to find this place and get himself here, let alone hide out in the woods. He must really be desperate."

"If he's so broke, how'd he pay for this trip?"

"Who knows?" I loosened my grip and tilted my head back. "Listen, I'm just glad I only had one photographer to contend with up here. Usually it's a herd of them. And even though he trespassed, it could have been a lot worse. He could have taken pictures through the windows."

"I wonder why he didn't," Xander said.

302

"Wouldn't he have gotten a lot more money for those?"

"Let's not look a gift horse in the mouth." I took his hand again and started walking back toward the cabin. "I should start packing up, get the cabin in order. I have to be back in Nashville tomorrow."

"What time do you want to leave?"

"About seven a.m. Is that okay?"

He nodded. "I'll make it work."

We reached the porch, and Xander pulled the door open for me. "I'll help you get this place cleaned up, and then we'll need to go to my house so I can grab a few extra things."

"Of course," I said. "Maybe we can have dinner in town. What was that place you wanted to take me before I left?"

"Mo's Diner. You definitely can't leave Cherry Tree Harbor without having a burger and milkshake at Mo's."

I clapped my hands. "Then let's do that."

"I'll clean out the fridge. Do you have instructions for trash?"

"Yes. One second." I headed over to the kitchen counter, where I'd left my phone, and pulled up my email. Scrolling through my inbox, I found the message Jess had forwarded with all the check-in and check-out instructions. "Here. Everything is listed in this email."

He glanced at it and nodded. "Okay. I'll take care of it. Did you change your password yet?"

"No, but I will do it tonight. I promise." I gave

303

him a quick kiss on the cheek before hurrying into the bedroom, where I experienced a catch in my chest as I began to repack my clothes in my suitcase. This trip definitely hadn't been what I'd envisioned for myself—solitude, silence, reflection—but I was leaving with a renewed sense of myself and my self-worth, and I supposed that had been the goal all along.

Funny how Xander had made all the difference after I'd tried so hard to get rid of him. Now I was so grateful he'd come into my life.

Guess I'd have to rewrite our song.

Austin, Veronica, and the kids met us at Mo's Diner for dinner. It was the quintessential fifties-style hot spot, complete with black and white checkerboard floor, an old-fashioned counter lined with red vinyl and silver chrome stools, signed movie star head-shots on the wall, and a juke box in the corner.

Ari was our server, and she recommended the Bollywood Burger, sweet potato fries, and a vanilla milkshake. Sitting in the roomy booth between Xander and Adelaide, across from Austin, Veronica, and Owen, I felt so light and happy, it was like gravity didn't exist.

When we were done, I hugged Ari and thanked her for the best burger I'd ever had.

"You're welcome," she said, taking a little bow. "The Bollywood Burger was my idea. I'm trying to get my parents to stir things up around here. The menu has been the same forever."

"Well, it was delicious," I told her. "And the sweet potato fries were perfect with it."

"Thanks. It was really nice meeting you. Do you think maybe you could send an autographed picture for our wall?" She gestured to the photos above our booth.

"Of course! I'd be honored to grace the wall next to Dashiel Buckley."

Ari made a face. "I'll give you a better spot."

I laughed. "Uh oh. Not a fan of Malibu Splash?"

"It's complicated." She waved a hand in the air. "But anyway, thank you so much for coming in! I promise to come to a concert on the next tour."

"You better! Here, let me give you my number. Just text me what show you want to come to, and I'll get you good seats and backstage passes." We exchanged phone numbers and another hug before saying goodbye.

The kids wanted ice cream for dessert, so we wandered down the street, the guys up ahead with the kids, Veronica and I ambling a little ways behind.

"So you're leaving tomorrow," she said. "And Xander's going with you?"

"Yes. He's going to drive my rented minivan, and then fly home next week."

"Are you glad to be going home?"

"Kind of." I shrugged. "I'm excited about the

awards show performance, but I also wish I didn't have to cut my trip short. I really love it here."

"You can always come back to visit," she suggested. "I'm sure Xander would like that."

"Oh, I don't know. He'll probably be glad to be rid of me."

She glanced at the guys ahead of us. "My gut tells me that is not the case. Austin told me earlier he has never seen his brother like this over a girl."

My face warmed. "Really?"

"Really. Escorting you back to Nashville just to make sure you're safe there when his bar is opening at the end of next week?"

I winced. "I do feel bad about that."

"Don't. Xander is doing exactly what he wants to do." She leaned into me, nudging me with her shoulder. "Because he cares about you."

"I care about him too."

"So why not make an effort to see each other again?"

I studied Xander's back for a moment, and my stomach muscles tightened. He glanced over his shoulder at me, as if he wanted to make sure I was still there, and I waved before dropping my eyes to the sidewalk again. "Lots of reasons," I said.

"Name one."

"Distance. Nashville and Cherry Tree Harbor are not close."

"You can afford flights, right?"

"I'll be back on tour by early next year."

"He could come to you."

"He's just starting a business. He can't be leaving it all the time to follow me around the country."

"Lots of people have to date long-distance these days. It's possible."

I shook my head. "I don't think either one of us wants that. We'd never see each other. It would get frustrating. He'd probably be worried all the time. And I have some trust issues," I admitted. "It would be hard for me not to wonder what he was doing when we weren't together."

"I get that. But maybe you could have an open relationship. You know, like you agree to be together when you're together and not be exclusive when you're apart?"

"No way could I do that," I said. "It sounds modern and progressive, but I know myself. I'm old-fashioned when it comes to relationships. And probably a bit unrealistic and starry-eyed."

"How so?"

"I'm a romantic. I want someone to fall for me and only me. I want to be the love of someone's life." I laughed a little. "I've probably read too many fairy tales and watched too many romantic comedies."

"I get that," she said with a sympathetic smile.

"You'd think I'd be jaded after seeing my parents' dysfunctional marriage—my dad sort of comes and goes as he pleases and my mother just puts up with it. Maybe that's why I know I could never be okay with an open relationship. I know what it felt like as his daughter every time he left. I know that feeling of hope rising every time he came back." My throat grew tight. "And I know the crushing disappointment of being abandoned again, wondering if it was my fault."

Veronica put her arm around my shoulder and squeezed. "I get that too."

"And then of course, I spent three years with someone who treated me the exact same way."

"Some people think we seek out our childhood trauma and try to relive it," she said, "hoping for a better ending."

"That did not happen for me." We walked for another minute in silence. "Xander and I actually talked about love," I told her quietly. "We have very different ideas about it."

She looked surprised. "Tell me."

"Well, he's looking for a comfortable, easygoing kind of thing. He wants someone laidback, someone who makes him laugh. He doesn't believe in lightning-bolt love, the kind that just—BOOM!—strikes you in the heart and changes your life forever. He says that kind of love doesn't last and it's too unpredictable."

"Oh, Xander," she sighed.

"In his defense, he's not one of those guys who never wants to settle down. He does have this vision of himself as a husband and father—he just sort of wants to approach finding a wife the way he'd shop for a T-shirt or something. Comfort over style."

Veronica snickered. "Durability over looks."

"Definitely she needs to be durable." I lowered

my voice even more. "Xander is built like a battleship and likes the fight."

She burst out laughing, making the guys turn back and look at us. Attempting to be quiet, she cleared her throat. "I know exactly what you mean."

We reached the ice cream shop, and Veronica tugged my arm. "If you're not getting ice cream, come sit with me on the bench."

I looked at Xander, who looked up and down the nearly empty street and shrugged. "It's okay. We'll be out in a minute."

The guys went inside with the kids, and Veronica and I parked our behinds on a bench near the corner that faced the water. The sun was setting, and the light was golden warm on our faces. I took a breath, savoring the scent of this place—the bay, the fudge, the evergreen trees.

"I wanted to say one more thing." Veronica pulled her heels up to the bench and wrapped her arms around her legs. "Because I went through this with Austin too. Losing their mom so young affected them in ways they don't like to talk about."

I looked over at her. "Actually, he has talked a little about that with me."

Her eyebrows shot up. "He has?"

"Yeah. He said how he'd sort of prided himself on never being afraid of anything before that happened, and then losing her made him afraid. He hated that feeling."

"Wow. He really opened up to you.

That's . . . that's kind of amazing. Xander doesn't usually admit to weaknesses or fears."

"No, he doesn't," I agreed. "But we've been pretty open with each other." I laughed a little. "When you're alone with someone twenty-four hours a day, you tell a lot of your stories."

"So maybe it's fear holding him back when it comes to falling in love in that lightning-bolt way. Maybe he's afraid of it."

I shook my head. "Xander has told me a million times, he's not afraid of anything anymore."

"Do you believe him?"

"I have no reason not to."

Veronica nodded, then looked at the sunset again. "Sometimes lies protect us from feeling things we don't want to feel. I lived a lie for a long time and almost married the wrong guy because of it. But in my experience, the universe tries very hard to show us we'll be happier once we admit the truth."

"What was the truth for you?" I asked curiously.

"That I deserved better," she said with a smile. "And sure enough, I found it that very day."

Half an hour later, I gave each twin a squeeze, told them to be good, and invited them to come see a concert sometime if they wanted—my treat.

"Can we?" Adelaide looked hopefully at her dad.

"Sure," said Austin. "As soon as the tour schedule comes out, we'll take a look."

"I don't get all the way up here, but I do come to Chicago," I said. "Would that work?"

Austin nodded. "Definitely doable."

"Great!" I gave Austin a quick hug, then rose up on tiptoe and threw my arms around Veronica—she was a lot taller than me. "Keep in touch, okay? You have my number. I want to hear all about the dance studio opening."

"Okay." She spoke softly in my ear so no one could hear. "And call me if you need to talk about Xander."

I whispered back, "I don't think there's much to say."

We released each other and she shrugged, a tiny smile on her lips. "Maybe not," she said, "but I've got a feeling."

On the ride home, Xander asked me what Veronica meant. "What does she have a feeling about?"

"She thinks my career is going to get even better," I lied, too nervous to tell him what Veronica had actually meant. Xander and I had not discussed what would happen after he left Nashville, and I wasn't ready to have that conversation tonight. "She's really glad I'm going to start releasing music under my own name."

"Oh."

I wasn't sure if he believed me or not, and I felt guilty—I wasn't used to hiding the truth from him.

But my feelings for him were growing deeper and more complicated, and I didn't really want to wrestle with that out in the open. What if his weren't deep or complicated at all? What if he wasn't worried about missing me or saying goodbye? And even if he was willing to stay in touch, what would be the point? Would we have sex for a couple days and go our separate ways again? What would happen when he met that future wife, the mother of his three rowdy boys?

No. There were just too many obstacles in our way.

The timing. The geography. The views on love and relationships. Plenty of things were all wrong.

So I wouldn't let myself think about everything that felt so incredibly right.

CHAPTER TWENTY-TWO

xander

WE REACHED Nashville around seven o'clock the following evening. Crazy as it sounds, the twelve-hour drive seemed to fly by. I found myself easing off the gas just to prolong the time alone with her. Somehow, I felt like things wouldn't be the same once she was back in her celebrity world. Maybe she wouldn't want me the same way.

As we pulled up to the gate at the foot of Kelly's driveway, I rolled down the minivan's window. "What's the code?"

"My birthday. Twelve, twenty."

I took a second to glare at her. "That needs to be changed."

"I wanted something easy to remember," she said defensively. "But okay, we can change it."

I punched the numbers on the keypad and pulled into the driveway, which curved around in front of a large, two-story home built with pale bricks. It had a three-car garage on one side, tall arched windows on the first floor, and beautiful landscaping. "Nice place you have here."

"Thanks. I just bought it last spring. I'm not sure it feels like home yet."

"Sometimes that takes a while. Where should I park?"

"You can pull up by the front door. Jess will return the van, and I have cars you can use while you're here." She unbuckled her seatbelt as I put the van in park. But even after I turned off the engine, she stayed in the passenger seat, making no move to get out. She just stared out the window at her big, beautiful house.

"What's wrong?" I asked.

"I don't know. I just don't really want to go in."

"How come?"

"I can't even put a finger on it, really. Maybe it's just the whole going back to real life after being on vacation. Having to deal with people day in, day out." She looked at me. "I miss the cabin already."

I laughed. "I bet once you get inside this house, you won't miss it. You probably have at least four bedrooms—"

"Five."

"And five bathrooms too."

She smiled. "Six, actually."

"See? How about a kitchen table?"

"Yeah."

"And air conditioning."

"That too."

"And I bet you've even got a swimming pool. A grand piano. A fucking library."

She nodded. "Check, check, check."

"You won't miss that cabin, Kelly."

"Maybe you're right. I do like my piano." She took my hand. "I guess I'll just miss our time together."

My heart tripped over its next few beats. "Me too."

She kept looking at our hands. "Xander, I—"

"There you are!" A woman appeared in the front door of the house. "I've been frantically worried about you on the road all day!"

Kelly sighed, taking her hand from mine. "Come on. Time to meet my mother."

That night, we had dinner at the dining room table with her parents and her business manager, Wags. As we ate the chef-prepared meal, I mostly stayed quiet, observing the others.

Kelly's mom, Julia, was probably over fifty, but she had tight, clear skin that looked as if she rarely saw the sun and often saw the dermatologist. Looking at her, it was obvious where Kelly had gotten the fair complexion, red hair, and emerald eyes. But after meeting her dad, Connor, I saw where she'd gotten her full-lipped smile, the grit in her voice, and the gift of charming anyone she spoke to. He was exactly as she'd described him to me—handsome, outspoken, charismatic, with a firm handshake and a genuine good-old-boy grin that made him look younger than his age, which Kelly had told me was fifty-six.

I'd been prepared to dislike him but found it difficult at first, to be honest. He was good with words and had a quick wit, bantering back and forth with his wife, his daughter, her manager, even me. He didn't try to dominate the conversation like a lot of men would. He didn't seem interested in trying to prove he was the alpha at the table. He was easygoing and laidback, and when he asked you a question, he had a way of making eye contact as you answered that made you feel like he was really listening. Still, I knew what I knew, and I didn't trust him.

Wags, Kelly's manager, seemed like a good guy, sort of a second father figure. He wasn't charming like Kelly's dad, but he seemed solid and steady. My gut said he was a good guy.

"So you had a good trip, peanut?" Connor asked his daughter.

"Yes." Kelly took a sip of her water. "I wouldn't have cut it short if it wasn't for the awards show performance."

"What a lucky break," Julia said.

"It's not luck, it's talent," said Connor. "Right, Wags?"

"Right."

"And it doesn't hurt to have Duke Pruitt pulling

strings for you, either." Connor winked at Kelly and lifted his whiskey, which he liked neat.

"No, it doesn't hurt," she agreed.

"He thinks you should sign that PMG deal."

"You talked about it with him?" Kelly's tone took on a sharp edge.

"A little. He's got so much experience, you know? I figured it would be good to get his input."

"I don't need his input, Daddy. And I'd appreciate it if you didn't talk about me with him. We're not together anymore."

"Now, peanut, don't get upset. I'm only trying to help."

"I don't need your help with this. Or Duke's."

"You shouldn't go into those negotiations alone. When's the next meeting with the label?"

"I don't remember," she said stiffly, and I could tell she was lying.

"I think Duke mentioned it's coming up next month," Connor went on, swirling the whiskey in his glass.

"Could be."

"I'll be with her," Wags said. "No need to worry. She won't be alone."

"Good." Connor nodded. "I just don't want her to make a mistake she'll regret later."

Kelly stood up. "I'm tired after the long drive. I'm going to bed." She looked at me. "Xander, come on upstairs. I'll show you where your room is."

I gladly rose to my feet.

"Goodnight, Xander," Julia said. "Thanks for

keeping an eye on her in the woods, and for bringing her back safely. I was so relieved when she said she wasn't driving back alone."

"Of course."

"And you're going to stay a few days, is that right?" Wags asked. "Get new security measures for her in place?"

"That's right."

Her dad spoke up. "That seems like a big imposition on you, Xander. You know, Duke offered to send some of his guys over to—"

"I don't want Duke's help, Daddy," Kelly said sharply. "Xander is here, and he's going to handle it." She looked at me. "Let's go."

I followed her up the stairs and into her bedroom. She shut the door behind me and leaned back against it, squeezing her eyes shut. "Take me back to the cabin."

"Jesus. Do your parents *have* to live with you?"

She exhaled. "No. But I can't kick them out."

"I think maybe you can."

Pushing off the door, she moved toward me and looped her arms around my torso, laying her cheek on my chest. "My dad will be gone soon. He never stays around long. As soon as I tell him I'm not giving him the money for his new business scheme, he'll take off. And my mom isn't so bad."

I kissed the top of her head and stroked her back. "Your call. You did a good job of speaking your mind at the table, by the way. I was proud of you."

"I didn't say all the things I wanted to."

"Maybe not, but you didn't just sit there and let him treat you like a child. It's a start. Give yourself some credit."

"Thanks. By the way, I don't really want you to stay in a different room. I just didn't want their questions. Stay in here with me."

"I'll stay wherever you want me to."

"Right here. Please." Her body relaxed against mine. "My safe place."

Long after we turned out the light, got under the covers, and reached for each other in the dark, her words stayed with me.

I liked being her safe place. I worried about what would happen when I was gone. I hated the fact that I probably wouldn't see her again once I left town.

But there was nothing I could do about it except make sure she'd stay safe once I was gone.

Starting the next morning, I dedicated every waking hour to Kelly's security. I contacted Jackson Cole, my previous boss, and asked him for advice on hiring skilled, trustworthy guys, and he gave me the number of some people he knew in the area. I conducted interviews. I supervised the testing of every camera at her house, the motion sensors, and the alarms. I changed the code on her gate. I met with the guard at the gatehouse of her subdivision and asked a hundred questions about what safe-guards were in place. I performed background checks on her driver, her chef, her housekeeper, her landscaper, her agent, her stylist—even the pool guy.

My favorite candidate for Kelly's full-time security was a guy named Marius Boley, and not just because of his intimidating size. He was a former Navy guy (yes, I'm biased) in his early thirties, whose name I'd gotten from Jackson. Newly trans-planted from L.A., he'd provided security for a well-known actress for the last three years, and she'd given him glowing reviews. He had a wife and one daughter, and they'd moved back to this area to be closer to his wife's family. He'd take care of finding additional bodyguards for her tour when the time came, and he understood he was not to leave it to the record label or anyone else.

He had a firm handshake, good eye contact, answered all my questions correctly, and had experi-ence dealing with paparazzi.

Speaking of which, I'd also heard back from Zach Barrett. No surprise his contacts had discovered the car had been rented to a guy named Lawrence Hooper, who had a Tennessee driver's license with a Nashville address. "Need more?" he asked. "He must have flown in. I could get his flight information."

I thought about it for a second, then decided against it. "Don't waste your time. I know who Hooper is, and if I had to find him, I could."

"Okay. Let me know if there's anything else I can do for you. And good luck with the bar opening."

"Thanks. I appreciate it."

Every day, I maintained contact with Veronica and Austin, who were working hard to make sure Buckley's Pub could still open on time. Veronica promoted on social media, Austin and my dad spread the word around town, and I reached out to all my old high school buddies, letting them know there would be a new place to get together and watch the game. The fucking barstools still hadn't arrived, but if we had to, we could get along without them. We had everything else in place.

Kelly was busy with rehearsals and fittings and appointments every day, but when she'd arrive home in the late afternoon, we always took a run together, worked out in her home gym, practiced the self-defense moves, and often took a swim late at night. At first, we were careful not to touch each other romantically when others were around, but by the end of the weekend, we'd gotten fairly reckless, especially in the pool.

There in the dark, beneath the surface of the water, her arms and legs would twine around me, and my hands would seek out all my favorite places on her body. Our lips would meet, wet and warm and hungry, and we'd get so worked up, we'd race from the pool to the bedroom without even drying off, dripping through the kitchen, up the stairs, down the hall, and across the carpet.

We were usually good at being quiet, but sometimes I'd have to put a hand over Kelly's mouth while I fucked her because she'd get carried away and start to cry out.

Afterward, we'd lay in her bed, damp and breathless, submerged in whatever this was between us.

But we'd stopped talking late at night. Sometimes I even faked falling asleep quickly to avoid a difficult conversation.

We were getting too close to goodbye.

One week after I arrived in Nashville, I woke up and forced myself to face reality—Buckley's Pub was opening in three days, and I needed to get back. Marius was coming over later to meet Kelly, and if she liked him, he was hired. He would take over from here.

I looked over at her, and my blood warmed at the sight of her sleeping, naked and bed mussed. Immediately I rolled over and curled my body around hers, inhaling her sweet, summery scent. How many more times would I get to do this? What if I walked out of here tomorrow and never saw her again? What if I never met anyone who made me feel this way, like I wanted to keep her close to me all the time? What if I never met anyone who trusted me the way she did? Or whose trust *mattered* as much as hers did? What if I never found someone who challenged me like she did? Made me laugh like she did? Made me want to drop to my knees just so she didn't feel so alone?

How was I supposed to go from seeing her and talking to her and hearing her sing or laugh or whisper every single day and night to nothing at all? It would be like having an addiction and quitting cold turkey. I wasn't sure I could do it.

Suddenly I felt angry. Why the fuck had I let myself fall for her this way? Hadn't I known better? Hadn't I always been so careful to keep relationships casual? I'd been so fucking sure of myself, so cocky and carefree. Even when I'd imagined how I'd feel about my future wife, it was nothing like the way Kelly Jo Sullivan had knocked me off my feet. I didn't know which way was up anymore. I tried to picture my life without her in it, and I didn't like it at all.

But I didn't want to love this woman, with her world tours and sold-out shows and rabid fans and social media bullshit and dickhead paparazzi chasing her around. I wanted a laidback, small-town life. I wanted privacy and freedom. I wanted someone who'd belong to me, not the music industry. I didn't want to share.

And yet . . . here I was. Holding onto her like I was scared the world might end.

A celebrity. A fucking celebrity.

Served me right.

Around noon, I took Kelly's car—a tiny little BMW convertible I barely fit in, the thing was like a toy—and went out to grab some lunch. Her driver had picked her up earlier for a meeting with someone about a possible film project, and then she was heading to a dress fitting.

I parked in a public lot downtown and walked around until I found a sandwich shop on a quiet side street off Broadway. I ordered a combo, debated taking it to go, but ended up grabbing a table by the window facing the street. When I was done with my sandwich and chips, I gave Austin a call.

"You back?" he asked.

"Not yet," I said, fighting off guilt. "Soon. I booked a flight for Thursday morning."

"Cutting it close."

"I know, sorry. How are things there?"

"All good. Barstools finally arrived today."

"Fucking *finally*." Relief eased some of the tension in my neck and shoulders.

"They look great."

"Good. Thank you for everything. I owe you guys."

"Don't worry about it. That's what family is for. Veronica is there now if you want to call her."

"I will. Speaking of Veronica." I paused. "Can I ask you a question?"

"Sure."

Outside the window, a couple walked by, hand in hand. "If she'd gone back to New York, would you have tried to make it work?"

"Yes. But I'd have done everything in my power to convince her not to go." He paused. "Is this about Kelly?"

"Yeah. I'm just—" I groped for words that would encapsulate how I felt about her. "Struggling with leaving her behind."

"In Nashville? Or in life?"

"Both," I admitted. "But I can't see how it will work. Her career means everything to her. My bar is important to me. Our lives are so far apart." I frowned. "This is stupid. It won't work."

"You haven't even tried yet."

"Because what's the point? Would you want to date someone who lived twelve hours from you?"

"If that's what it took."

"It would drive me crazy, Austin, being so far away from her, not knowing what assholes are hanging around her, trying to get a piece of her. I'd worry about her all the time."

"When you're in love, fear comes with the territory."

"I'm not in love with her," I said quickly, but my heart knew it was a lie.

"You will be."

Exhaling, I watched a woman with red hair walk

past the window, and just the shade of her ponytail made my heart skip a beat. "I don't like this feeling. I don't like being afraid. I've worked so fucking hard not to be scared of anything. I've faced down every possible fear you can imagine—even death."

"No, you haven't."

I scowled. "Yes, I have, asshole. Remember that business about being shot twice in the leg?"

"I'm not saying you haven't looked death in the eye, brother. And I'll always be in awe of you for that. I'm saying you haven't faced down every possible fear in life. And I get it." His voice grew a little quieter. "I was the same way you are for a long time. I wanted complete control over everything, including my feelings. And realizing that I didn't have it was scary as fuck."

"Yeah."

"You want kids? Let me tell you, becoming a father is like jumping out of a plane without a parachute. You will worry about your children from their very first breath in a way you cannot comprehend before it happens."

"I believe it."

"But it's worth it," he said, his voice sure. "And I think if you meet someone you have feelings for— especially to the point where it scares you—it's worth at least trying to make it work. What have you got to lose?"

I didn't know how to answer that.

"I'll tell you what you stand to lose," he said, in true bossy big brother style. "The chance to make her happy. And if you walk away, someone else is going to grab that chance. How does that make you feel?"

"Like pushing that someone out of a plane without a parachute. After I beat the shit out of him for touching her."

Austin laughed. "Exactly."

"I've just never met anyone like her," I said. "When I'm with her, I just—I can't seem to—I want to just—" Again I fumbled blindly for the right words to convey how I felt. "And when I'm not with her, it's even worse."

"Believe me, I get it. You know what to do, Xander."

"Yeah." I watched a guy with a camera bag over his shoulder go by the window. He looked familiar, and a fraction of a second later, I placed him—Lawrence Hooper, the photographer who'd trailed Kelly up to Michigan. "I gotta go." Without saying goodbye, I ended the call, shoved my phone in my pocket, dumped my trash in the bin, and raced outside.

I caught up with him easily and fell in step beside him. "Lawrence Hooper," I said gruffly. "I'd like a word with you."

He turned in surprise, and when he saw my face, he panicked. "I've got nothing to say to you."

When he turned to keep walking, I grabbed his arm. "I think you do. I want to know how you knew exactly where Kelly was staying."

"I told you. Social media post," he said.

"What post? Show me." I still didn't believe this

guy's story. He just didn't seem sharp enough to figure out the exact location of the house from Kelly's single post showing the address.

"I don't remember which one it was." He wrenched his arm from my grip and kept walking.

I followed him. "Did someone tell you where she was staying?"

"Go away."

"Was it her assistant?"

"No."

"Her agent?"

"No."

"I still haven't forgotten how you trespassed on private property, you know. How you took photos not just of Kelly but of me."

"You guys let me go already."

"Kelly let you go. But she's not here."

"I can't tell you anything, okay? I'm in enough trouble as it is."

"With who?" I grabbed his arm again, although we'd reached the corner, and the intersection at Broadway was busy. "Goddamn it, with who?"

"Look, I like Kelly, okay? She's always been good to me. She should be careful who she trusts." Yanking his arm free, he melted into the crowd, disappearing in a sea of denim and cowboy hats.

I stood there for a moment, then pulled out my phone and shot a message to Zach Barrett.

> Hey, I changed my mind. Could you get that flight information to me?

He replied quickly.

On it.

I wasn't sure what I'd learn from it. Maybe nothing. Maybe the trouble Hooper had been referring to was his sick kid or his habit of trespassing or maybe his wife had thrown him out—*trouble* could mean anything. But the warning at the end that Kelly should be careful who she trusts? That had me on edge.

I didn't want to leave her.

CHAPTER TWENTY-THREE

kelly

"*KELLY.* YOU OKAY?" The seamstress looked up at me from where she knelt, pinning the hem of my awards show dress.

"I'm fine," I said. "Sorry, I zoned out. Did you need me to turn?"

"Yes. I just want to look at the back in the mirror."

Dutifully, I rotated ninety degrees and let her do her thing. I wasn't sure what was the matter with me. Everything for the awards performance was going well. After apologizing for his rudeness during our last phone call, Duke was treating me with polite friendliness. Rehearsals were running smoothly, we sounded great together, and the label and producers were thrilled.

Wags, my agent, my parents, and the rest of my team were all proud of me and excited to watch the show. Jess was back in town, and it felt great to have a buddy again. I told her all about Xander, and she almost choked, she laughed so hard. She thought it was hilarious that the bodyguard I'd tried so hard to fire turned out to be the best sex of my life.

The divorce scandal had run its course, so paparazzi were interested in me again, and there was a lot of are-they-or-aren't-they speculation about Duke and me since we were being heavily promoted as the opening act, but with Xander by my side whenever I was in public, I always felt protected.

I loved my dress—a long, glittering silver gown with a high slit—and I was eating healthy, drinking plenty of water, and despite my late nights with Xander, doing my best to get enough sleep so I'd look and feel my best on Thursday night.

And yet, with just two days to go before the show, I felt like I was constantly on the verge of tears.

"Okay," the seamstress said, rising to her feet. "Face the mirror one last time."

I did as she asked just as Jess and my stylist, Kayla, entered the room. Both of them ooh'd and ahh'd.

"It's so perfect," Jess gushed.

"I'm so glad we went with the silver," said Kayla. "It's so sophisticated."

"I think it's perfect for introducing Kelly Jo Sullivan to the world," said Jess.

"Thanks," I said. Then without warning, I burst into tears.

"Oh honey, what's wrong?" asked the seamstress. "Is it too tight?"

Blubbering, I shook my head. "It's not the dress."

Jess and Kayla came forward and helped me off the pedestal. "You're overwhelmed," Jess soothed. "This is a lot all at once. Let's get that dress off and then we can talk."

They helped me out of the heavy, sequined gown, which Kayla carefully took back to the seamstress. Once I was dressed in my jeans and top again, we walked up the street and ducked into a coffee shop. Jess and I grabbed a table at the back, and Kayla put in our orders at the counter.

A few minutes later, cold brew in hand, I tried to find words for what was wrong. "This is dumb, you guys," I said, dabbing at the corners of my eyes. "I have nothing to be upset about. Everything is going fine."

"Is it Duke?" Jess asked, ever suspicious of my ex.

"No. Believe it or not, he's actually been a gentleman all week."

"Is it that former bodyguard?" Kayla wondered. "I heard there was someone threatening to sue, of all the ridiculous things."

"He was threatening, but he backed off. It's not that."

"Is it your dad?" Jess asked gently. "I know it's hard on you when he comes and goes the way he does."

"That does get to me," I admitted, "but I don't think it's him."

"Is it Xander?" Kayla asked. "I haven't wanted to

pry, but what's going to happen when he goes back to Michigan?"

"I don't know." I fought off tears again. "But I suppose that could be it. Beneath all this great stuff is this fear that I'm never going to see him again, never feel as good as I do when I'm with him."

"Have you told him that?" Jess asked.

I shook my head. "No. It's just sort of understood that when we part ways, we'll part ways. I don't think either one of us is into the idea of a long-distance relationship."

"So it's all or nothing?" Jess cocked her head. "I mean, you guys just met. Maybe there's room to start slow and let it grow. See what happens."

"But I don't think I'd do well if we weren't exclusive. I'd hate the thought that when we're apart, he might be with someone else. Actually, it makes me feel physically sick."

"You need to talk to him," Kayla urged. "You'll be sorry if you don't. Trust me when I say the dating pool around here is shallow and scummy."

"I think your taste in men might be an issue," Jess teased.

"Tell me about it. It's like I'm only attracted to losers. 'What? You've got no money, no steady job, no car, and you're sleeping on your friend's couch? No, thanks. Oh wait, you play the guitar? Take my body.'" She shook her head. "Someday, I will like an actual grown-up man."

"Xander is definitely a grown-up man," I said. "As far as I'm concerned, he's got everything going

334

for him except that he lives far away. He works hard, he's devoted to his family, he makes me laugh, he's got a big heart, and he gets me like nobody ever has."

"He's not bad to look at either," drawled Jess. "And I've only seen him fully clothed."

"I can confirm he is quite nice to look at with no clothes on," I said, laughing. "Ten out of ten."

"Then what are you doing here with us?" Kayla prodded. "Go talk to him. Right now. Get out of here."

"But it's so scary." I chewed the end of my straw. "What if he doesn't feel the same way I do?"

"Then you'll know it's not meant to be," said Jess with a shrug. "But at least you won't always wonder what might have happened if you'd been brave enough to ask."

When my driver brought me home, Xander was there waiting to introduce me to my new head of security —a huge guy named Marius with dark skin, a deep but gentle voice, and sharp brown eyes. Xander had told me all about him, and after a few minutes, I could see why he'd been the favorite candidate. I especially loved his reaction when I asked to see a photo of his little girl—he immediately pulled out his phone and showed off pictures of an adorable baby just learning to crawl, as well as his beautiful wife.

"I can't wait to meet them," I said with a tired smile. "Welcome aboard."

He nodded, returning the smile. "Thank you."

"Tomorrow, Marius and I will go over to the auditorium where the awards are taking place and check things out. I spoke to Wags about getting us security clearance. He says it won't be a problem."

"Okay." My voice cracked, and my throat felt dry. I needed some water. Maybe some ibuprofen too. I had a headache.

Xander was looking at me carefully, like he knew something was wrong. Could he tell I'd been crying? He turned to Marius again and held out his hand. "Thanks for coming today. I'll see you at nine tomorrow, and we can do the paperwork after that."

"Sounds good." He shook Xander's hand and nodded at me. "See you tomorrow."

After showing him out, Xander took my elbow and led me straight up to my bedroom. Closing the door behind us, he took me by the upper arms and looked at me with serious dark eyes. "What's wrong, baby?"

I opened my mouth to start the conversation, but instead of the careful words I'd rehearsed on the way home, I burst into tears and threw myself into his arms. Face in my hands, I sobbed against his broad, comforting chest while he held me, saying nothing. He stroked my hair and my back. He rocked me gently. He made deep, soft shushing sounds that sounded like waves on the shore. I cried it out until my eyes went dry and his shirt was soaked, and all I had left in me were a few leftover shudders.

Finally, he kissed the top of my head. "Did the dress not fit?"

I laughed and hiccupped at the same time. "No. It fit fine."

"So what's this about?"

Tell him now, I thought. *Just say it. Be brave.*

I took a deep, shaky breath. "I'm worried about what will happen when you leave."

"You've got nothing to worry about. The cameras work perfectly, and Marius is familiar with the system. Your alarm system is working, your doors are all secure, your staff all passed background checks. I did ask your landscaper about getting a taller fence for around your pool, and he's going to work on that. When it comes time for your tour, Marius is going to hire a couple more guards. You're safe, or I wouldn't leave you."

"That's not what I meant."

His hands stilled on my hair.

"Just listen for a moment, Xander, okay?" Leaving my head tucked beneath his chin—it was easier if I didn't meet his eyes—I spilled my guts. "I know what I'm about to say sounds crazy. My life and business and family are here in Nashville, and your life and business and family are up in Michigan, and trying to make something work between us would be hard. We'd always be saying goodbye to each other. I'd miss you all the time."

"I'd miss you too," he said quietly.

"And it's not just the distance between Nashville and Cherry Tree Harbor. In a few months, I'll be on tour again, and the separation might feel even worse. I mean, I've got trust issues. I've got deep-seated insecurities that have nothing to do with you and aren't your fault. It would be hard."

"The separations would be hard."

"Plus, we've only known each other a few weeks. Maybe what I think I'm feeling isn't really what I'm feeling. Maybe it's just that the sex is so good. Maybe it's just that I trusted you so fast and so completely. Maybe it's just that I feel so damn safe when I'm with you, and I'm scared to lose that feeling. I don't know what I'm saying . . ." I pulled away and looked up at him. "I just know I don't want to say goodbye."

His eyes were smoky and serious. "Then fuck it. Let's not say it."

My heart stumbled over its next few beats. "What?"

"Let's not say goodbye."

"You . . . you mean it?"

"I mean it. I feel the same way you do. And I agree—all those reasons you listed why this might not work are valid. The distance and the time apart won't be easy. But I can't walk away from you without a fight."

"You can't?" Tears filled my eyes, and I snuggled back into his warm, solid chest.

"Fuck no. I don't know what you did to me, Kelly Jo Sullivan, but I kinda like it."

"Does it feel like you've been hit with a hundred million volts?" I asked instead.

He laughed. "That's exactly what it feels like."

"Good." I squeezed him tight. "So what do we do now?"

"I'm trying to figure that out. I'm wondering if I should ask Austin and Veronica if they can cover Buckley's opening."

"No!" I leaned back and placed my hands on his chest. "No way. You're going back up there to open that bar yourself. I will not have it any other way."

He frowned. "I have some concerns about the—"

"Xander, no. This relationship doesn't mean we stop following our dreams. I refuse to be the reason why you were not there the night Buckley's Pub opens its doors. Did you book a flight?"

"Yes. For Thursday morning."

"Good. You're going to be on that flight, and that's that."

He quirked his brow. "Now who's bossy?"

"You must have rubbed off on me."

His eyes lit up, and he opened his mouth, which I quickly covered with my fingers. "No dirty jokes. We're having a very sweet conversation."

"Fine," he mumbled. He kissed my fingers, then took me by the wrist, removing my hand from his lips. "But I want it on record that I don't feel right leaving the day of your big show. I want to be there for you."

"You'll be there in my heart, and you can watch on TV," I said. "Hey, I have an idea! Let's come up with a little sign that I can give so you'll know I'm thinking of you."

"How about this?" He mimed giving a blowjob, fist in his face, tongue poking the inside of his cheek.

"Um, *no*, I will not be doing that on camera. I meant something like this." I tapped my chest three times, right over my heart.

"Yeah, your idea is probably more appropriate," he said with a shrug. "Let's go with that."

"Perfect. Look for it on Thursday." I sighed. "I promised Duke I'd let him pick me up so we could arrive together. I wish I hadn't."

Xander growled, his eyes narrowing.

"I know, I know. I'm sorry. But I will make it very clear to the media we are *not* back together. Believe it or not, Duke has actually honored his promise to keep things casual between us."

The lines in Xander's forehead deepened. "I don't trust him. I never will."

"But you trust me, right?"

"Yes." His face relaxed and he kissed my forehead. "Of course I trust you."

"Good." I leaned back again, cringing when I saw the giant wet spots on the front of his T-shirt. "Yikes. Sorry about your shirt."

"Fuck my shirt. Are we good?"

"Definitely." I smiled and met his eyes, tapping my chest three times. "We have an understanding, you and I."

I was too wiped out to go on our usual run, so I told Xander to work out without me. Instead, I did some slow, easy laps in the pool, then wrapped myself in a towel and lay in a lounge chair. Eyes closed, I took deep, calming breaths. Imagined myself surrounded by warm, golden light. Thought about all the things I was grateful for.

Xander was at the top of the list. I was so proud of myself for telling him the truth about how I felt. Even if I hadn't had the nerve to say those three scary words, I'd still taken a risk—and it had paid off.

It would be hard, sure, but my gut told me we could make it work. We were that good together. It would take effort and sacrifice on both sides, but it would be worth it. I smiled, imagining Kevin's reaction to the news that I was in a relationship with the man whose life he'd saved—the man he'd hired to protect me. I hoped I'd get to tell him in person so I could see his face. I was definitely grateful for my brother's choice, no matter how much I'd fought it.

I was also grateful for my voice. My health. My family. This house. My career. My team. My fans. The opportunities I'd been given. The opportunities yet to come. I even found space to be grateful for the hardships I'd experienced, whether emotional or physical. Everything I'd been through had gotten me where I was today, and I was okay. If I wanted to make changes going forward, I could. I didn't have to let fear stand in my way.

I hadn't backed down when that James Bond guy wanted money. I'd stood up to Duke. I'd admitted my feelings for Xander. And when it was time, I'd stand my ground with PMG. If they wouldn't let me make the record I wanted to make, as Kelly Jo Sullivan, I'd leave. The music was what mattered to me.

A shadow fell across my face, and I thought it was Xander. "You're always blocking my sun."

"Sorry, peanut."

My eyes flew open to see my dad standing there. "Daddy." I sat up and swung my feet to the ground, wrapping the towel tighter around me.

"Don't get up. I didn't mean to disturb you." He sat down on the chair next to mine, facing me. Hands on his knees. "Whatcha thinking about out here?"

"Lots of things."

"Big week, huh?"

"Yeah."

"Have you given any more thought to the PMG deal?"

"Some." I tested the waters. "I might walk away."

He looked offended. "Why would you do that?"

"Because I want to make music that means something to me. And I'm tired of not having a say in that."

"But they've been good to you. Duke thinks you'd be crazy to—"

"I don't really care what Duke thinks," I said firmly.

He rubbed a hand over his jaw. "I just think you ought to listen to him. He cares about you."

"I doubt it."

"You two have history," he said pointedly. "And history matters."

"Yes, history matters. And he wasn't good to me, Daddy." I met his eyes. "No matter what he says now, he wasn't good to me then. He hurt me."

Anger flashed in my father's eyes. His spine straightened. "He hurt you?"

"Not with his fists. It wasn't physical."

"Oh." As if my emotional pain was just a trifle, he relaxed again. "All relationships have ups and downs."

"He wasn't faithful to me."

"But he still loves you. I know he does."

"That's not enough, Daddy." My chest was so tight, I could barely breathe. "It's not enough to just love someone. You have to *show* them you mean it. You have to stay."

His jaw ticked. "Some people just aren't meant for it. So you take what you can get when you can get it."

I knew his warped philosophy on love stemmed from his own upbringing, and I nearly backed down. But then I remembered what I'd said to Xander in the car the night we'd danced at The Broken Spoke. The words I'd practiced.

"That's not the kind of love I want, Daddy. It's not good enough."

"Is that why you won't give me the loan? Because I wasn't a good enough father?"

"It's more complicated than that."

"Nobody's perfect, Kelly Jo," he argued, like I'd known he would. "That's your problem. You expect perfection. You can't handle it when the people who love you are flawed."

"Yes, I can, Daddy. I can accept your flaws. And I love you, I honestly do." I stood up. "But I deserve better."

Leaving him there, I walked into the house. My legs trembled, my chest ached, and my eyes were filled with tears.

But I'd done it.

What the fuck was this *day*?

I went straight to the gym in my basement, where I found Xander doing pushups on the mat like his life depended on it. When he saw me, he popped to his feet, his expression concerned. "Hey. You okay?"

I threw my arms around him. "I'm okay," I said breathlessly. "I had the chance to say the words to my dad, and I said them. I said them!"

"Holy shit. Did you really?" He held me a little tighter. "Your entire body is shaking."

"I know." I peeled myself off him and hitched up my towel. "But I did it."

He tucked a strand of damp hair behind my ear. "I'm proud of you. How do you feel?"

"Better. I mean, I don't think he's going to change. He is who he is. But I don't feel like a trampled-on doormat right now, and that's a good thing."

He pulled me close again. "That's a very good thing."

Closing my eyes, I inhaled. "You smell like sweat. I kinda like it."

"Why don't you take off your towel and suit and I'll get it all over you?"

I laughed. "I've got a better idea. Why don't we go up and take a shower together? Then we can order in and bring dinner upstairs to my bedroom and ignore everyone for the rest of the night."

"Hmph. Your idea involves more patience."

"But it lasts longer."

"True. I guess I can be patient for you." He pinched my ass, making me shriek. "I'll need the practice."

On Wednesday, Duke and I had a final rehearsal, during which I used every shred of acting ability I possessed to appear as though I was still in love with my ex, a woman desperate for a second chance. I

345

held his hand. I moved in close. I looked into his cool blue eyes and pretended I was lost to them.

On the inside, I felt nothing, maybe even a faint repulsion. Yes, he was handsome, but beyond what he'd done to me emotionally, he held zero physical appeal for me. He was tall and wiry, with none of Xander's carnal brawn. His icy blue eyes lacked the warmth and depth of Xander's smoldering brown. His teeth were too white, his hair too blond, his clothes too stylish, his voice too smooth, his jaw too weak, his cologne too strong.

When we were done and the mics were off, Duke gave me an impersonal hug and took me by both hands. "I'm so glad we're doing this. Thanks so much for filling in."

"Thanks for asking me."

"You sound amazing," he said. "Never better. It's like there's something different in your voice. It's richer, more mature."

"Thank you. It's a great song."

"Hey, Duke?" a producer called. "We've got a question on something."

"I should go," I said. "I've got one last fitting this afternoon."

He nodded. "I'll see you tomorrow. Pick you up at four?"

"Fine. But we make it clear we're just friends, okay?"

"Just friends," he said with a wink. "I promise." He gave my shoulder a squeeze and moved past me.

I didn't love that wink, but I decided to forget

about it—I just wanted to get through my fitting and go home, eager to spend every last minute I could with Xander before he left.

He still hated the idea of leaving me, but I had a surprise for him. As soon as I could clear it with Marius, I planned to book a flight to Michigan so I could be there for the Buckley's Pub opening. I knew Xander would be frantically busy the whole time, but that wouldn't bother me. What mattered was supporting each other's dreams.

I had a feeling we'd be good at that.

CHAPTER TWENTY-FOUR

xander

"MAYBE I WON'T GO." I was lying on top of her, our bodies still damp with sweat, my cock still inside her. If I was going to make my flight, I needed to leave for the airport in half an hour.

She beat her hands on my back. "Xander, if you don't get out of this bed right now, I'm going to kick you out."

"Try."

She dug her heels into the backs of my thighs. "Listen, I know some *moves*."

I laughed. "Unless you have some I didn't teach you, I can anticipate all your moves."

"Xander. You need to *go*. I need to get up and start getting ready anyway. My glam squad will be here shortly."

"Fine, I'll go." I gave her one last kiss and reluctantly extricated myself. "But only because a glam squad sounds terrifying."

I took a quick shower, trying hard to shake the

feeling that leaving her today was the wrong decision. But she fought back every time I suggested staying today and leaving tomorrow. *Xander, don't be ridiculous! The opening is tomorrow. What if your flight is delayed? What if there's a last-minute emergency at the bar? What if there's a decision to be made that only you can make?*

She was right, but fuck if that pit in my stomach wouldn't close up. I'd told her about the run-in with Hooper, but she blew it off. "Face it—I posted a photo that broadcast my address to millions of people without even realizing it. We're lucky he was the only one to show up."

"But don't you think that's weird?" I asked. "Why was he the only one?"

"Maybe I'm just not that popular," she joked. "Maybe I should be glad Hoop even bothered."

I got her in a headlock for that one, rubbed my knuckles against her scalp.

But all jokes and foreboding feelings aside, I did hate saying goodbye to her, even if it was only temporary.

"We have to get used to this," she said at the front door. "We're going to be coming and going a lot—no pun intended."

I smiled, but I still felt uneasy as I kissed her one last time. "Kick some ass tonight. I'll be watching."

"Thank you. I'll try." She touched her stomach. "I'm nervous."

"You're going to bring them to their knees." I

pressed my lips to her forehead. "Just like you did to me."

"Be safe," she whispered. "And I will too."

"Call me when you can." I opened the front door, words I wanted to say sticking in my throat. "I'll see you soon, baby."

She blew me a kiss, and I forced myself to walk out.

I should have trusted my gut and stayed.

CHAPTER TWENTY-FIVE

kelly

AFTER SHUTTING the door behind Xander, I went into the kitchen to grab a cup of coffee. I found my mother sitting at the counter in her bathrobe, her eyes bloodshot and her face puffy. A wad of tissue was balled up in her hand.

"Mama?" Alarmed, I sat next to her and touched her shoulder. "What's wrong?"

"He left again. He's gone."

Every time, it hurt. Every. Single. Time. "I'm sorry."

"He said—he said—" Her chest hitched, and she dabbed at her eyes with the tissue. "I guess it doesn't matter what he said."

"Not really." I rubbed her shoulder and spoke softly. "He speaks without meaning things a lot of the time."

"Not every time," she said, astonishing me once more by defending him.

"Not every time," I allowed. "But enough so that

353

we really shouldn't trust what he says about turning over a new leaf."

Her eyes closed, and she nodded, a tear slipping down her cheek. "I wish I didn't love him," she said. "I wish I didn't care so much."

"Me too." I hugged her arm and tipped my head onto her shoulder. "But maybe what we have to do is love him at a distance." I took a breath and said what I'd been thinking for a while. "I think maybe we shouldn't keep letting him come back home only to disappoint us over and over again."

She was silent a minute. "He told me what you said."

I froze. Was she going to blame me for his leaving?

"And I was proud of you," she finished.

My throat closed up. "Thanks, Mama. I was proud of me too."

"And I think you're right. Next time he tries to come home, we lock the doors and turn on the alarm. I need to at least *try* to respect myself more."

"I think so too."

"You might have to remind me I said this."

I laughed through a sniffle. "I can do that."

She kissed the top of my head. "Did Xander leave?"

"Yeah."

"You okay?"

"I'm okay."

"He seems like a good man."

"He is the best kind of man."

354

"Are you in love with him?"

"Madly."

She laughed softly. "I can tell. So he'll be back?"

"I certainly hope so. And how would you like to go up to Michigan sometime and see where he lives? Cherry Tree Harbor is a beautiful town. I think you'd love it."

"But what about the bears? And the gray rat snakes?"

"Never saw a single one."

"Okay, then. I guess that sounds nice."

"It will be." I gave her arm one final squeeze and stood up. "Now I better get some caffeine in me. It's going to be a long day."

"Caffeine!" My mother looked horrified. "That will make your skin dehydrated and saggy. You don't want that today. Let me make you some herbal tea instead."

"Okay, Mama." I smiled and sat down again. "I'd like that."

The rest of the morning and afternoon passed in a blur. I showered, shaved, shampooed, conditioned, exfoliated, masked, and moisturized. The glam squad showed up and did my nails, hair, and makeup. The designer's assistant and my stylist helped me into the stunning silver dress. The emerald and diamond jewelry I'd been loaned for the occasion sparkled around my wrist, at my throat, in my ears.

A few minutes to four, I took a final look in the mirror. I was happy with what I saw in the glass. My hair flowed down over my shoulders in big, loose waves. My green eyes popped from beneath dramatically long false lashes. My skin looked luminous, my cheeks bright. My lips were painted a deep cherry red. "Well?" I asked the team. "What do you guys think?"

"Perfection," said Kayla.

"You look gorgeous." Jess smiled. "Xander is going to see pictures and lose his mind."

I met her eyes in the glass. While the glam squad performed their magic, I'd told her and Kayla about my conversation with Xander, and how we'd agreed to try to make it work between us. "Thank you."

My mom entered the room. "Duke is here," she said. Then she looked at me and gasped. "Oh, baby. You look so beautiful."

"Thanks, Mama."

She came over and took my hands. "I'm so proud of you, Kelly Jo. You're still my baby, but you've taught me so much about persistence and resilience and staying true to yourself."

"Stop it, Mama." I pulled a hand back and fanned my face. "Don't make me cry right now."

She laughed. "Okay, okay. You go and wow them. I'll be watching."

"Thanks." I took a deep breath and one final look at my reflection. I might have been all done up, but beneath the hairspray and lipstick and gems, I knew who I was and what I was doing. I felt like me in my skin.

And I wasn't afraid.

"You look ravishing," Duke said for the tenth time in the back of the black SUV with tinted windows. "I can't take my eyes off you."

"Thank you." I scooted a little closer to the door so his leg, which was lolling to one side, wouldn't touch me.

"Are you ready for the reactions when we hit that carpet? It might be chaos."

"I'm ready."

The car slowed, and I kept my eyes straight ahead.

"You know, you look different somehow," he said thoughtfully. "Gorgeous, but different."

"Must be all the makeup."

"No. It's not that. There's just something about you that's different. I can't put my finger on it."

Good, I thought.

The car came to a stop. "Well, what do you say, Pixie girl? Are you ready to give them what they want?"

"Please don't call me that. I'm Kelly Jo Sullivan tonight. And moving forward."

"Has the label okay'd that?"

"They will," I said, more confident than I had a right to be.

The door on Duke's side opened. He got out, then offered me a hand. With some difficulty in the heavy silver dress, I slid across the seat and placed my palm in his, already aware of the screaming crowd outside the vehicle.

I took one last deep breath, pasted on a smile, and stepped out.

Duke's arm immediately circled my waist.

Tight.

CHAPTER TWENTY-SIX

xander

"DAMMIT," I muttered after getting the update on my phone. My flight was delayed *again*.

We'd already been delayed twice. It was close to three p.m. now, which meant I'd been sitting at this fucking airport for more than five hours.

I was tired and cranky, Kelly hadn't been in touch, and my stomach was tied in knots. Maybe I was hungry. I hadn't eaten since breakfast.

Tossing my carry-on over my shoulder, I left the gate and walked around the terminal until I saw a restaurant that had a couple open seats at the bar. I went in and sat down, and when the bartender came over, I ordered a beer and a club sandwich.

"Coming right up," she said with a smile. Her black collared shirt had Kate stitched on it in gold letters.

While I was sitting there, a text came in from Zach Barrett with Lawrence Hooper's flight information. I scanned it quickly. No surprises—he'd flown in on

Thursday, the same day Kelly had arrived, the day she'd posted the selfie that revealed the house address. He must have seen the photo and jumped on a plane first thing.

Then I looked a little closer.

The days made sense, but the *times* did not. His first flight had left Nashville around nine a.m., long before Kelly had posted that photo.

What the fuck? How had Hooper known where she was going? Who'd tipped him off?

I recalled asking her who knew she was coming up here, and her answer had been her parents, her assistant, her manager, and Duke. But that was Friday afternoon, and according to Kelly, Duke had only learned of her whereabouts that day. And she'd claimed everyone else could be trusted.

So who'd leaked her location? And why? For publicity? Money? To keep tabs on her? It was going to gnaw at me until I had an answer. I needed to get ahold of Hooper and convince him it was in his best interest to be up front with me. But how was I going to find that asshole?

While I was thinking about it, the guy next to me held up his credit card and waved it around. "Hey, can I get my check?"

"One second," Kate answered, typing something into the computer. When she returned, she took his credit card and looked at it. "James Bond? Is that really your name?"

"Sure is, sweetheart."

James Bond?

I gave the guy a sidelong glance. White skin. Blond hair. Tall and beefy, like a bouncer. Was this the asshole who'd tried to get ten grand out of Kelly?

"Cool name," I said. "So are you a spy?"

He looked over, his eyes raking over my build and my tattoos. He sat up a little straighter, puffed up his chest. "No. I'm in private security."

Boom.

"Oh yeah? Like a bodyguard?"

"Yeah." He tried to suck in his gut.

"So have you ever guarded any big name celebrities?"

"Tons of them," he boasted. "But they all suck."

I laughed like he'd said something funny. "Anyone I'd know?"

He rattled off a few people I'd never heard of. And then. "I worked for Pixie Hart too. The singer."

"Oh yeah? My kids like her. She seems nice."

"She's a bitch just like the rest of them," he said, and I had to fight the urge to punch his fucking lights out. "She fired me for no reason."

"Seriously?" My beer arrived, and I wrapped my hand around it so tight I thought the glass might splinter.

"Yeah. Couple of the other guys on the team were doing some shady shit, taking money for tipping off the paparazzi and whatnot, but it wasn't me, and I got fired anyway."

"So the paparazzi were paying the security team for tips?"

He shook his head as he signed his check. "Fuck

no, those guys don't have any money. It was her ex-boyfriend paying the guys to leak the info."

Deep breaths. In through the nose. Out the mouth. "Her ex-boyfriend paid the security team to leak information to photographers? Why?"

"Who knows?" He put the pen down. "Probably just to fuck with her. The guy's a douche bag."

"The world's full of them," I said, getting off my chair. Tossing money onto the bar without even waiting for my food, I bolted from the restaurant with my phone to my ear. Kelly's voicemail picked up, and I left a message. "Hey, baby, it's me. Please call me when you can." Then I tried Marius and got his voicemail too.

Fuck!

Following the signs for luggage claim, I ran as fast as I could for an exit. Waiting in line for a cab seemed to take fucking years. While I was standing there, I tried to connect everything. Duke had paid her dipshit security guys to tip off photographers, but how was *he* getting the information? Was someone in her inner circle feeding it to him? Was it her shithead dad? Would Wags betray her like that? Would her assistant? I found it hard to believe either Jess or Wags would do that to her. Maybe someone else at the record label, a PR person or something, had caught wind of her whereabouts and thought it would be good publicity.

And Duke. When I thought about him, I saw red. If that asshole thought he could continue to fuck with her now that I was in the picture, he had another thing coming. Every time I thought about him at her side today, the way she was trusting him to be a decent fucking human being, I wanted to kick his ass.

"Motherfucker," I seethed, causing the guy in front of me to cast a wary eye over his shoulder.

Ten minutes later, I was in a cab heading for the theater. Unfortunately, it was rush hour, and the traffic around the city was gridlocked. Closing my eyes, I cursed myself for ignoring that gut feeling that told me not to leave her.

Never again.

CHAPTER TWENTY-SEVEN

DESPITE HOLDING me a little too close on the red carpet, Duke generally behaved as promised.

"Just friends," he'd shout out when reporters or photographers asked if we were back together. But I could hear the insincerity in his voice, like his answer was a joke that everyone was in on.

We did a live television interview right before we entered the Milton. The reporter asked the usual questions about who we were wearing and what made this night so special. Duke kept that arm around me, and I tried not to squirm uncomfortably in his grasp.

"So, of course, I have to ask, are the rumors true?" The reporter smiled at us with big red lips and shiny white teeth. "Are you two back together?"

"You shouldn't listen to rumors, Carrie," Duke teased. "Pixie and I are just good friends."

"Is this true?" Carrie asked, putting the microphone in my face.

Angry that he'd called me Pixie when I'd specifically asked him to refer to me as Kelly today, I managed a smile. "It's true. We're just friends. I'm actually dating someone else."

Carrie's eyes about popped from their sockets. "Who is he?"

"Keeping it secret for now," I said, sensing Duke going stiff with fury beside me.

"Ooooh, a mystery man!" Carrie laughed and spoke to the camera. "You heard it here first. Back to you, James."

Duke marched me into the Milton and pulled me aside. "What was that all about?"

"What?" I said innocently. Marius was standing nearby, so I wasn't scared.

"You're dating someone? Who?"

"None of your business."

He pressed his lips together and exhaled through his nose. "I don't appreciate being ambushed, Pixie."

"It's Kelly," I said. "My name is Kelly Jo Sullivan. Remember that, please."

"Duke?" His publicist tapped his shoulder. "We need to get backstage." She glanced around. "And this is very public."

"Give us a minute," he snapped. He held up his palms. "Look, I'm sorry. Tension is running high today. We can talk later. Let's just give them all a good show."

"Fine," I said, although I had no desire to talk with him later.

I missed Xander already. I was sorry I'd told him to go.

Backstage, Duke went one way, and I was ushered in the other.

In the dressing room, the hair and makeup crew touched me up, and I was happy when Jess walked in. "Hey! Could I see my phone real quick?"

"Sure," she said, taking it from her bag.

But there was no service. "Shoot. I can't even send a text."

"This place is the worst," the hair stylist said. "It's like a Dark Ages dungeon in here."

Sighing, I dropped my phone back into Jess's bag. "I guess I'll have to wait until later."

When I was ready, Marius walked with me to the stage door, where someone dressed in black wearing a lanyard and holding a clipboard told him he could wait for me there in the hall. I'd exit the wings through this same door.

Marius looked at me. "You want me to come back there with you?"

"That's not allowed," said the skinny guy with the clipboard.

My bodyguard looked at him like he was a bug. "I didn't ask you."

"I'm fine, Marius." I touched his forearm. "You can wait for me here."

He wasn't thrilled with my answer, but he nodded. "Okay."

Clipboard guy brought me backstage, and my stomach began to jump.

Duke opened the show with a little patter, delivered with his signature Southern drawl and playboy charm. To be honest, I was shocked when he introduced me as Kelly Jo Sullivan. For some reason, I'd been convinced he wasn't going to do it.

"We're here tonight to celebrate our city, our history, our musicians, our songs, and relationships that inspire them," he said. "And now I'd like to bring out someone very special to me. You might know her by a different name, but she's still country music's sweetheart. Please help me welcome Miss Kelly Jo Sullivan."

My heart hammered in my chest as I joined him on stage, and as the band behind us played the opening bars, I tapped my chest three times, just in case Xander was watching. Then I let the music fill my soul, the energy in the room lift me up, and the lyrics tell the story. I played the role of a woman longing to go back in time, to forgive and forget, to fall in love again. To deliver the most compelling performance I could, I thought about Xander, about our days in the cabin, about the way he made my pulse race and my skin warm and my heart open. I might have been looking at Duke, but every note I sang, every word I uttered, was for another man.

But it was also for myself. I knew that this performance was the start of something big for me. I felt it in my bones. I gave that song my all, and when it was over, the entire auditorium echoed with thunderous applause.

Duke took my hand and squeezed it hard. When I looked up at him, he smiled, and I smiled back. A glimmer of goodwill flared in me. Of affection for this community. Maybe he and I could be friends. Maybe I could find it in me to forgive him for the way he'd treated me, and we could just move forward. I didn't want Duke Pruitt as an enemy. Perhaps this fence could be mended.

So when he kept my hand in his, leading me to exit stage right instead of stage left as planned, I went along. When we reached the wings, he turned to me. "Got a minute?"

"Don't we have to get to our seats?"

"I'd really like to talk to you. Please. It's important. And it will only take a minute."

I hesitated, then gave in. "Okay."

He took my hand. "Come upstairs with me. I keep an office here. We can talk there."

"I should let my security know," I protested as he opened a door and pulled me into a dark, narrow stairwell.

369

"No need. You're with me." He began going up the steps. "You're perfectly safe."

An alarm bell went off in my head. "Where are we going?"

"I told you. My office."

"Slow down, Duke. I'm in heels. And this dress isn't easy to move in."

"Sorry, darling." He moved a little slower. "You were amazing out there. Never sounded better. Our voices blend perfectly, don't you think?" He opened a door into a well-lit hallway after only one flight of stairs, and I breathed easier.

"Thank you. Yes, I thought it went well."

"*Well*?" He laughed as he led me down the hall and opened the last door on the left. "We brought down the house. Didn't you hear the applause?"

"I heard it." I entered the room and looked around. Corner office. Desk. Chairs. Couch. Window overlooking the city. Framed records on the wall. "This is nice."

"Can I get you anything?" he asked, closing the door behind him. "Are you thirsty?"

"No, thank you." Aware I was alone with him and no one knew where I was, I started to get nervous. What if I had to run back down the hall? Scramble down those stairs? I slipped my heels off. "You know what? My feet are a little sore. Maybe I'll just take these shoes off for a minute."

He smiled as he came toward me. "Yes. Get comfortable. Take the whole outfit off. Or I can do it for you."

I backed up until my butt hit the desk. "That's not funny."

"It wasn't a joke." He moved closer and braced his hands on either side of my hips. "Why do you think I brought you up here?"

"You said it was to talk. You're too close, Duke." I pushed against his chest, but he didn't budge.

"Stop fighting this." His hands moved to my hips. "We belong together, sweetheart. And the sooner you admit it, the sooner we can stop all this cat and mouse bullshit."

"What cat and mouse bullshit?"

"These games. Trying to hurt each other. I know that's why you went away with someone else. Why you're dating someone else."

"I've never done *anything* to hurt you."

He gripped my hips harder. "The guy in the photographs Hoop took. Is that your new boyfriend?"

Icy cold fear slithered through my veins. "How do you know Hoop took photographs of us?"

"God, you're so naive. That's why you need me. You'll be eaten alive without me to protect you." His smile was patronizing and sinister. "I knew he took the photos because I sent him up there to do it."

"How did you know where I was? Did my dad tell you?"

"Your dad?" He looked surprised I'd asked. "No. Your dad did not prove as useful as I'd hoped where you're concerned. But I didn't need him to tell me where you were. I almost always know where you

371

are, darling." He tucked my hair behind my ear. "Because you left your email open on my laptop, and you never changed your password. See? Naive *and* careless."

"Fuck you!" I tried to knee him in the balls like Xander taught me, but because of my dress and my short stature, I was only able to get him in the thigh.

But it was enough to stun him, and he loosened his grip on me enough that I could make a run for the door. Unfortunately, without my heels on, the damn dress was too long, and my toes got stuck in the hem, sending me tumbling to the floor.

He was on me in an instant.

CHAPTER TWENTY-EIGHT

xander

WHEN I FINALLY ARRIVED AT the auditorium, I jumped out of the cab and ran around the building as fast as I could to the back door by the loading dock. Some guys from the crew were standing around outside smoking, and I saw several who'd been here yesterday.

As luck would have it, one of them was a Navy guy named Javier I'd spent a little time talking to, and he recognized me. In very few words, I explained the situation and said I had to get inside.

The rest of the crew looked doubtful, but Javier nodded. "I'll get you in," he said confidently. Then he looked at another guy. "Curtis, give me your badge."

Curtis shrugged, took off his lanyard, and handed it to me. "There you go. But if I get fired, I'll need a new job."

"I'll find you one," I said, ditching my bag and slipping the lanyard over my head. "Thanks."

Once I was in the building, Javier and I managed

to make our way into the backstage hall, where I saw Marius arguing with a skinny guy holding a clipboard.

"Marius, what the fuck? Where is she?"

"I'm trying to figure that out," he said, giving clipboard guy a menacing look. "They told me she was coming out this way."

"She was supposed to come out this way," said the clipboard guy, looking distressed at having to face down the three of us. To be honest, I wouldn't have wanted to do it either. "But she must have gone off the other side."

"Is there a door on the other side?" I asked.

"There is, but it would have led right back to this hallway."

Suddenly Jess careened around the corner, running at full speed. "I can't find her, Marius. She's not in her seat."

"Okay, if she didn't come back through this hallway and she didn't go right to her seat, does that mean she's still backstage? On the other side?" I asked.

Javier was already moving in that direction, the rest of us on his heels. When we reached the door, he knocked on it, and as soon as it opened, Marius and I charged backstage.

With producers and crew shushing us left and right, he and I swept the area and quickly determined she wasn't there. What the fuck? She hadn't just disappeared into thin air! Where was she? Adrenaline, fury, and terror had my heart racing, and sweat was dampening my clothes. Why the fuck had I left her? If anything happened to her, I'd blame myself.

Then Javier grabbed my arm, jerking his head toward a door at the back. We ran for it, and when it opened onto a dark, narrow stairwell, somehow I knew that's where he'd taken her.

I raced up, three at a time, Marius and Javier right behind me. We reached the first landing and I threw the door open. "You keep going," I told them. "There's at least one more floor."

They continued hurtling up the stairs, while I took off down the hall, opened every single door onto empty offices.

Then I heard her yell, "Fuck you!"

I rocketed toward the sound.

CHAPTER TWENTY-NINE

HE FLIPPED me onto my back and sprawled over me, his hands pinning my wrists to the carpet.

"I gave you what you wanted tonight," he said, like all this made perfect sense. "And now you're going to give me what I want."

"Like hell I will." Instinct kicked in. I bent my knees and bucked my hips, sending him sailing over my head. He was *much* easier to toss than Xander! Just as planned, he released my arms to break his fall and save his face.

Immediately, I swept my arms down and hugged his torso tight, remembering to turn my head so his chest didn't smash it. Xander's voice was in my head. *Climb the tree. Wrap the arm.* I scooted up, hooked my left arm around his right bicep, and rolled him onto his back.

Then I delivered a blow with my right elbow to his cheek and a second one to his gut. Both landed with satisfying thumps, and I quickly tried to scramble to my feet.

Unfortunately, that fucking dress was not made for easy movement. I hadn't quite managed to stand up when Duke regained his strength and popped up. He was coming toward me with pure evil on his face when suddenly the door behind him flew open, and he was jerked backward and tossed to the ground like a marionette. Then he took a blow to the face that was much harder than the elbow I'd delivered—it landed with an explosive *crack*!

"Motherfucker!" Xander yelled, standing over Duke like an angry god. "I should fucking kill you for putting your hands on her!" He clutched the front of Duke's white shirt—now splattered with blood from Duke's nose—and hauled him up to his feet. "Fight back, asshole! Or do you only get rough with people smaller than you?"

"I'll fucking—!" Duke sputtered, but I never got to hear what he was going to fucking do because Xander caught him in the solar plexus with two more sharp jabs. Duke fell to the floor and cowered, gasping for air, while Xander cocked his fist again.

"Xander, no! I'm okay," I said, pulling up the hem of my dress and rushing over. "I'm okay!"

He immediately abandoned Duke and took me in his arms. "Are you sure? He didn't hurt you?"

"He didn't hurt me," I said. "I promise, he didn't. Did you see my bridge high, throw low?"

"No." He looked at me with awe. "Did you use it?"

"It worked," I said excitedly. "It really worked."

Then I burst into tears.

Later, after I'd filed a police report, returned the jewels, ditched the dress, washed off my makeup, hugged my mother, and told her the story over a couple of very strong cocktails, I let Xander tuck me into bed and crawl in beside me.

"I'm so glad you're here," I said, pulling him close, laying my cheek on his chest. Would anything ever feel as good as lying naked with him? Feeling his warm, hard body against my skin? Hearing his heart beat so close to mine?

"I'm so sorry I left," he said. "I knew something wasn't right. When I think about what might have happened if I hadn't gotten there, it fucking kills me."

"Were you scared?"

"Hell yes, I was scared."

"*What?* Big, bad Xander Buckley is admitting he gets scared?"

"I guess he is. Keep my secret."

"Want to know one of mine?" I kissed his chest.

"I want to know all of yours."

I picked up my head and looked down at him, my pulse pounding. "I'm in love with you."

"I—"

I covered his lips with my hand before he could get another word out. "No, don't say anything. I don't need any words in return. I just wanted you to know how I feel and how grateful I am for you."

He pushed my hand away. "When am I allowed to do the same thing?"

"Maybe tomorrow."

"That's nice of you."

"I *am* country music's sweetheart."

Even in the dark, I sensed his smile. "Tell me again."

"I love you."

"I like the way it sounds when you say it. Sometimes I just want to sop your voice up with a biscuit and swallow it whole."

My entire body tingled, right down to my toes. "I missed you so much today. I know we won't always be able to be there for each other, even on the big days, but it really didn't feel right without you there."

"I will do my best to be there on the big days, I promise."

"Me too," I said. "I'm so happy we're flying back together tomorrow."

"You don't have to, you know. The opening of my bar is not the same as a big performance. And I won't have a ton of downtime over the weekend."

"Hush. I'm coming, and *that's that*." I poked his chest twice. "You're sure it's okay with your dad if I stay with you?"

"Yes. It's safer than a hotel. And I promise, I'm going to look for a house soon."

"Get the bar up and running first. The house can come later."

"I wish our flight tomorrow wasn't so early," he said, his hands beginning to stray beneath the covers. "We have to get up in like six hours. And I'm sure you're tired. I want you to get some sleep."

"I can sleep on the plane," I told him, rolling onto my back and pulling him on top of me. "And I can nap when we get there. I can nap all day if I have to."

He settled his hips between my thighs. "Does that mean I can keep you up a while longer?"

"I'd be very *unsatisfied* if you didn't."

"I can't leave you unsatisfied, can I?" He lowered his mouth to my neck. To my shoulder. To my chest. "You might write a song about it. My reputation would be ruined."

I giggled as his beard tickled my stomach. "Speaking of ruined reputations, I cannot wait for Duke's mugshot to make the rounds tomorrow."

Xander picked up his head. "Do we have to talk about him?"

"With that giant black eye and his broken jaw— which he deserved."

"He deserved worse," mumbled Xander, pushing my thighs apart.

"The tabloids are going to have a riot," I said glee-fully, sighing with pleasure when Xander's tongue made a slow stroke up my center. "Especially when that video footage gets out."

It turned out that every office in the Milton had security cameras, and the footage from tonight clearly showed Duke assaulting me. Even better? It showed me fending him off with my bridge high, throw low. I hoped that video was shown on every website, social media app, and television news outlet tomorrow. Duke would deserve every bit of vitriol and ridicule he got.

"Agreed. Are we done talking about him now?" Xander's tongue worked its magic over my clit, and I buried my fingers in his hair.

"I'm done with everyone and everything but you," I whispered. "You're all I need."

He knew exactly what my body craved and gave it to me with endless patience and superb skill. No teasing tonight, no holding back, no denying pleasure. He was more gentle than usual, as if he was worried I might not be in the mood for rough, aggressive sex after what I'd been through tonight. After making me come with his tongue, he moved up my body and eased inside me.

"Fuck, this feels good," he whispered. "But are you sure you're okay?"

"Yes," I told him, sliding my hands down his back. "Trust me. Nothing has ever felt so right."

"I do trust you," he said, beginning to move his body over mine. "I just want to take good care of you."

"You do," I said, my eyes closing softly as I fell deeper into the dream. "You will."

I could have sworn I'd just drifted off to sleep when I felt Xander shake me from behind. "Hey. Kelly. Wake up."

"Mmph. Is it time to get up already?" I curled into a tighter ball.

"No."

"Then why do I have to wake up?"

"Because it's tomorrow."

"Huh?"

He tugged my shoulder, pushing me onto my back. "It's after midnight," he said, brushing my hair off my face. "That means it's technically tomorrow, so it's my turn to talk."

I started to laugh.

"Excuse me, but I don't think you're supposed to find it funny when a guy is trying to tell you he loves you for the first time."

My heart hammered with pure joy. "No?"

"No. Especially when he's never said those words to anyone. He's not even sure he's ever *felt* them for anyone. And he certainly never intended to feel them for a celebrity he'll have to share with the world."

"Really?"

"Really." He cradled my face with one hand and rubbed my lips with his thumb. "You took me by surprise, Kelly Jo Sullivan. But I wouldn't change a thing."

"You know, lying here with you right now, I'm so happy I feel like I could walk away from all the celebrity bullshit and the music industry and even the money and be totally fine."

"I'd love you either way. You know that, don't you? And I'll never ask you to give any of it up for me."

"I know. And I don't *really* want to give it all up, not now. I still love music. I still want to sing. I still love performing. But knowing I have you, my safest place in the world, waiting for me when I walk off the stage or leave the recording studio—it means everything."

"I'll be there. Every time."

I smiled. "I love you."

"I love you too." He kissed my lips. "This is only the beginning."

The following night, I attended the grand opening of Buckley's Pub. It was crowded from the moment the doors opened, full of family and friends, locals and tourists, neighbors and strangers. I stayed out of the way, sitting with Veronica at a little table against the wall, sipping drinks and chatting with people who popped over to say hi. I wore a ball cap and ponytail and tried to stay under the radar, but I was recognized fairly quickly. Although the crowd wasn't my usual fanbase, I did get requests for autographs and photos for people's kids.

I said yes each time, but I was careful to ensure my presence there wasn't a huge distraction. If it had been, I would have left—I wanted the focus to be on Xander.

He was busy all night long—everyone wanted to shake his hand, or give him a hug, or hear all about the renovations he'd done—but he checked on us whenever he could. Watching him work the room, I thought my heart might burst with pride and excitement. This place was going to be a success, I could feel it.

Around eleven, Xander came over and dropped into the chair next to me, draping his arm over my shoulders. "Is it over yet?"

Veronica laughed. "Not yet."

I patted his leg. "You must be exhausted."

"I'm fine. You doing okay?" He glanced around. "I saw some people ask you for photos."

"I'm totally fine. My goal is to be such a regular around here that it's no big deal when I'm spotted. I want to be old news in Cherry Tree Harbor."

He laughed and kissed my temple. "I want that too."

When Xander got up again, Veronica's eyes were huge. "I still can't get over it," she said. "You guys look so happy together."

"It took us by surprise too," I said with a laugh. "But in the best possible way."

"So now what? Will you guys go back and forth?"

"We're talking it out. Actually," I said, pulling my ponytail over my shoulder, "I might stick around here for a while."

Her jaw dropped. "Seriously?"

"Yes. I'm in sort of a transitional space in my career, where I want to move away from the whole Pixie Hart persona and do something more personal and meaningful to me, and I think maybe taking a little time off might be good before that kind of reinvention."

"That makes sense," she said. "So will you rent a place in Cherry Tree Harbor?"

"I think so," I said tentatively. "Xander and I talked about it on the flight here, and we think that's the best plan for now. I really like it up here, and plenty of people in the industry don't live full-time in Nashville."

Veronica picked up her gin and soda and took a sip. "Have you decided what you'll do about your record label?"

"If PMG won't give me more creative control, I'm out," I said firmly. "I'm reaching out to several people I know who left their big labels behind in favor of going indie, and even though it means less money and exposure, it also means more freedom, which feels more important to me right now. I really want to love what I do."

"I bet they give you what you want," Veronica said confidently.

"We'll see." I shrugged. "They're definitely going to have their hands full doing damage control for Duke, so they might not want the headache of losing me at the same time. And I have some other projects in the works. I just had a meeting with a Hollywood music director about contributing some songs to a soundtrack, and we clicked really well. I'm excited about it."

"That's amazing. You have to follow your heart, you know? Money is nice, but it isn't everything."

"I agree," I said. "It's the music that matters to me. And the people I love."

Xander caught my eye across the room. He lifted his hand and tapped his chest three times.

I smiled and tapped mine too.

epilogue

KELLY: ONE YEAR LATER

BEFORE THE LAST song of the night, I paused to take it all in.

The hot glow of the stage lights. The electric hum of the equipment. The sea of faces filling the open-air amphitheater. The thousands of phones held high, waving like stalks of wheat in a field. The starry late summer sky beyond them.

It was the final show on my tour—my first as Kelly Jo Sullivan. And despite the label's dire warnings about the name change, the different sound on my new album, and my insistence on working with mainly up-and-coming female producers instead of their usual stable of aging good old boys, my professional renaissance had been successful beyond my wildest dreams.

I adjusted the strap on my guitar and moved closer to the mic. As always, I tapped my chest three times before beginning my closing song—my biggest hit yet—which I'd written for Xander. It was called

"Lightning Bolt Love," and it was about meeting your soul mate when you least expected it. About realizing there was someone alive who could bring you to your knees. About how no matter how hard you fought it, love would always win.

He wasn't here, and the show wasn't being televised, but he often saw videos people posted on social media, so I sent him our sign every single night. Despite the distance and time we were forced to spend apart, we'd only grown closer over the last year. There was no doubt in my mind he was the one for me. We hadn't talked much about the future in concrete terms—mostly we just tried to be together as often as we could and made the most of every single minute we had. We never took a single moment for granted.

When I strummed the opening bars, a tsunami of cheers rushed toward me from the audience—they knew every single word, and they'd sing it along with me, just like fans had done at every show all over the country.

My eyes teared up as I began the song. Tonight was bittersweet for me. I was saying goodbye to a phase of my life, but I was also eager to take a break. I'd been working nonstop for the last ten months, and slowing down for a while was going to feel so good.

So would waking up next to Xander every morning.

Last fall, we'd agreed that we'd try not to go more than three weeks without seeing each other, and so far, we hadn't gone more than two. Within a few days of the Buckley's Pub opening, I'd rented a small, fully furnished home on a quiet street within walking distance of downtown Cherry Tree Harbor and the waterfront. The owners only used it during the warmer months, so it would be mine until the end of April.

Xander moved in the following week, and we agreed that he'd stay there full-time while I went back and forth from Nashville as needed. He started looking for houses, and in February, he found one he loved and made an offer. It needed work, but with his dad and his brother's help, he completed enough of it that we were able to move in when my lease was up. My brother had some leave time, and he flew in and helped us move. We'd told him about us as soon as he was back on the grid. Xander had been a little nervous, but not only was Kevin happy to hear the news, he wanted credit for introducing us!

Between the bar and the home renovations, Xander's free time was scarce, but he came to Nashville with me as often as he could, and he always made the trip if something important was happening. Like the day last October when I had the meeting with PMG. He didn't even tell me he was coming—he just surprised me by showing up at my house the night before. "I know you can handle this on your own," he said as I hugged him tight, "but I want to be there in your corner."

While I was recording my new album, he visited often, and when my tour began, he tried hard to make it to a few shows each month. But I never felt like we had enough time together, and I couldn't wait to have days on end to spend with him. He was anxious to have me all to himself too—he worried about me every day when we weren't together. But Marius was still with me, and his team had been amazing during my tour. I always felt safe in their keeping, and we hadn't had a single security mishap.

Which was why it was odd, as the last note of the song was drowned out by cheering, that I sensed someone walking onto the stage from the wings. I glanced to my left and noticed a tall, muscular man moving toward me. He wore jeans and a fitted black T-shirt, impressive biceps testing the sleeves.

I blinked. It *couldn't be.* Xander wasn't in California—he was back in Cherry Tree Harbor. And he usually stayed out of the spotlight, unless he was escorting me to an event. Even then, he'd take a couple photos with me and then move off to the side.

Yet there was no doubt in my mind who it was walking across that stage—I knew that body like I knew my own. I dreamed about it every night we were apart and lost myself to it every night we were together. He was my safest place in the world.

I squealed with joy as he got closer, then I lifted the guitar strap over my head and set my instrument aside. "Y'all," I said in the mic, my eyes locked on Xander's, "I want you to meet my person. This is Xander."

The crowd had been going crazy already, their screams and whistles ringing in my ears, echoing in the night, but somehow the noise level rose when Xander reached my side.

"Hey," he said, a sexy, mischievous grin on his face.

Laughing, I shook my head. "What on earth are you doing here?"

He dropped to one knee. "I'm looking for a wife."

My jaw dropped, and the fans lost their minds as Xander uncurled his fist to reveal a ring box hidden in his huge palm. I slapped my palms over my cheeks as the gorgeous diamond solitaire sparkled in the lights. It wasn't fancy or fussy like the luxury pieces loaned to me for big events, but I'd never loved anything more.

"Kelly Jo Sullivan," he said loudly, so I could hear him. "I'm crazy in love with you. And my dad says that only happens once. So what do you say? Will you marry me?"

I nodded, because my throat was too tight to speak. Tears ran down my face as Xander slipped the ring on my finger—it fit perfectly. Then he stood up and took me in his arms—*we* fit perfectly. Lifting me right off my feet, my red boots dangling as he crushed me to his chest, our lips and hearts melded together.

He set me down and rested his forehead against mine. "For the rest of my life, all I want to do is make you happy. You and our five rowdy kids."

"*Five*?" I laughed as happiness flowed through my veins.

"We'll talk," he said with that grin I never could resist.

Later, as we lay next to each other, skin to skin, my head on his chest, I held my hand up in the dark of my hotel room. "I love my ring so much."

"You can't even see it," he teased.

"But I know it's there, and I love it. Not just because it's beautiful, but because of what it means."

He kissed my head. "I love you."

"I love you too." I wrapped my arm around him again. "When do you want to get married?"

"I don't know. Tomorrow? We could go straight to Vegas from here."

I laughed. "I'd like a church wedding, please. And a big party with all our friends and family there."

"Then that's what we'll do."

Sighing, I let my eyes drift closed so I could dream about the future. "Xander?"

"Hmm?"

"We won't really have *five* rowdy kids, will we?"

He chuckled softly. "I guess we'll have to wait and see."

epilogue

XANDER: ONE MINUTE LATER

OF COURSE WE WOULD.

want more xander and kelly?

If you loved Hideaway Heart, subscribe to my mailing list using the QR code below, and the first thing you'll get is a bonus scene from Xander and Kelly's future!

Find out if they had those five rowdy kids...

also by melanie harlow

The Frenched Series

Frenched

Yanked

Forked

Floored

The Happy Crazy Love Series

Some Sort of Happy

Some Sort of Crazy

Some Sort of Love

The After We Fall Series

Man Candy

After We Fall

If You Were Mine

From This Moment

The One and Only Series

Only You

Only Him

Only Love

The Cloverleigh Farms Series

Irresistible

Undeniable

Insatiable

Unbreakable

Unforgettable

The Bellamy Creek Series

Drive Me Wild

Make Me Yours

Call Me Crazy

Tie Me Down

Cloverleigh Farms Next Generation Series

Ignite

Taste

Tease

Tempt

The Cherry Tree Harbor Series

Runaway Love

Hideaway Heart

Co-Written Books

Hold You Close (Co-written with Corinne Michaels)

Imperfect Match (Co-written with Corinne Michaels)

Melanie Harlow likes her heels high, her martini dry, and her history with the naughty bits left in. The author of over thirty contemporary romances, she writes from her home outside of Detroit, where she lives with her husband and two daughters. When she's not writing, she's probably got a cocktail in hand. And sometimes when she is.

Find her at www.melanieharlow.com.

Milton Keynes UK
Ingram Content Group UK Ltd.
UKHW042031230124
436531UK00004B/57